END OF THE ROPE

Jackie Calhoun

Bella
BOOKS

2010

Bella Books, Inc.
P.O. Box 10543
Tallahassee, FL 32302

Printed in the United States of America on acid-free paper
First Edition

Editor: Medora MacDougall
Cover Designer: Stephanie Solomon-Lopez
Front cover art is based on an original watercolor entitled "Rush Hour" by Ann Singsaas (www.annsingsaas.com) from her Horse Series.

ISBN 13:978-1-59493-176-5

Dedication

In memory of all the horses that passed through our barn, with special mention going to Tangy Bevin, our best pleasure horse, and Rhubarb, our big pleasure pony.

Acknowledgments

Thanks to my first readers—
My good friend, Joan Hendry
My sister, Chris Calhoun

Thanks also to Ann Singsaas (annsingsaas.com) for the great cover—"Rush Hour."—from her Horse Series.
And special thanks to those who work for Bella Books, who made this book possible.

About The Author

Jackie Calhoun is the author of the following Bella Books: *Wrong Turns, Roommates, The Education of Ellie, Obsession, Abby's Passion, Woman in the Mirror, Outside the Flock, Tamarack Creek, Off Season* and *Seasons of the Heart* (reprint). She also wrote *Crossing the Center Line*, an Orchard House Press book, and ten novels published by Naiad Press. Calhoun lives with her partner in northeast Wisconsin.

For more info on her and her books, go to her Web site at www.jackiecalhoun.com.

For comments and questions e-mail her at jackie@jackiecalhoun.com.

Chapter One

Precariously balanced on rickety scaffolding, Meg Klein was spraying the old barn a bright red when the Subaru drove in. She turned because she heard the dog yapping, which was a sure sign that Nicky Hennessey had arrived. Her heart took a leap, partly because the board she was standing on bounced under her weight and partly because Nicky did that to her.

"That looks dangerous." Nicky was peering up at her, her eyes shaded with one hand. "I think you should come down."

"It's terrifying." The scaffolding could collapse any minute or she might misstep and fall. Either was a real possibility, but how else could she paint the barn? "Wait a minute." She emptied the spray gun and ran paint thinner through it.

Nicky hushed the little dog, a black curly-haired mixed brand of poodle and cocker, and held the ladder while Meg climbed down. When Meg reached the bottom, she leaned forward and kissed Nicky's cheek. "Thanks for coming."

Nicky touched her cheek and looked Meg up and down, "Have I got the right day?" Her dark eyebrows lifted in question.

Meg nodded, taking off her gloves. "I'll just change and get Tango. Want to come inside? Get a drink of water or something?"

The old Wisconsin farmhouse was hot, even though every window was thrown open. Scrappy rushed into the kitchen and paused to glance around as if remembering he had once lived there. They laughed.

"He's a smart one," Nicky said, opening a cupboard.

Meg headed for the bedroom to change into her show clothes. As she was pulling off her paint-spattered T-shirt, Nicky appeared in the doorway with two glasses of ice water.

"It must have been hot up on that board."

"Hot enough. Thanks." She drank half the water before setting the glass down. "I need to take a shower. I'm a sweatball."

"Hey, you look good sweaty."

"Yeah?" Meg smiled at Nicky, taking in her dark blue eyes, noticing the gray strands in the nearly black hair that curled around her ears. She wondered if Nicky was thinking about their first bedding in this room all those years ago, of how Meg hid in the closet when Beth showed up in the middle of it and how they'd laughed guiltily when their eyes met outside afterward. Had she fallen for Nicky a decade ago and only realized it when it was too late?

"While you get ready, I'll take a look at the horse. Where is he anyway?"

"In the barn. I gave him a bath." She glanced at the dog, whose tail wagged his whole body. His little teeth showed briefly. "Nice smile, Scrappy, but it won't charm Tango. It might be better if he stays in the house for now, Nicky. Most horses don't like dogs much. Remember?"

Nicky nodded. "I'll get my camera. You stay, Scrappy."

"Does he listen?"

"Sometimes. See you outside."

At Nicky's wink, Meg lifted an eyebrow. "You can get into trouble that way."

Nicky laughed. "I *have* gotten into trouble that way."

"Go. I'll hurry.

Meg jumped in and out of the shower in record time. She brushed her tangle of wet hair smooth, fastened it in a ponytail, and dressed in a long-sleeved shirt, clean jeans and cowboy boots. *Not bad*, she thought, as she tucked her fair hair under her western hat in front of the mirror. She shut the screen door in Scrappy's surprised face on the way out of the house, admonishing him to "be a good dog."

Nicky stood near the gate, her camera bag hanging from her shoulder, a smile on her face. "Who is the little guy?"

"Dan's goat, Pete."

"What's under that mound out there? It's so green."

Meg didn't have to follow her finger. "That's where Brittle and Tawny are buried. Tawny was Lucy's horse. You met Lucy, didn't you? Callie's daughter?"

"I should have guessed. I loved Brittle too." The smile was gone. "That's why you bought the place from Callie, isn't it? It's a money pit, you know."

Meg did know, probably better than Nicky imagined, even though Nicky had owned the house and land before moving in with her long time lover, Beth Forrester, and selling the place to Callie. "I couldn't stand the thought of a bulldozer driving over my horse." She blinked away tears. It had been nearly a year since Brittle and Tawny had been struck by lightning.

Nicky put a comforting hand on her shoulder. "I'm ready any time you are."

Meg tied Tango in his makeshift stall. She brushed him, combed his mane and tail and sprayed him with fly spray. His head shot up. "Easy," she said and slid his show halter over his head. Outside, the horse blinked in the sunlight and trotted sideways next to her. He spied the goat and whinnied loudly.

3

"Shush," she said, putting a hand over his fluttering nostrils. "Open the gate, Nicky, will you?" She was standing in the pen outside the barn. The goat bleated, his little legs churning as he raced toward them. When Pete was inside the pen, Meg dumped a handful of grain on the ground for him and led Tango into the field. "Now shut it quick."

"He looks like Brittle, but he doesn't act like him," Nicky said, keeping a respectful distance from the horse.

"He's young." Meg led him to the willow tree next to the creek and stroked his neck, calming him. "He's Brittle's baby brother."

Nicky was all business when she did photo shoots. Meg knew that. She moved around Tango and Meg, snapping as she went. "Good, that's good," she'd say. "How about a smile now?"

"Me or Tango?" Meg was sweating under her clothes, especially the hat. She kept Tango's attention by flipping the end of the lead whenever he tried to move or his ears began to droop. He'd have to stand with four legs squarely under him in a halter class anyway, so he needed to learn.

"You want some pictures of you on his back, don't you?"

"I do. I'll take him out to the horse trailer and saddle him and put my chaps on. It'll just take a few minutes." She led the horse out of the pasture to the trailer, threw a show pad and saddle on his back and pulled his show bridle over his ears.

Nicky followed her and zipped Meg's chaps when she buckled them on. "I haven't seen you like this in a long time. You look good, Meg."

"I look sweaty. Let's get this over with." She put a foot in the stirrup and threw a leg over Tango's back. He chewed on the bit, crow hopped a little and moved off sideways before she settled him down and rode to the willow.

Nicky again walked around the two of them, snapping photos as she went. When she was done, she said, "Okay, I've got enough," and packed her camera and lenses in the bag.

Meg rode to the trailer and took the tack off the horse. She turned him loose in the field and let Pete out of the pen. The horse and goat walked off together, looking ridiculous, one so small, the other so large.

"Want a beer?" she said. When Nicky glanced at her watch, she hid her disappointment behind words. "That's okay. It's kind of early."

"Got any good stuff?" Nicky asked with a smile that melted Meg's defenses.

"You bet. Let's go imbibe. I want to get out of these clothes."

"I love you in your show clothes. Did I ever tell you that?"

She hadn't. Meg shook her head. Unable to resist Nicky's charm, she felt a smile creep across her face.

They sat on the porch, nursing their Pale Ales, Scrappy stretched out at their feet.

"This is the best room in the house," Nicky said. "I lived out here spring, summer and fall when I owned the place. Why are you painting the barn, Meg? And why did you want photos?"

"For advertising. I'm going to board horses." She hoped to, anyway. That was how she planned to pay for the place. She felt Nicky's gaze on her. "Want to help build stalls?" She was only half kidding.

"Sure. I'm good with a hammer."

"Okay. Great. Do you think Beth will be all right with that? How is she anyway?"

"She won't care. She's gone a lot." Nicky looked away.

The heat shimmered above the grass. Meg knew things weren't going well between Nicky and Beth. Meg had practically moved into their condo after Brittle died, when she couldn't stand to look at the pile of dirt covering her horse. She knew how often Beth claimed an out-of-town conference or a late meeting.

"You almost never came out here when I was renting the upstairs from Callie."

"I know. That's because you came over to my place instead. I believe Callie had a crush on you."

Meg laughed. "I think I turned her into a lesbian."

"You could burn the paint off a statue, Meg," Nicky said.

Meg's heart twisted a little.

"Sometimes I think we made the wrong choices all those years ago."

She assumed Nicky meant when Meg had gone back to Denise and Nicky had chosen to stay with Beth. How old had she been then, thirty-three? Nicky would have been thirty-five. She and Denise had lasted two more months before Meg fled, leaving nearly everything behind. But Beth and Nicky were still together. She couldn't blame Nicky. Elegant and smart, Beth practiced law in a firm made up of women attorneys. Beth and Nicky had been college roommates. How did you break a habit like that?

"Are you hungry?" she asked. The sun hung over the treetops, dusting the fields with gold.

"Scrappy certainly is." At the sound of his name, the dog put his front paws on Nicky's knees.

"I have dog food and treats." She'd bought the food for times like this, to keep Nicky around a little longer. Was that pathetic or what?

"Okay. Let me call home first."

Meg got up. "I'll go feed Tango."

Nicky met her eyes and nodded, but her attention was already elsewhere.

Meg went through the house and out the kitchen door. The screen door slapped shut behind her.

Tango and Pete were hanging around the gate, and on a whim she slipped a halter over Tango's ears. After tying the free end of the lead to the halter and throwing the rope over his head to use as a rein, she stood on the rim of the water tank and slid onto his back. She'd done this often with Brittle.

She squeezed him, and Tango broke into a trot that turned into a canter. They loped around the field until they reached the stream, where the horse threw on the brakes and skidded to a stop. Unprepared, she pitched forward onto his neck. As she scrambled back, Tango lowered his head and arched his spine. She wrapped her fingers in his mane, thinking she could ride out a few bucks. But when Tango left the ground and landed stiff-legged three times, she felt her legs losing their grip. "Whoa,

whoa, whoa," she yelled, even as she flew through the air.

She landed on the rock-hard ground with a grunt and lay sprawled on her back, trying to breathe. When she made a move to get up, her vision blurred. Tango and Pete were grazing not far from her. She had to get the lead rope off the horse before he put his leg through it and panicked. Even though spasms of pain coursed through her, she rolled over and pushed from her hands and knees to her feet.

"Damn horse," she whispered in Tango's ear, grimacing as she took the halter off. The gate looked a mile away as she plodded toward it, willing herself to go forward. Her body contorted as it catered to the pain that literally took her breath away.

Nicky, who had been walking toward her, started to run. "What happened?"

"Tango threw me." Her voice came out whisper thin.

"I'll get the car. You stay here."

"No!" She didn't want the horse and goat to escape. That would be more than she could handle. "Let's get out of the field first."

"Take my arm."

Normally she would have refused. Now she leaned on Nicky and focused on the car.

Nicky helped her into the front seat. "I'll call Dan. He can take care of Scrappy."

"Ask him to feed Tango. One scoop of grain and a flake of hay." The words came in gasps. How could it hurt to talk? What stupid thing had she done to herself? She didn't know Tango well enough to ride him bareback with only a halter for control.

Nicky slid behind the wheel and started the car before flipping open her phone. "Hey, brother-in-law, can you do me a favor?" Meg heard the rumble of Dan's voice. Nicky filled him in on the situation and asked him to take care of Scrappy and Tango. More rumbling. "I'll call you as soon as I know something." Nicky closed the phone and headed down the driveway, hitting all the holes in the gravel. She shot Meg a worried look. "How are you feeling?"

"I'll live," she said, stiffening against the rough ride.

Nicky looked grim. She was clutching the steering wheel with both hands and leaning forward as if that would help the car move faster. "You don't have to be tough around me, Meg."

But she did. The last thing she wanted was for Nicky to see her as vulnerable. After a few minutes, she said, "Can you slow down a little? I want to get there alive."

"Too rough, huh?" Nicky stepped on the brakes, bringing the car to a crawl. She turned on the hazard lights and flinched as they hit another break in the blacktop.

Meg smiled a tight little smile. "On the other hand, it *would* be nice to get there before tomorrow."

Nicky pushed the speedometer up to thirty-five. "How's that?" A pickup sped past them, horn blaring. "Bastard," she muttered.

Meg said nothing. She stared straight ahead and moved as little as possible. She wondered if her core was broken and thought about all the things she wouldn't be able to do—ride, fix the barn, go to work.

Thirty minutes later, Nicky dropped her off at the front door of Immediate Care on the north side of the Fox Cities and went to hunt for a parking spot. Inside, Meg focused on the admitting desk and walked slowly toward it, barely noticing the people slumped in chairs lining the walls. The pain was nearly unbearable. It worried her.

The woman behind the desk smiled at her as Meg passed over her insurance card. "What happened?"

"My horse threw me. The ground is like concrete. I'm pretty sure I fractured some ribs. I just hope one of them hasn't poked a hole through something important, like a lung. I can hardly breathe," she said in that whispery voice.

"Ouch." The woman copied the card. "Find a seat. I'll get you in as soon as possible."

Meg made her way to where Nicky had snagged two chairs and was patting one. She sat down carefully, her attention briefly caught by the talk show yammering away on the TV at the far end of the room. "Places like this are breeding grounds for communicable diseases, you know," she said in a stab at being funny.

"You're the medical technician. You should know. I steer away from them as much as possible. Maybe you'll get one of your doctors."

"Maybe." She worked at First Physician's Care, and the doctors rotated shifts here. "Thanks for helping, Nicky."

Nicky looked her in the eyes. "I'll always help you." She watched as Meg tried to find a comfortable position. "I'm going in with you."

"Hey, I may be a few years younger than you, but I'm over forty."

"You think you're immortal. You need someone to look after you."

"Do you want the job?" she asked. "It's available."

"It won't always be."

"Better snatch it then."

When the nurse called Meg's name, Nicky went with her to the examining room, A thirty-something doctor asked questions as she gently probed Meg's midriff before sending her for X-rays and a urine sample. Nicky waited behind.

Shortly after Meg's return, the doctor reentered the room and shoved the X-rays under a clamp on the wall. She turned and smiled at them. Her hair was shiny black, her eyes a soft brown. Her nametag read Dr. Christina Rodriguez. Meg had never heard of her. "The good thing is that there was no blood in your urine, which means your kidneys are not affected. However, three ribs are cracked, here in the back. They have not punctured any organs, but I'm afraid you'll have to stay off your horse until they heal, Ms. Klein. Don't pick up heavy things. Try not to jar yourself. The ribs will mend on their own, but they need a little time."

Meg looked at the woman's hands, the warm fingers that had touched her. There were no rings. "How long till they heal?"

Dr. Rodriguez shrugged. "One or two months."

"Two months!" Meg cried out and winced, then asked, "What about work? I work in a lab. I'm a med tech."

"Two months is the worst-case scenario. When the pain is under control, you can go back to work. Your body will tell you when you can ride again and when you can pick up anything over ten pounds."

"Like a saddle or a bale of hay or a horse that's going to jerk you around," Nicky added.

"She's right. You don't want to do anything to tear the healing," the doctor said. "If you don't have any more questions, tell me about your horse. I always wanted one." Her words carried a slight accent as if English might not be her first language. She laughed, a bell-like sound. "Now I have money but no time."

The pain turned Meg's laugh into a gurgle. "He's young, not as well broke as my last horse. Riding bareback with only a halter was stupid."

"Very," Nicky said.

She started to shrug, but even that hurt. "By the way, doctor, this is my friend, Nicky Hennessey," she said belatedly.

"Are you a photographer?" Dr. Rodriguez asked Nicky.

"Should I know you?"

"I went to an exhibit at the art center. I think you were one of the artists exhibiting there. I bought a photograph of a field of wildflowers by a Nicole Hennessey. Would that be you?"

"Yes." Nicky was smiling now.

"I love your photos," the doctor said.

"Thanks. That means a lot."

Dr. Rodriguez handed a prescription to Meg. "This will help with the pain."

"If you ever get that horse you wanted and you're looking to board," Meg said, "come see my place. Actually, we're just now building stalls in the barn." She turned to Nicky. "Do you have anything to write on?"

Nicky fished a wrinkled business card out of her pocket and handed it to Meg, who took a pen off the nearby counter and wrote her name, address and cell number on the back. She gave it to the doctor. "Just in case."

In the car Nicky said, "Think she'll show up?"

"I doubt it," Meg grunted.

"You're really serious about boarding horses, huh?"

"That's how I hope to pay for the place."

"Well, this is definitely the wrong way to network."

"I know," she whispered.

Nicky stopped at the pharmacy on the way back to Meg's. She also picked up a pizza. When she said she was staying the night, Meg grunted her thanks. She opened the bottle of pain pills, popped a couple in her mouth and worked up enough saliva to swallow them. Then she leaned back against the headrest and closed her eyes, waiting for them to go to work.

They left the Fox Cities and drove the eight miles home in silence. Nicky helped her out of the car and opened the door to the house. Scrappy was waiting inside, tail wagging in welcome. Meg headed straight for the porch. Nicky joined her, ear to her cell phone.

"Dan fed Tango and Scrappy. He said for you to stay off the scaffolding. He took the paint gun and put the paint away." She pocketed her phone.

There was no way she could hold the sprayer, much less climb a ladder. "I'll call the rental company and tell them to pick up the scaffolding," Meg said. "I have to call work, too. Don't let me forget."

"How about some pizza?"

"Sure."

After choking down one piece, Meg waved away a second. "I'm not hungry."

"You should lie down. I'll get some ice to put on your back."

"Okay." She tried a deep breath and gasped. Dr. Rodriguez had said deep breaths would help keep pneumonia at bay. In bed, still dressed, she lay carefully on her stomach.

"Want to get this off?" Nicky said. She unhooked Meg's bra without waiting for an answer and gently put the towel-wrapped bag of ice on Meg's T-shirt.

Meg winced at the cold, but soon the pills kicked in and she fell asleep. When she awoke, the only light in the room came from the moon. She briefly wondered why it felt as if someone were kneeling on her back before deciding she needed a couple more of those pain pills. When she turned over, she nearly blacked out. "Whoa."

"Hey, how do you feel?" Nicky said from the other side of the bed.

"God awful. Do you know where the pain pills are?"

"Don't move." Nicky gave her a glass of water and a couple of tablets. "Here. Do you have to pee?"

"I can't stand up. The room is spinning."

"I'll help."

When they returned from the bathroom, Nicky helped her out of her clothes and pulled an undershirt over her head. "Go back to sleep. I'll be right here." She stretched out next to Meg.

"Did I ever tell you I love you?" Meg said.

"I know. Me too." Nicky's hand closed over Meg's wrist and Meg drifted into a drug-induced sleep.

Chapter Two

Early the next morning Nicky went outside to put Tango in the barn, leaving Meg and the dog in the house. She stood by the open gate inside the pen, rattling grain in a small pail as the horse bore down on her. When she feared he was not going to stop, a strangled scream escaped her and she dumped the grain. She shut the gate behind him but not before Pete squeezed through. As the horse crunched the feed with his strong yellow teeth, she managed to get the halter over his head. Pete followed them into the barn and slipped into Tango's makeshift stall with them, forcing Nicky to wrap the lead rope around the goat's neck and drag him out of the stall and into the next one. By the time she'd finished watering and feeding and made her way back to the house, her legs and heart were trembling.

From her bed Meg asked, "How'd it go?"

"A piece of cake," Nicky said, dreading having to do this day after day and night after night until Meg was able to take over. "I'm going home now and check my e-mail. I'll be back in the afternoon. Can I fix you some breakfast?"

"A couple pieces of toast and some water would be good," Meg said. Her hair had spilled out of its tie, and her gray eyes followed Nicky's every move.

"I'll get some more ice to put on your back," Nicky said, sure that Meg wanted her to stay and just as certain that she would never say so.

Meg sat on the side of the bed and chewed on the toast till she managed to wash it down with water. "You eat the other one," she said, and Nicky gobbled it down.

She helped Meg lie on her belly and heard her gasp as she put the fresh ice on her back. Although she needed to follow up on a photography job lead, she sat next to the bed near the open window and watched Meg sleep. Twice she reached out to lift the fair hair sticking to Meg's face, smoothing the strands in with the rest that spilled over Meg's pillow.

The morning passed slowly. In the early afternoon Meg got up on her own and shuffled to the bathroom and the kitchen. "I'm all right now, Nicky. You can go."

"I'll come back with food tonight and take care of the animals. Don't you try to do anything, okay?"

Meg nodded. "Would you tie my hair up first? I can't seem to lift my arms."

"Yeah, sure. Should I brush it?"

"No, that's okay. Just get it off my neck."

She gathered the thick, blond hair in both hands, noticing the slender neck beneath. It looked so vulnerable. She wrapped the elastic band loosely around the ponytail. When she left with the dog, Meg was sitting at the kitchen table, looking out the window.

At the condo, she found a note from Beth on the table. It read, *Dinner meeting tonight. Won't be home till late.* She climbed

14

the stairs to her office in the loft and turned on her computer. The follow-up e-mail she was looking for, the one about filming a wedding, was sandwiched among all the pleas for money and the petitions for her to sign. A friend of the family, an amateur photographer, had offered to take the photographs for cost, it said. Sorry, but they wouldn't need her services.

She felt a little desperate and called her old friend, Margo, hoping to hear better news. "Hey, how are you? Anything selling?" Before Margo's divorce had forced her to sell the building and move some of the better prints into her home, she had owned a framing and art gallery where Nicky had worked. Now she sold art and photos through a site on the Internet.

"Someone bought the kestrel on the fence post yesterday. It was one of my favorites."

"Mine too," Nicky said. "Thanks, Margo. I'll print you another and bring it out." She had to get back in the field, she thought. And soon. She couldn't rely on selling the same prints over and over. She had to find more of those elusive photo opportunities, like the kestrel.

Margo said, "You should be teaching classes on photography."

"I applied for a job at the Tech once. They only consider people with degrees in photography."

"Well, now that you're an established photographer, they might change their minds. At the very least you should have your own Web site. You need to get your name out there. You could link up to my site. I'll sell more of your art that way."

"Okay. When I come out tomorrow, I'll bring my laptop. Maybe *you* should be working at the Tech."

Margo laughed. "I'd rather work from home. I like what I do."

Nicky picked up Chinese takeout at five and took it out to Meg's. "I'll clean stalls, feed Tango and Pete and put them out. Okay?"

"Okay," Meg said. She was back in bed. Her eyes looked

sunken and her skin washed out. Nicky began to worry. Maybe this was worse than she thought it was.

She took Scrappy with her to the barn, thinking he had to learn to watch out for himself. Tango leaned his head over his stall door and nickered at her. Pete tried to climb out of the other stall.

While she was waiting for Tango to finish his grain, Dan Schumaker walked in. "I thought maybe Meg needed some help, but I guess you're taking care of things."

"You could put them out when they're done dining," she said.

"Not a problem. I'll work on stalls while I'm waiting."

"I'll help," she said, not because she wanted to, but because she thought she should.

When she finally went inside, Meg was asleep and the Chinese takeout was stone cold. She transferred the food to different containers and popped them in the microwave before taking them to the bedroom. "Sit up. You've got to eat something."

"I don't want to eat here," Meg said.

Nicky took the food to the porch, where Meg ate one crabmeat rangoon and fell asleep. Nicky drank a beer and nearly finished off the food before rousing Meg and helping her back to bed.

Nicky lay down beside her. "You can't lie in bed all day, Meg, and you have to eat. You need to keep your strength up. Remember what the doctor said about pneumonia?"

"I know," Meg said. "Could you get me a couple of pain pills?"

"That's why you're sleeping so much. You look like a druggie—unwashed, uncombed, hollow-eyed."

"Thanks," Meg said with some of her old asperity. "You're so sympathetic."

"My life is falling apart, Meg. No job, no money, no partner."

"Where's Beth?" Meg said and then asked again for the pain pills.

"One. You can have one." Nicky fished one out of the bottle. It was almost empty. "Hey, what happened to these? You been

16

taking them around the clock? What happens when they're all gone?"

"There is one refill."

Nicky put the bottle on the dresser. "Come on, Meg. You're going to have to wean yourself off these."

"When they're all gone, I will." She swallowed the pill. "Lie down with me."

After a while, Nicky fell asleep. She dreamed she'd taken Meg's pain pills and Tango was galloping toward her, neck snaked, ears pinned. He was making a whining sound and she couldn't move because she was so tired. She awoke with a start. The room was dark.

It was Scrappy, wanting out. She got up to go with him. Sometimes to dispel a dream, to not fall sleep again and continue dreaming the same dream, she had to make herself stay awake for a while. She crossed her arms for warmth and craned her neck skyward. Clouds moved over stars flung against the black sky. A sliver of moon hung low in the west. She heard Scrappy retching and walked barefoot toward him through the damp, prickly grass. The dog heaved up a pile of food with green stuff in it. She caught him by the collar and pulled him away from the mess before he could chow it back down.

"You ate the rest of the food, didn't you, you little bugger." She shooed him into the house and cleaned up after him. By then, she was wide-awake. Back in the house she threw away the empty fast-food boxes, washed the dishes and returned to bed.

Nicky left the next morning after feeding the animals. At home she found an annoying note taped to her mail, which was piled on the island in the kitchen.

Patricia Robson is coming for dinner tonight. Would you please do something with the stuff on the counter?

She hadn't seen Beth in days, and this is how she greeted her? In a burst of anger she tore through her mail, throwing most of it away and putting the rest upstairs in the office. "No 'Hello, how are you?'" she said to Scrappy as if he were Beth. "No 'I miss you? Why don't you come home?'"

17

The dog wagged his tail and showed his little white teeth, and Nicky gave him a rub. "At least *you* appreciate me." After checking her e-mail, which once more held no answers to her job inquiries—she was sending résumés by e-mail—she looked through her framed photos and called Margo.

"I've got time if you have."

"Get your butt over here. You understand this is not a one-hour or even one-day thing?"

"I'm on my way."

Margo's house was across the street from the river. She was a big woman, with dyed blond hair and kind eyes. Her husband had left her for someone younger. Nicky never understood what the other woman saw in him—a paunchy man with little hair—except that he had money.

"Hey," she joked, walking through the open door onto the large enclosed porch, which, lit by many windows and track lighting, served as an art gallery. "I'm making off with all these pictures."

Margo appeared in the doorway. "Let me see what you have." She looked through the photos Nicky was carrying and hung a print of a pair of bluebirds building a nest in the space on the wall vacated by the kestrel. "I'll just hang onto these others. Okay? When one sells, I'll put another up."

Nicky regularly uploaded her photos to Margo's Web site, where the images would be easy for both of them to access. Many of the files were in raw form, the digital equivalent of undeveloped film, which she tweaked using Photoshop. The rest were JPEGs that were ready for printing in which she'd adjusted color settings, contrast and other elements to let each image's essence shine through.

She set her laptop on a folding table next to Margo's computer desk. For the next hour they studied Web sites, including Margo's.

"We'll use Go Daddy. It's a web-hosting site. Okay?" Margo said.

By the time Nicky left, they had put together a Web site of

sorts—a pretty basic home page—but it was a start. The artist in her wanted to design a more complicated page, colorful and eye-catching, something she could picture mentally but lacked the skill to do.

"This is time-consuming," she said, packing her computer in its case.

"Anything worth doing takes time, doesn't it?"

"I should be out taking photos. Why don't you design me a Web site and I'll pay you?" Maybe she could trade a photo for the work.

"You have no patience, Nicky." Margo walked her to the door.

Nicky thought of the many hours it had taken to find the nesting bluebirds and how she'd waited at least another hour for the light to be just right. "I have patience. Not for this, though."

At home, she found an Acura parked in front of her side of the garage. She unlocked the front door and stepped into the small foyer. After leaving Margo's, she'd taken a short trip out of town. She'd been lucky enough to find a family of four sandhill cranes poking around in Dan's cornfield and gotten some good shots. She also called Dan to ask if he'd take care of Tango and Pete and check in on Meg. She told him she'd be by later in the evening.

"Hey, it's hot out there," she said as she walked into the kitchen.

Scrappy slurped thirstily from his water bowl before turning his attention to Beth, who absentmindedly ran a hand over his furry back. Still clad in a suit skirt and blouse with an apron tied around her, she said, "You two know each other, don't you?"

Patricia wore a suit too and heels. She stood up from where she'd been sitting at the table and shook Nicky's hand, then bent over and cooed a little over the dog.

Nicky backed toward the stairs, feeling like a misfit. "I shall return clean," she promised and scurried upstairs. She took a quick shower and hopped out to find Beth standing in the doorway.

"Are you staying for dinner?"

"Do you want me to?" she asked.

"If you like. It's all about business. You'll be bored," Beth said.

Nicky looked at Beth for a long moment, at her hazel eyes with the long lashes, at the thick hair and great figure under the elegant clothes. "Sure, I'll stay. I have to leave right after we eat, though. I told you about Meg."

"How is she?"

"Still in bed."

"Well, I have to finish dinner." Beth started out the door.

"Want some help?"

"I'm good."

Nicky had the distinct feeling that Beth wanted her to leave, which was one reason she decided to stay. The other was the aroma emanating from the kitchen. Beth was a wonderful cook.

Beth had been right about the conversation, though, which centered around work at the law office and what was on the docket in court. Nicky *was* bored. How would they react, she wondered, if she broke in to say she'd gotten some great pictures of sandhill cranes that afternoon? Imagining their blank stares kept her silent.

After dinner, Patricia and Beth moved into the den. Nicky cleaned up the dishes before poking her head in the door to say, "I'll be late."

"Stay if Meg needs you."

"Okay, I will." Seething, she threw a few clothes in an overnight bag and scooped dog food into a plastic container.

At the farmhouse, she found Meg showered and dressed and standing out by the pasture. "You're out of bed!" she said with surprise.

"Guess who called?"

"I don't know. Ellen DeGeneres?" The Meg she'd left had morphed into her old self, or so it seemed until she looked closely.

"Dr. Rodriguez. She's on her way over."

"That's what's prompted this metamorphosis?" She was a little put out that Rodriguez's impending visit could bring about such a change when she hadn't been able to get Meg out of bed, much less outside.

Meg was leaning on the fence. "I'm a little dizzy," she admitted.

"What does the doctor want?"

"She wants to look at the place. She's thinking about buying a horse."

"Couldn't she wait till you can stand up on your own?"

"Hey, I need the money. Maybe you can show her around."

A black BMW was bouncing down the driveway. Nicky watched as the doctor got out of the car and walked toward them. At work she'd worn a white jacket and tied her hair back severely. Today she wore tightly fitting jeans and a T-shirt and her hair fell to her shoulders in a thick, black wave.

"Hi, Dr. Rodriguez," Meg said with a smile that to Nicky looked more like a grimace.

"Please, call me Tina," the doctor replied, quickly adding, "I should have waited. You're not up to this, but I was so excited."

"You got her on her feet, at least. That's good." Nicky smiled.

"I live right down the road." The doctor pointed to the east where a new subdivision had cropped up a year ago.

Urban sprawl, Nicky thought unkindly.

"Tell me about the horse," Meg said.

"One of my patients has lost her job. She has to sell her horse, and I wondered if you would look at it with me. She said the horse is kind and gentle and easy to ride."

"Can you wait a week or two?" Meg asked.

"Of course. As your doctor, I insist that you sit down immediately, before you fall and further injure yourself."

Ashen faced, Meg looked like she just might do that. Nicky took her arm. "Come on. Sit on the stoop. I'll show Tina around."

"I want to tell her what the barn is going to look like when it's done."

"I'll tell her." She turned toward the doctor. "There are going to be five stalls with a small arena at the end. We just haven't had time to finish them." She smiled tightly. "Would you like to see the barn?" she asked, although she thought that might scare her off. The interior still looked like cows lived there.

"Right now we just have a couple of portable stalls," Meg added. "So there is room for another horse."

Tina shaded her eyes and looked into the field. "Is that your horse?"

"Yes. That's Tango."

"He's gorgeous. This horse is called Sienna Sam."

Meg looked surprised. "Mary DeBruin's horse?"

"Yes, that's the name of the owner."

"He's a great horse. I used to show against him and Mary."

"Then I'll tell her I'll take him, and we'll pick him up as soon as we can." She was now looking at Meg's stock trailer.

"You have to ride him first. You can't just buy a horse over the phone."

"I'll put something down on him then, so that she will hold him."

Nicky looked at Tina closely. She seemed sincere.

"Listen. You go back inside. You can show me around when we go get the horse." Tina started toward her car. When she got there, she turned back. "Should I give you a check to hold the stall for me?"

"You haven't got the horse yet. I'll hold the stall. I promise." Meg put a hand over her heart.

Tina gave a little wave, got into her car and drove away.

Nicky and Meg were silent for a moment before Meg said, "I'm taking her advice and going back to bed. Do you think she's for real?"

"She wants to put money down on a stall to hold it for a horse she hasn't bought. Hey, that sounds like my kind of boarder." Nicky steadied Meg and stayed close to her until she was lying down.

"I think I better stop taking those pills."

"That a girl. How about something to eat? I can fry an egg."

"Maybe later. Do you have to go home?"

"No." She wasn't sure what was going on between Patricia and Beth, but it was clearly something they wanted to keep under wraps. Did she care? Yes, but it was easier to let it go right now. Sooner or later she'd find out.

Dan knocked on the door at near dark. When Nicky opened it, he handed her a warm casserole dish. "Dinner," he said with a smile. "Compliments of your sister."

"How lucky you are to be married to such a great cook. Tell her thanks. Want to come in?"

"No. I fed and turned the animals out. How's Meg doing?"

"I think in a couple weeks she'll have a boarder."

His ruddy face lit up. "Good for her. We'll have to get the barn ready."

"We'll have to do it without her. She's hurting."

He kicked at the step, then looked at her and grinned. "We can do it. We just have to clean out the inside and build stalls," he said, like it was no big deal. "I'll be out in the barn."

Meg ate a little of the casserole while Nicky watched. "Would you get me some ibuprofen from the bathroom?" she asked, handing Nicky her plate.

"You're going off the pain meds cold turkey?" She went to get the pills without waiting for an answer.

"I can do it." Meg swallowed two. Her face was pale and shiny with sweat.

"I'll be out in the barn for a while. Call my cell if you need me." She thought it a clear indication of how badly Meg felt when she didn't ask why Nicky was going to the barn, when instead she closed her eyes and nodded.

Nicky and Dan worked for a couple of hours, knocking down stanchions, the metal posts that had held the cows in place while they were being milked. Set in concrete years ago, they soon lay on the floor, the cement smashed into chunks around them.

"Will you be around tomorrow night?"

Nicky nodded. "If you're going to be here, I will, especially if Nattie sends over dinner again." She watched as her brother-in-law got in his truck and drove away. The night was warm, the sky cloudy. Heat lightning flashed in the distance. Maybe it would rain. She stood in the yard until the mosquitoes found her. They whined around her head, sending her hurrying inside.

After a quick shower, she checked on Meg, who opened her eyes and said, "Lie down with me."

As Nicky fell into an exhausted sleep, she felt Meg's hand close over her wrist.

Chapter Three

Meg set her coffee mug carefully on the truck's steel bumper. She had just backed under the gooseneck trailer. It had been three weeks since her accident. She'd gone back to her job at the end of the first week. Working in the lab was easy. Handling Tango or building stalls were another matter. Sudden moves tore at her healing ribs. She was pleased how every day she was able to do a little more, like jacking the trailer down onto the ball in the bed of the truck.

Tina's BMW purred down the driveway in a cloud of dust, and the doctor got out. "Can I help?"

"Nope." She picked up her coffee and smiled at Tina in the morning light. "I'll show you how the barn is progressing. Nicky should be here any minute." Nicky was riding with them. Just in case Meg needed help, she'd said.

"You're going to help *me* with a horse?" Meg had asked in astonishment.

"Hey, in your condition any horse might be too much for you," Nicky had shot back.

The barn was bare of stanchions now and swept clean. The two portable stalls, bedded with straw, looked lonely in the empty interior. "You did this?" Tina asked.

"Well, no. Nicky and Dan Schumaker, who is the neighboring farmer and Nicky's brother-in-law, did most of it. I helped a little." She had driven Dan's loader tractor, creeping along, carrying the broken posts and chunks of concrete outside and dumping them in Dan's truck. Nicky's sister had fed them. It had almost been a family affair.

"Wish I'd had time to help," Tina said almost wistfully.

"Hey, you're the boarder. You're not supposed to have to get the place ready for your horse. Besides, you haven't bought him yet." They walked out into the sunshine as Nicky drove in.

"Am I late?" Nicky asked, joining them.

"Nope, but now we can go. Tina, I think you should brush, saddle and ride Sam before you buy him. He's a great show horse, but sometimes show horses go ring sour."

"What's that?" Tina stuffed her hands in her back pockets.

"It's when the horse no longer works in the show arena, when it behaves badly, like it's fed up with showing." It had never happened to Brittle, though.

They climbed into the truck, making a sandwich of Tina on the wide front seat. "It still runs okay, I see," Nicky said, as they turned left out of the driveway.

"It broke a hundred twenty-five thousand miles a few weeks ago." She turned to Tina. "I bought the truck from Nicky when she sold this place." Then, of course, they had to explain to Tina that Nicky had once owned the house and few acres that Meg had bought from the previous owner, Callie.

As they passed the subdivision a mile later, Tina said, "I live in one of those houses with my mother. She's just visiting for the summer. We sort of rattle around in the place, but I really wanted to live in the country."

The subdivision sat in a former cornfield, and the only trees were fingerlings planted by a nursery. It wasn't Meg's idea of living in the country, nor, Meg was sure, was it Nicky's. How could you call it country living when you had neighbors a few yards away?

They pulled into Mary DeBruin's driveway, passing the FOR SALE sign in front, and drove up to the tidy barn behind the house. Sienna Sam stood in the paddock, ears perked, watching them. Mary emerged from the house as they piled out of the truck.

"Hi, Doctor," she said, and then smiled at Meg and Nicky. "Long time."

Meg, who had lost more than once to Mary and Sam, thought that today it was Mary who looked defeated. "The doctor lives right down the road from me," she said in explanation.

"I know Sam will have a good home then," Mary said, her voice stretched thin.

She'd never seen Meg's place, of course, but Meg's stock trailer should have been a dead giveaway that it wasn't anything special. Meg couldn't afford a color-coordinated truck and enclosed trailer like many quarter horse people owned. Mary had had a matched set, but Meg saw no sign of either on the grounds.

"We'll take good care of him," Meg promised. It was all too easy to put herself in Mary's shoes. She knew how she would feel if she'd had to sell Brittle or even Tango.

"My husband lost his job too. We're moving into a rental we own in town."

"I'm sorry," Tina said.

Meg toed the ground. "That sucks."

Mary snorted, part sob, part laugh. "Doesn't it, though." She paused, then continued. "I heard about Brittle. I'm sorry, Meg." Tears welled up and she blinked.

It was too much for Meg. She turned away to hide her emotion. Nicky squeezed her arm.

"I hear you bought a new horse," Mary went on.

"I did. He threw me a few weeks ago. Broke some ribs. That's how we met Tina. Nicky took me to Immediate Care."

"Funny how things work out or don't, isn't it?" The bitterness was evident in Mary's tone.

"Life isn't fair," Nicky said.

They went into the neat little barn, and Mary led the horse in from the paddock. "You'll want to ride him."

"Yes," Meg said.

"No. I'll take him as is. Meg said he's a great horse." Tina smiled tightly, and Meg thought she would have bought him no matter what.

Sam eyed them over the top of the Dutch door. Mary took him out of the stall into the aisle and stood him up. A lean, sleek bay with a long neck and pretty head, he was show-ready. His tail nearly touched the floor. A few weeks out in the field would roughen his coat and give him a belly, Meg thought. The goat would probably chew on his tail.

Mary handed Meg the lead rope and disappeared into the tack room. She came out with his quarter horse papers and an already signed transfer form.

Tina handed her a check and took the paperwork. "You ever want him back, give me a call."

Mary nodded. "Do you want to buy the tack, too?"

Tina said sure.

If they didn't get out of there soon, Meg realized, they'd all be crying. She loaded the horse in the trailer, while Mary put the gear in the tack compartment. When she fastened his head, Sam was chomping on the hay Meg had put in the manger.

As they turned onto the road, Nicky dug a tissue out of her pocket to give to Meg, whose nose was running. "That was hard."

"Worse than hard." Meg's heart contracted as she watched Mary grow smaller in the rearview mirror.

At home, Meg shut Tango and Pete in the pen, where Tango whinnied and Pete bleated at the intruder. She asked Nicky to throw the saddle on Sam and tighten the girth. Tina managed to get a foot in the stirrup and, using the horn, pulled herself onto his back.

Meg wanted Tina's first ride on Sam to be a good experience. "Keep light contact with his mouth. Steer him by laying a rein on the side of his neck. He'll move away from it. Gently squeeze him into a walk. He's sensitive to your leg and mouth cues. Just relax and let him take you for a walk along the fence line." When Tina looked scared, she added, "I know that's a lot to digest, but Sam's a pleasure machine. You're as safe as if you're sitting in a chair as long as you don't ask him to do anything but walk."

"I saw the check, Meg," Nicky said once Tina was out of earshot. "It was for fifteen thousand."

"He's worth more."

"Maybe, but someone has to be willing to pay that much."

"I'm going to have to keep him inside during the day. Otherwise, he'll get sun bleached and potbellied. I'll keep Tango in with him."

"Pete will be lonely."

Meg looked at Nicky. "She looks good on him, doesn't she?"

Nicky said, "I guess. She looks sort of small up there."

"Sam will take care of her."

"How about some champagne to celebrate?" Meg had bought and chilled two bottles for this occasion, thinking she was on her way to financial independence. Maybe a glass or two would help her forget the sight of Mary disappearing in the rearview mirror.

No adornments or plants hung from the walls or sat on the counters in the sunlit kitchen. It wasn't so much that Meg liked the Spartan look, she just couldn't be bothered with decorating. She opened the fridge and removed one of the bottles, while Nicky searched the cupboards for suitable glasses.

"Do you think they'll be all right out there?" Tina asked. The horses had been turned out together and, after much snorting and pawing and mock rearing, they had settled down to graze.

"We can see them from the window."

"I don't know much about horses." Tina laughed, maybe because it was so obvious.

"Could have fooled me," Meg said dryly, popping the cork on a bottle of Brut. "I'll teach you." She poured the foaming liquid into three glasses.

Nicky held up hers. "Here's to Sam and Tina."

Meg opened a bag of chips and set it on the table, then sat down where she could keep an eye on the animals. She had always wanted her own stable. She doubted she would be able to quit her job, but maybe boarders would pay Tango's bills. When it occurred to her how this was going to tie her to the place, she tucked the thought away where she kept things she didn't want to think about.

Meg's cell was ringing the next morning when she came in from the barn. She put it to her ear before it could roll into voice mail.

"Hi, this is Jeannette Bailey. Remember me?"

Meg did, of course, though the call was so unexpected it took her a few moments to place her. She'd shown against Jeannette and her horse, Jack, just as she'd shown against Mary and Sam.

"How about Midnight Jack? Do you remember him?"

"Of course. I remember you both. How is he? How are you?" were all Meg could think to say.

"He's great. Mary DeBruin told me her doctor bought Sienna Sam."

"Yes," she said cautiously.

"Well, Jack is for sale. Do you know anyone else who is looking?"

"Did you buy another horse?" Meg asked.

"No. I'm getting a divorce. I can't keep Jack anymore, and I haven't had any luck finding a buyer."

"Well, if I hear of anyone, I'll let you know." But all the people she knew who might be interested were the same people Jeannette knew.

"Do you have room for him?"

"For Jack?" she said in surprise. "In maybe a couple weeks I will. Right now we're working to get the barn ready. I got hurt and can't do much. Are you looking to board?" she asked, wondering where the conversation was going.

"I can pay something for board."

There was a pause while Meg remembered how little she liked this woman, a poor loser who sometimes took it out on her horse. Jack would be better off without her, but what would Meg do with him? "What did you have in mind?"

"I hear Mary got fifteen thousand for Sam. Jack's every bit as good, but people are selling, not buying." Jeannette sounded bitter, and Meg wondered how much moxie it took to ask her a favor like this. Jeannette had always looked down her nose at her and her old mismatched truck and trailer.

She also knew a horse was only worth as much as someone would pay for it. She wouldn't say this, though, because she too thought Jack was worth as much as Sam. "How long before you have to find a place for him?"

"A couple of weeks. Can you take him on consignment? I've talked to everyone else I know."

"Yeah, I could probably do that," she heard herself say. Was she crazy? "How much can you pay?"

"Maybe a hundred a month and ten percent of the selling price."

There was no profit in a hundred a month. She opened her mouth to say that wasn't enough and couldn't get it out.

"I don't want him to go to just anybody. He might end up in a can of dog food."

Chills raced across Meg's skin. Although she couldn't be sure, she thought Jeannette was yanking her chain. And that bit about having to get rid of Jack in two weeks was probably because she had said she'd probably have room in two weeks.

When she hung up, her mind was racing. She called Dan and told him she might have to make space for a third horse in a couple of weeks.

"We'll get those stalls built," he assured her.

31

Another week went by. She was feeling pretty good. She hadn't ridden yet, because when she'd tried to throw a saddle over Tango's back, the pain had left her breathless. She was healed enough to handle the horses, though, turning them out on grass for a couple of hours at night. Dan had taken Pete home, reducing a little of the wear and tear on the pasture, which was in danger of turning into a dust bowl.

Tina was riding her horse in the new outdoor arena that Dan had fenced outside the smaller pen. Meg leaned against the top board and called out instructions. She was thinking about how much money she'd put into this place already. The board Tina paid couldn't begin to catch up with it. She sighed and glanced at her watch. It was five o'clock, about the time Nicky and Dan usually showed up to work on stalls. They were building their own, using odd-sized oak two by sixes because they were cheaper, but they had to pre-drill the nail holes because the wood was so hard.

Scrappy barked once at Sam and, tail wagging, sat down next to her. He leaned against her leg and looked up at her from dark eyes hidden under bushy black brows. "Hey, cutie," she said, and he showed his little teeth in a smile.

Nicky joined them. "He always announces my arrival." She nodded at Tina and the horse. "She's bouncing a lot, isn't she?"

"Yeah, she is." Meg raised her voice. "Tuck your behind into the saddle, Tina, and take the jog with your legs. Good. Bring him back to a walk now and ask for a canter. Touch him with the outside leg. Remember he moves away from pressure. Hear the three beats? The foreleg that touches the ground last is the lead you're on. It's the leg that reaches furthest." As Sam lifted himself into a canter, Meg said, "You want the horse to take the inside lead, so he's not off balance. If you were going in the other direction, you'd ask him to take the other lead. You'll need to know what lead you're on when you show in any class."

She looked at Nicky, happy to see her. "When did you become an expert on riding?"

"It comes from hanging around you. I'm bound to learn something." Nicky winked at her. "You're going to be hoarse if you keep this up."

"I know. I hate yelling." She winked back. "It's dusty out here," she teased.

Nicky laughed and said, "I am bored stiff with my Web site. How do people sit for hours in front of a computer?"

Meg smiled. "You're asking the wrong person."

"It's great of Margo to help me, but I'd rather pay her than do it myself."

Meg looked into Nicky's dark blue eyes and tucked a bit of dark hair behind her ear. "Pay her then."

"I would, but I've got the shorts."

"Don't we all," Meg said. She turned back toward Tina and Sam. "Time for a walk. Just shorten the reins a little and say whoa. Do you think I should take him in?" she asked, meaning Jack.

"It's your call. I'd get Jeannette's offer of a commission in writing before you do, though."

Meg knew she was right.

"Whoa," Tina said, catching their attention. "I have to leave. It's my mother's birthday. I'm taking her out to dinner."

"When are you bringing her over to meet Sam?" Meg opened the gate.

"She wants to come, but she's not so steady on her feet." Tina dismounted, jumping the extra foot or so to the ground. "I guess I'll bring her next time I come." She gave them a bright smile and disappeared into the barn.

"She's kind of cute, isn't she?" Meg said once Tina was out of earshot.

Nicky winked at her again. "You're sexier."

Meg laughed. "Yeah, sure," but she knew she was. She'd seen it in too many faces not to know. "Time to go to work, I guess. Want me to drill for you?" She couldn't wield a hammer yet or hold up the heavy boards.

"I guess. I'd rather build stalls than look at a computer."

When Dan ducked into the barn later, Scrappy ran to greet

him. "Hi, little fellow. Hey, girls, are you getting those boards on square?"

They had both reached an age where they didn't mind being called girls. "The horses don't care if they're square."

Dan smiled. "Just so they're close enough together. You don't want a stuck hoof."

"Hey, I thought we were pretty good at this," Nicky said.

"You're getting there."

While Meg and Nicky worked on boarding in the third stall, Dan turned on the lights in the barn and framed in the fourth. During the day natural light slanted across the floor from the small windows. It made Meg feel good to know that the horses could look outside when they were in their stalls. All the windows were open tonight, as were the doors. A hot breeze swept through the open barn, amplified by the furnace fan Dan had brought over.

After turning the horses out in the pasture for a few hours, their wrapped tails ghostly appendages in the dim light, she went inside. Nicky was standing in front of the open fridge.

"Got anything to eat?"

Meg was thinking how nice it was to have Nicky with her. "Sure. Macaroni and cheese and baked beans."

"Sounds like my kind of meal."

"I bet it ranks right up there with one of Beth's gourmet dinners."

Nicky set a beer in front of Meg and took another for herself. "I figure I earned this."

Meg sat down. She still tired easily. "You certainly did. The macaroni and cheese and beans are in the cupboard."

Nicky found them and began rummaging through drawers.

"What are you looking for?"

"A can opener. Ah, found it." She opened the beans and dumped them in a pan. "You should be doing this. You know where everything is."

"I will. You can clean up. Just give me a minute."

A floor fan blew hot air around their legs. Meg's shirt stuck to her skin.

"I have to remember last winter to appreciate this heat," Nicky said. "One of Beth's partners came to dinner again last night. I'd eat macaroni and cheese and beans any day rather than listen to their conversation about work."

"Was it Nancy Brown?" Meg asked.

"No. Patricia Robson. She's head of the firm."

"What happened to Nancy Brown?"

"She joined a firm in Madison."

The water was boiling. Meg threw the macaroni in and set the timer before turning to face Nicky. "You can eat here anytime. I love the company, but you know that."

"You're a lot more interesting, except when you go on a roll about horses. I suppose talking about photography bores people too."

Meg shrugged and drained the macaroni and stirred the butter and milk and cheese in it. She dressed up the beans with onions and brown sugar, then got down a couple of plates. "Come on. Help yourself."

Nicky heaped food on a plate. "I think Beth relates better to her peers."

"You're her peer, Nicky."

"I'm not an attorney. I didn't even get my degree. Come on, let's eat on the porch." Scrappy had finished his small bowl of dog chow a long time ago, and his eyes were riveted on Nicky's plate. She nodded toward him. "Do you think he remembers when he was really hungry before he moved in with me?"

"I do." Meg followed Nicky and the dog to the porch. "You're an artist," she said, returning to their conversation. "That's better than a lawyer."

"Oh, sure. I make a pittance compared to Beth. She foots most of the expenses." Nicky sat on a chair and put her plate on another. "Go lie down, Scrappy. Stop staring at my food." She took a bite of beans and said, "The thing about Beth is I've known her forever. She's a habit."

Meg said nothing. She was listening to a whippoorwill's monotonous call and thinking how lonely it sounded. A little bit of hope, she thought, was sometimes worse than no hope at all. What a dope she was to think that maybe she was beginning to be Nicky's habit.

"My mom couldn't come today," Tina said as she brushed Sam. Hair and dirt flew around the two of them, landing on both. "Maybe next time. She loves horses and wants to meet you."

Meg was listening to the sound of a vehicle coming down the driveway, sure that it was Nicky or Dan or both.

It was neither. Jeannette came through the open door instead. "Hi, I brought Jack."

Meg was speechless. She hadn't called Jeannette, nor had Jeannette called her. "I didn't know you were coming."

Jeannette gestured with her hand. "I'll just go get him." When Meg only stared at her, she said quickly, "It's hot in the trailer." She walked out the door, and in a few minutes came back in with the horse. Born black, Jack was now a dark gray. He was tall and leggy and excited. He whinnied and Sam and Tango answered. Jeannette tied him to an empty stall.

"Here," she said, handing Meg a check for one hundred dollars along with Jack's quarter horse papers. "You can show him if you have these. It might help sell him. I really do have to go. I have an appointment with my lawyer."

Meg looked at the check and then at Jack. He was nervous. This was the part of the horse business she hated. The buying and selling of animals as if they were chattel, as if a horse didn't feel panic when it was taken away from all that was familiar. She hadn't written up any agreement about receiving ten percent of Jack's selling price either. Now there was no time.

Jeannette pointed at the check. "My cell number is on the memo line. I'll call in a day or two to see how Jack's doing." She turned and looked Tina up and down. "Are you the doctor who bought Sam?"

"Yes. Tina Rodriguez." Tina put out a small hand. Jeannette looked at it for a moment before shaking it.

"Know anyone who might be interested in a really good show

36

horse like Midnight Jack?"

"I'll ask at the clinic." But she looked doubtful.

"I've got to go now. Is it okay if I leave the trailer here?"

"Let me put Jack in a stall first." Meg didn't want Tina alone with two horses to handle, and she had to make sure the trailer was out of the way. It was collateral.

Jeannette's trailer was a silver and gray three-horse gooseneck with dressing room. Her truck bore the same colors. She climbed into the cab in dressy slacks and blouse and taupe sandals.

"I'll unhook it. Just get the trailer as close to the barn as you can," Meg said and directed the backing. It would be good advertising, she thought as Jeannette maneuvered it into place. She climbed into the bed of the truck, unhitched the ball and folded it down, then jumped out to let the legs down and jack the trailer high enough for Jeannette to drive out from under it. Jeannette leaned out the window to say that she would keep in touch and drove off with a wave.

Nicky pulled in while this was going on. "Nice trailer," she said admiringly.

"Bitch," Meg said angrily. "She just put the horse in the barn and left."

"You didn't know she was coming?" Nicky opened the door to the dressing room and peeked inside. "It looks like a miniature house in there."

She shot Nicky a frustrated look. "She didn't say thanks or how are you or is this okay. She gave me a hundred dollars and Jack's papers. I can show him anyway."

Nicky followed her inside the barn. When Meg grabbed the wheelbarrow to bed a stall for Jack, Nicky took it away and headed for the pile of sawdust in the corner of the indoor arena.

"He's gorgeous." Tina looked over the stall door at Jack.

"Isn't he? And he's show-ready. He's one in hundreds, like Sam." She had two of the best western pleasure horses in the area in her barn. How often did that happen? Her heart swelled a little with pride. "When can I start riding again?"

"Whenever it doesn't hurt."

When she could throw a saddle on again, she thought. She'd have to give it a try. She made a mental note to call Callie, her former landlady, and ask if her daughter could ride Jack and help around the barn. Tawny had been Lucy's horse. She'd been heartbroken when he died.

Chapter Four

Meg was picking sawdust out of Nicky's hair when Nicky's cell rang. They both jumped at the sudden noise, and Nicky fumbled to get the phone out of its case. It was Beth. Beth seldom called her anymore. "What's up?"

"Are you coming home this evening? I've got a pork tenderloin marinating in the fridge."

"Sounds good. What time?"

"I get home at five thirty. Where are you?"

"At the barn." She glanced at Meg, who was now untying Jack, and moved out of earshot. In the ten years she had known Meg, she hadn't been able to shake her attraction for her. When Beth had left her marriage nearly ten years ago, though, and they

39

had bought a condo together, she had taken care to maintain only a friendly relationship with Meg.

"I've got an appointment with a client in five minutes. I'll see you tonight."

Beth was standing in the kitchen when Nicky came through the garage door. Dressed in jeans and the blouse she had worn to work, she looked as lovely as she had at college. However, now she carried an aura of self-assurance that seemed unshakeable. She smiled. "Would you like a glass of wine?"

"I think I'll take a shower first." She studied Beth a moment, remembering their passion as roommates at the university. Later, after Beth had married Mark and moved to the Fox Cities, they had only seen each other a few times a week. Sex had been sporadic and exciting. Did passion usually peak and then go downhill? Was it always more exciting when it was on the sly?

The condo they shared was a sunny place with high ceilings and many windows. It had seemed so friendly at first, so light and airy. Now the rooms echoed with the unspoken grievances that were whittling away at their relationship. Where once they had so much to say to each other, there was now silence. When had they stopped being best friends, Nicky wondered, and become polite companions?

When she came downstairs, Beth was putting the food on the table. Besides the tenderloin, there was a pasta salad, a green salad and rolls. Although Nicky's mouth watered, she was wary. She couldn't remember the last time she'd come home to a meal like this, unless Beth had invited someone like Patricia to join them. "Are we celebrating something?"

"Pull up a chair." Beth poured two glasses of an expensive cabernet.

She sat down, her stomach clenching and not just from hunger. NPR was turned down so low she couldn't hear it. "What's going on, Beth?"

Beth sat down opposite her. "Let's eat. Then we can talk."

She took a bite. The tenderloin was delicious, as was the rest. In spite of a sense of impending disaster, she scarfed down everything on her plate, only then leaning back to sip the wine.

Beth looked amused. "That was quick. Would you like seconds?"

"I'd like to know what prompted this dinner. You hardly ever do this anymore."

"You're hardly ever here," Beth said mildly.

"You're the one who goes to conventions or eats out or works late."

"I don't want to fight with you, Nicky." Beth put down her knife and fork and looked at Nicky for a long moment. "I want to talk to you."

"I'm listening."

"How's Meg?"

"Is that what you want to talk about?" Nicky asked.

"Not really. You spend a lot of time at her place, though."

"Yeah. Life with you is lonely, Beth."

Beth waved away her statement with an impatient gesture. "I know. I don't blame you. Besides, you always had a thing for Meg. I'm glad now." She looked at Nicky over her wineglass. One eyebrow was slightly arched.

"And you had a thing for Nancy Brown and Patricia Robson," she shot back, her heart lurching painfully. Had they come to a crossroads? She felt as if she might vomit.

Beth shook her head and compressed her lips, and Nicky braced herself for what was coming next. "Nicky, Patricia is the senior partner in the firm. When she came to dinner a few weeks ago, she was giving me her support. I admit I went overboard trying to please her, but it's not her I've been seeing. It's Mark."

"Mark?" she said with dismay and disbelief. "Your ex-husband?"

Beth smiled wryly. "Yes, Mark. I'm sorry, Nicky. I should have told you, but you were spending most of your time with Meg."

"And you were always gone someplace where I wasn't invited."

"You're right, but those were meetings, nothing more."

"Why are you going back to Mark?"

"I'm not going back to Mark. He's running my campaign to replace Warren Hamner as county judge." She paused, but Nicky was speechless with surprise. "I trust you, Nicky."

"Trust me?" She stared at Beth, trying to understand. "Why didn't you tell me this if you trust me?"

"My opponents are going to say I'm a lesbian."

"And you're going to deny it?" Memories of her and Beth making love flashed through her mind.

"No. I'm just not going to talk about it. There are other issues."

It hurt terribly to not have been privy to this information. That must have shown on her face, because Beth said gently, "Nicky, you're not sure what or whom you want. I know what I want. I want to be a judge. I can make a difference. The system needs new people. Hamner's been behind the bench so long he's mildewed. He puts people away for years for minor offenses." It sounded like a campaign speech.

Nicky's vision blurred as she put things together. "I'm a liability, aren't I?"

Beth looked at her for a long minute before admitting it. "Yes."

"You want me to leave, don't you?"

"It will look better if we don't live together. I'll buy you out, of course."

"Couldn't you have just said so?"

"I tried. I was kind of angry about you and Meg, but I'm grateful too. At least, you won't be alone."

"*You* will be." She stood up and walked to one of the windows. A sob was working its way up her throat. She struggled to regain control. How long had she been involved with Beth? Twenty-five years? Her voice trembled when she said it aloud. "Twenty-five years."

Beth came up behind her and put her hands on her upper arms. "Nicky, this is my chance. Who knows when I'll get another?"

"So you feed me one of my favorite meals, like a convict before execution." At the moment it seemed an accurate statement, although a bit dramatic.

"I'm sorry, Nicky. I'm committed now."

"I thought you were already committed…to *me*." Nicky turned to face her.

Beth surprised her with a kiss. "One more time?"

Later, as they lay in a tangle of arms and legs, Beth said, "Stay the night."

When dawn lit the sky, her eyes popped open. Beth lay on her side, her back to Nicky. Nicky's eyes traced the curves from the bare shoulders to the slender waist to the rise of hips covered by the sheet. She slipped out of bed and into the bathroom. When she returned, Beth hadn't moved.

She dressed quickly, but not before Beth began to stir. "What time is it?" she asked.

"Early," Nicky said.

Beth leaned on her elbow and peered at Nicky. "Are you leaving?"

Nicky stared at her breasts. They had never been much more than a handful, but they were firm. Blue veins ran through them like rivers. The small nipples hardened under Nicky's gaze. "Yes," she said.

"Come back to bed. Please?"

So she did.

She showered after Beth left for work and then wandered through the condo looking at the framed photos that lined the walls. Margo could sell the ones Beth didn't want. She wouldn't have to worry about money for a while anyway, although she knew she should sock away her settlement, if that was what it was called. She checked her e-mail, then put her laptop in its case and carried it and the expensive large-format printer she used for her photos out to the car. Scrappy was lying by the door, patiently waiting for her to leave. She was in no hurry. Meg was at work. She wouldn't go to the barn till after five.

Numb with disbelief, she was unable to keep a thought and moved as if she were in a fog. She would return to the condo later for the rest of her belongings, she decided as she gathered her summer clothes and shoved those that wouldn't fit in her suitcase into paper bags. She packed her bathroom stuff and some books she hadn't read and looked around but saw nothing else she wanted.

She desperately needed someone to talk to, someone to help her digest what had just happened. How could she have been so blind and single-minded as to not see beyond her suspicion that Beth was having an affair?

Anger began to stir, working its way through the lethargy. She called Margo.

"Hey, are you busy?"

"No more than usual."

"I'll be over."

Margo opened the door and looked at her with concern. "What's the matter?"

She started to tell her and then remembered Beth saying, "I trust you." Instead she said, "I'm okay. I thought maybe you could help me with my Web site."

"Aren't we pretty well done with that?"

"Yeah. I think I'll go hunt for photos."

"It's raining, Nicky. You're all wet. Has something happened?"

"We need rain," Nicky said, knowing she wasn't making much sense. "Can I just stay here a while?"

"Of course. Have you got your computer? You can tweak your photos."

But she couldn't concentrate. After she jumped out of her chair a few times and walked around with Scrappy on her heels, Margo said, "Okay. That's enough. Tell me what happened."

"Beth and I are splitting." She watched Margo's face for surprise or dismay and saw neither. It was as if Margo had expected this to happen.

"I see. You can stay here if you like."

"Thanks, Margo." *Damn*, she thought, struggling not to cry. "I have a place to stay, I think, but if I get thrown out, I'll come here." She sat down again next to Margo, who patted her hand.

"I don't know what to say, Nicky. I know how it hurts."

"You do, don't you?" She gripped Margo's hand for moment.

She left for Meg's around five. Rain was falling in sheets. Lightning streaked toward the ground, followed by crashing thunder. Scrappy cowered on the floor. They needed rain so badly, yet this downpour would wash onto the roads and into streams and be gone. She turned onto the driveway behind Meg's truck. With her baggage in one hand and Scrappy tucked under the other arm, she sprinted toward the house. In the mudroom the little dog shook, sending spray flying. Nicky rubbed him down with an old towel, then slipped out of her shoes and padded into the kitchen, suitcase in hand.

Meg asked, "Are you moving in?"

Nicky set down the luggage and looked into Meg's questioning eyes. "How would you like a roomie?"

"You took me in. Why wouldn't I take you in? What happened?"

"She's buying me out, so I'll be able to pay rent. That's the good news, not having to worry about money anymore."

"What's the bad news?" Meg crossed her arms and tilted her head. Her hair and clothes were soaked from her own short run to the house.

"Even when you're all wet, you're one damn good-looking woman."

Meg laughed. "I think I'll change into something dry. How about you? We can talk then. Where do you want to put that suitcase?"

"Where do you want me to put it?"

Nicky moved her clothes into the downstairs bedroom Meg pointed at, then changed into dry clothes and fed the dog before going out to the barn. With Meg, the animals always came first.

The rain had stopped by the time they came inside to eat. A yellow smudge marked the horizon as the sun slipped out of sight. Meg pulled two beers out of the fridge and a pizza from the freezer. She doctored up the pizza and put it in the oven while

Nicky made a couple of salads.

Only then did she say, "Tell me what happened, Nicky."

Nicky twisted the cap off the beer and took a long drink, suddenly realizing how parched she was. She filled Scrappy's bowl with fresh water.

"If you don't want to talk about it, that's your choice."

Nicky took a deep breath. "Beth and I are splitting."

"I already know that much." Meg's gray eyes darkened.

"What else is there to tell?" Nicky shrugged. She really didn't want to talk about this right now. She might cry, which was something she absolutely wanted to avoid in front of Meg.

"You could tell me why you're splitting."

"It wasn't what I thought at all, Meg." The words, suddenly released, rushed from her. "She's not having a fling with Robson or anyone else. She's going to run against Judge Hamner next year." She met Meg's eyes, which still looked puzzled.

"So? She's ambitious."

"And I'm a liability."

Understanding dawned on Meg's face. "Because you're a lesbian?" She sounded astonished.

Nicky nodded and took another long drink. "I was blindsided too, but it makes sense. She'll lose if she's living with me."

Meg took the pizza out of the oven and set it on a hot pad on the table. "She's still a lesbian, even if she isn't living with you. Do you think you and Beth were a secret? That no one knew? My god, you've been living together for how many years now? Nine, ten?"

"This is confidential, Meg. Don't talk about the two of us in the same sentence to anyone else. Okay?" Beth's words "I trust you" kept repeating like a mantra in her mind.

"Someone will. Aren't you angry?"

Yes, she was angry and sad and disillusioned, but she wasn't going to cry. She shrugged and looked away. "Sort of, but it's done and I never had a clue. I thought she was having an affair. Guess who's working on her campaign behind the scenes?"

Meg was slicing the pizza. "Who?"

46

"Her ex-husband, Mark."

"How could she?"

Nicky went on the defensive for Beth. "I guess he and Robson want her to be a county judge. Actually, it's pretty big of him."

"Really?" Meg met her eyes. "He got her back from you, didn't he?"

She hadn't thought of it that way. Her lower lip trembled, and she grasped it between her teeth. She slugged back the rest of the beer and got another from the fridge.

Meg put a gentle hand on her arm. "Hey, don't wallow in beer. You'll hate yourself tomorrow."

"I'm just having another one with the pizza, for chrissake."

The ground steamed. The temperature had dropped, so they ate in the kitchen instead of on the porch. Nicky hardly tasted the food. After three pieces, she stopped trying to force it past the tight place in her throat. She leaned back in the chair, trying not to look miserable.

"How long has it been?" Meg asked.

"What? How long has what been?" She met Meg's gaze and saw the knowing smile. A little jolt passed through her. She raised her eyebrows. "Are you talking about sex?"

"You're free now. No guilt involved. It's a better way to forget than drinking beer."

"Ten years?" she said.

Meg got up and took her hand. "Come on."

"Shouldn't we clean up first?" There were dirty dishes and half the pizza on the table.

"I'll shove the pizza in the fridge. We can finish it later."

She looked at Meg's fair hair spread across the pillow, her undershirt and panties hinting at what was underneath and felt only a terrible sadness. She hadn't the heart. Sex with Beth had become infrequent and hurried, but last night's lovemaking had been poignant and passionate, probably because they both thought it would be the last time. She wanted what she had lost.

"I can't, Meg."

"Yes, you can." Meg covered Nicky with her body. They were

the same length. Her hair fell on Nicky's face, forcing Nicky to bury her fingers in its thickness. Meg smiled. "You've had back-to-back sex before and risen to the occasion." Meg's voice was gravelly, her eyes hooded. "I was there."

Nicky rolled her over till she was on top. "How did you know?"

"I guessed." Meg pulled Nicky's face down and kissed her. Her lips were warm and supple. "That's just a preview. Do you want more?"

"Maybe a little more." Nicky said. She'd tried so hard to resist Meg. Now there was no need.

"Take these off then." Meg tugged at her clothes.

Kneeling on the bed, Nicky stripped off her clothes, watching as Meg did the same. The passion they'd suppressed for years leaped to life. Meg's hands were gentle, her tongue warm. Nicky staved off climax with difficulty. "Come before I suffocate," Meg growled. When it was over and they were lying side by side again, they looked at each other and laughed as if intimacy between them was the norm.

Nicky signed a quitclaim deed in the title office, receiving a check from Beth in the amount of twenty-five thousand dollars. Beth had been generous. Nicky had put down seventeen thousand dollars on the condo, the amount she received free and clear from the sale of the farmhouse and land. She had also paid half the mortgage payment each month, although much of that was interest. Beth was buying the condo and contents, except for a few things Nicky wanted—a bed, a chair, a table and lamp.

"Is it enough?" Beth had asked.

"It's more than I should get. Is it guilt money, a thousand dollars for every year we've known each other, or are you buying my silence?" she said meanly and was immediately sorry.

Beth scanned her eyes coolly. "You can look at it any way you want. I think I owe it to you for all those years."

Their love affair was over, sealed with a check. She drove away from the title office while Beth was still inside, feeling set adrift by the quickness of their disentanglement. She had moved her few belongings from the condo. Now she turned into the credit union parking lot and deposited the check into her savings account. It boosted the balance to thirty thousand. Beth had been her safety net. Though, to be truthful, she told herself, her dad was her rescuer of last resort.

Could she keep this from her mom and dad? Probably not, since they knew Beth's parents. They had finally accepted Beth into the family. How ironic was that? They had moved to Florida, so she only saw them when her dad sent money for her to fly to Orlando. Here she was in her mid-forties and her dad was still sending her checks. Was she pathetic or what?

She phoned Margo. "Sold anything lately?"

"I've got an offer on the prairie chickens dancing. You've got a price of one seventy-five on it. They're offering one twenty-five."

"Hold out, will you, Margo?" She'd sat in a blind for hours, starting at predawn, waiting for just the right exposure, and practically the whole time she'd had to pee.

"You have some world-class nature photos here. You know that? You should charge more," Margo said.

"Then I'd sell nothing. I'll talk to you later. I'm going hunting for that elusive perfect photo." It was the best way she knew to make her feel good about herself. Right now she badly needed a boost in self-esteem.

Chapter Five

When Meg got home from work, and discovered a horse tied to one of her fence posts, she stepped out of her truck in disbelief. She walked toward the gelding, dismayed by what was in front of her eyes. The scrawny horse wore a filthy halter attached to a frayed rope. He stood in the hot sun, head hanging. His jutting hips, the ribs visible under the rough brown coat, tore at her heart. He swung his long, skinny neck and bony head her way, perhaps to see what was in store for him now. His brown eyes looked at her dully.

As she moved to put a hand on the horse's neck, a dog shot out of nowhere—a ball of barking, growling fury. Heart thudding, she backed away. "Easy," she said. The dog's black-and-white coat was matted and tangled with burrs and what looked like its own excretions. Its dark eyes peered out from under shaggy brows. It reminded her of Scrappy, except Scrappy was all black and when he'd shown up at Nicky's doorstep, he was friendly.

She went into the barn, pulled on an old pair of cowboy boots and leather gloves and returned with two small buckets of water. One she put down for the dog, the other she held up for the horse. Both drank greedily.

"C'mon, guy, let's get out of the sun." When she untied the frayed rope and led the horse toward the barn, the dog stood in front of her and growled. "You can bite my boots or you can come with us. Your choice," she said, brushing past the dog, which slunk along behind her.

The horses nickered and tossed their heads as she passed with the new horse, which nickered in return. Tying him outside the empty stall, she bedded it deeply. When she tried to take the filthy halter off and turn him loose in the sawdust, she saw to her horror that his skin had grown into the fabric, holding it fast. She would have to get the vet out to remove it. Speaking softly to the horse, she filled his water pail halfway and gave him a flake of hay. She had no way of knowing how long it had been since he'd eaten or had much to drink.

The dog edged its way into the stall with the horse. She looked at it for a moment. It looked back, even as it lifted its leg to pee.

"Ah, you're a guy," she said. "You're supposed to do your business outside. What am I going to do with you two?"

When she closed the stall door, the horse was munching on the hay and the dog was lying in the sawdust, chewing on his matted coat. She called the vet on her cell and went inside to change clothes and get some of Scrappy's food for the dog.

She set a bowl in a corner at the front of the stall. The dog was curled in a motley heap, its gaze fixed on her. She turned away and began cleaning stalls. *Nicky should be here by now*, she thought. She would have finished at the title company hours ago. How long did it take to sign a quitclaim deed? Maybe she was

51

out taking photos. When Meg had to work something out, she got on a horse. Nicky disappeared into the countryside with her camera.

Meg twitched the horse while the vet carefully cut the halter away from its face. She focused on the animal's nose, twisted into a knob by the rope at the end of the twitch's handle. It made him concentrate on breathing instead of the discomfort of having his skin freed from the dirty vinyl. Dr. MacIverson carefully washed and swabbed the skinned places with some dark liquid.

"Better worm him and give him a tetanus shot while I'm at it," MacIverson said. He was a small man, good looking, and tough and kind. He spit into the sawdust.

"Have you ever seen this horse?" she asked, as he carefully worked a tube up the horse's nostril and down into his stomach.

Mac, as everyone called him, poured the worming solution into the tube, held the tube high and then pulled it slowly out. Meg unwound the twitch and rubbed the horse's nose. The horse snorted and shook its head, spraying snot and worming solution. "Nope. I'd have reported the abuse if I'd seen him." He injected the horse with tetanus vaccine. "What are you going to do with him?"

She stroked the long skinny neck. "Fatten him up."

"Better have the blacksmith trim his feet."

"The dog probably needs attention too." She gestured toward the small animal in the corner.

Meg tied the horse inside the stall, and she and the vet approached the dog warily. Backed into a far corner, the dog growled. "We won't hurt you, fella," Mac said as he slipped a choke collar over the dog's head in a lightning quick movement and pulled it tight with the attached rope. The dog whined and fought, twisting against the collar. "You'll be all right," the vet soothed as he quickly slipped a muzzle over its nose. The dog gave up the fight, cowering and shaking and choking. "Hold the rope," Mac told Meg, who ached for the dog. He gently examined the small animal's body, looked in its ears, put a thermometer up his behind and checked his teeth as best he could. "He's mostly hair, not much meat on his bones. I'll give him his shots."

When Mac removed the muzzle and collar and backed away from the dog, the animal still trembled. It made Meg hate whoever had done this to these two. The horse was beaten down with hunger, the dog starved and neglected. "If you can't handle him, give me a call." He handed her a bottle of shampoo. "It'll get rid of the rest of the fleas."

"Thanks. What do I owe you?" she asked, untying the horse, hoping its presence would comfort the dog.

"I'll send you a bill," he said, looking in each stall. "You've done a good job with the barn, Meg."

"I've got Dan and Nicky to thank for that."

He paused in front of Jack's door. "Isn't this Midnight Jack?"

"Yep. Jeannette is looking for a buyer. You know anyone?"

He shook his head. "I'll pass the word, though. He's a good horse." He nodded at Meg and smiled. "Everyone needs a horse like Jack."

Nicky walked into the barn after MacIverson left. Scrappy made a beeline for the new horse's stall. He got down on his belly and was wriggling under the door, when she said, "Hey, get out of there."

Scrappy looked at her and began wriggling again. Meg caught him by his middle and dragged him out. "You might get eaten alive in there." She took a lead rope and clipped it to the dog's collar.

"Whose horse is this?" Nicky asked, eyeing the brown horse. "What happened to its face?"

"Take a look in the stall."

"Where did they come from?"

Nicky listened to the tale with disbelief on her face. "Poor guys," she said when Meg finished. "Are they both guys?"

"Yep. How did the closing go?" She studied Nicky closely.

Nicky met her eyes. "Beth was very generous." She arched a brow. "I love you in shorts and cowboy boots. Have I told you that?"

She smiled. "Yes. Now what really happened?"

Nicky's dark blue eyes looked almost black. "It went smoothly. I'm twenty-five thousand dollars richer. Life is all about money, isn't it?"

"Do I hear a little bitterness?"

"I think I've been bought off."

"I think I've been taken advantage of," Meg said, gesturing at the new horse and dog. When she wasn't looking the dog had eaten the bowl of dog food she'd given him. He had now retreated to the far corner where he eyed them suspiciously. "Already I've got a vet bill."

"I can help with expenses now." Nicky's mouth twisted wryly.

"The whole idea was to make the stable pay for itself, not to become a dumping ground for unwanted animals." For a moment she felt desperate, as if she were on her way to bankruptcy. What would happen to the horses then?

Nicky peered into the stall at the bony horse and filthy dog. "Can I let him meet Scrappy now?"

"I wouldn't advise it. The vet gave him something for fleas. They're probably abandoning ship right now."

"We should give him a bath."

Meg scratched her leg absentmindedly. "He bit my boot. Imagine what he'd do to our hands."

"I'll put Scrappy in the house."

"Buy a muzzle and choke collar. We'll bathe him tomorrow." She went into Tango's stall and took him out to the eaten-down pasture. Her cell was ringing when she came back to get Jack. It was Tina, saying she was coming over with her mother. "Do you want me to leave Sam in his stall?"

"Please. My mother will want to see him and the others. She uses a cane to get around."

Meg put Jack out with Tango. Tina's mother could look at them from afar. Alone, Tango would run like a ninny and tear the field up. She watched the two horses for a moment as they walked away together, noses to the ground. It was Jack who was

54

ready to show, his coat sleek, his wrapped tail nearly dragging the ground.

She had yet to ask Callie if Lucy could ride Jack. She hadn't seen Lucy since she bought the house and land from her mother. Actually, she missed the three of them—Callie and her kids. She made another mental note to call them. Lucy could ride out on the weekends with her brother Tony, who was working for Dan.

Tina's BMW was making its way down the driveway, stirring up dust. She parked near the barn, got out and opened the passenger door. Two legs emerged from the car, and Tina helped an older woman to her feet.

Meg walked over to greet Tina's mother. She was shorter than Tina with flashing black eyes and salt-and-pepper hair brushed into a smooth bun. Her ankles were swollen, and she leaned heavily on her cane. Meg held out her hand. "Hi. I'm Meg."

Tina's mother transferred the cane to her left hand and gave Meg a surprisingly strong handshake and a disarming smile. "My name is Rosita. Call me Rosie. Finally my daughter brings me to meet you and her horse."

"He's in the barn."

Rosie shook free from Tina's grip. "I'm not so old I can't walk alone."

"Okay, Ma, but you have to watch the ground. It's not smooth like a floor."

"I know," Rosie said and tripped over a mole tunnel. "I'm okay," she said, as Tina grabbed her arm. "My Tina worries too much."

"No, Mama, I care too much," Tina said.

Meg smiled wryly, thinking how different their relationship was from the one she had with her parents. Her parents had barely hidden their dislike of Denise. She didn't blame them for that. When they met, Denise had told them she and Meg were life partners. They had chosen not to believe her. She wished now that she had not tried to force her sexual orientation down their throats. What she had wanted was acceptance. What she got was denial.

When her parents retired and moved to Arizona. Meg had flown alone to their home in Scottsdale, had gone with them to the Grand Canyon and taken the mule ride down to the river. They had not asked about Denise and she'd not spoken of her. She would love to raft the Colorado River, but now she supposed she never would. Unless they came here, she probably would see them only in an emergency.

Rosie made her slow way to Sam's stall, where she stood looking at him for a long time. He thrust his head over the door, and Rosie ran a hand down his face. He tossed his head, and she said, "I think he wants to go outside with the other horses."

"Isn't he pretty, Mama?" Tina asked.

"He's handsome. Whether he's worth five thousand dollars, I don't know. I will have to see you ride."

Meg caught Tina's pleading glance and nodded. Five thousand? Tina had lied to her mother about how much she'd paid for Sam, but hey, so would she. "There's a bench by the tack room if you want to sit while Tina saddles Sam."

Rosie looked at Meg. "Is this horse worth five thousand dollars?"

"He's worth at least fifteen thousand," Meg said without hesitation.

The older woman smiled. "You lie, both of you. But if he makes Tina happy, it is okay."

The new horse, which had been lying down, struggled to stand, saving Meg and Tina from any further denials or explanations. Tina hurried over to his stall. The mangy dog backed into the corner and barked. "Who are these two?"

Meg was explaining when Nicky came into the barn. They crowded around the stall. The horse came forward, and Meg got him some hay.

"He is so thin."

"We'll fatten him up." That is what she'd said to the vet too, but Meg knew that fattening him up wouldn't be cheap. She went into the stall and immediately began scratching. She got out fast.

56

"The fleas are abandoning the dog. I better put new bedding in there and spray it." She'd have to wash the horse with flea soap too.

"Wait till I get the muzzle. We'll wash them both," Nicky said. She then introduced herself to Rosie, who shook her hand.

"Poor things," Tina said. "How could someone just abandon them?"

"Because they had no money?" Nicky suggested.

"You are right," Rosie said, "but the dog cringes and the horse's face shows the abuse."

Nicky's camera bag was slung over her shoulder. "May I take your picture, Mrs. Rodriguez?"

"My name is Rosie." The older woman brushed her hair back with her hands. Not even a strand had escaped the bun. "Why you want to take my picture?"

"I'm a photographer," Nicky said.

"That's what you do for a living?" Rosie asked.

Meg didn't hear Nicky's answer. She was cleaning Tango's stall. When Tina led Sam out to the riding arena, she put down the pitchfork and helped Nicky carry the bench from the tack room to the arena.

Sam craned his head, eyeing Tango and Jack in the field and ignoring Tina. "Wake him up," Meg said. "Pull his head down gently but firmly and tap him with your heels." The horse settled down then and walked, trotted and cantered around the rail at Tina's commands. "Good job," Meg said when Tina, cheeks glowing, dismounted. She took Sam inside to take his tack off and turn him out with the others.

The brown horse nickered as Sam left the barn. Meg wouldn't turn him out yet, not until he was free of fleas. Then she would put him out with either Sam or Jack.

Tina and her mother left soon after, and Meg said, "I wish my mother was more like Rosie."

"I'll bet she was a fireball in her day."

"And a beauty," Meg added, remembering the swollen feet and cane, hoping neither would be in her future.

She fed the brown horse a small scoop of grain, and Nicky

gave the stray half a cup of Scrappy's dog food. The dog slunk forward and emptied the bowl in a matter of seconds.

They went inside. The events of the day had caught up with her. Tina was the only one paying more than enough for her horse's keep. Meg might break even on Jack but the new horse was costing her money and the dog had bitten her. She slumped in a chair. "You'd think I was running one of those rescue operations."

Nicky took two Subway sandwiches out of the fridge and put them on the table along with two cold beers. "It's damn bad luck, but what if they'd been dropped off somewhere else? The horse would sell for what little meat is on him and the dog would end up at the Humane Society where he'd probably be put to sleep for biting someone."

"Well, when I run out of money, they will anyway," Meg said gloomily.

"I've got money now." Nicky put a hand on her shoulder. "Come on, eat something. You must be hungry. I am."

"You need to put that money away, Nicky." She twisted off the cap on the beer and took a bite of the tuna sub. Only then did she realize how hungry she was. "Thanks for picking these up."

"One of us has to go to the grocery store soon."

Meg sighed. "I know. It's my least favorite thing to do, next to cooking."

"I'll do it, but we have to have a menu."

"Planning ranks only a little higher than grocery shopping." She hadn't the energy to even go out on the porch. "I'm tired, Nicky." *And worried*, she thought, but then so was Nicky. She straightened her spine. "Okay. Let's do the menu. Then we can fight over who cooks."

"We'll take turns." Nicky got a piece of paper and scribbled down spaghetti sauce and pasta, burgers and buns, chicken and barbecue sauce, lettuce and red peppers and dressing, peanut butter and bread and butter, chips and salsa, and beer. "That'll keep us for a few days."

Meg got up from the table. "I'm going to bring the horses in and go to bed."

"I'll help," Nicky said, even though her heart still nervously skipped beats when Meg handed her a lead rope with a horse on the other end.

They fell asleep on their sides, hands on each other in an unfinished embrace. It was too hot to get any closer. When Meg awoke in the night, she was lying on her back with Nicky's arm over her. Gently, she moved the arm and turned onto her side. In the morning they were side-by-side, arms and hands and hips touching. It felt right. It felt good. It bothered her, though, that Nicky was bouncing from Beth to her without taking any time to grieve.

"Feel better?" Nicky asked, looking at her.

"Just like they say, everything looks brighter in the morning."

Scrappy put his paws on the bed. "I better let him out."

"Watch him so he doesn't go see the other dog." Meg set her feet on the floor. Time to feed and pick up stalls before taking a shower and going to work.

The lab was buried in the basement of the same building that housed the primary physicians. All day she led patients to her work area and drew blood to be tested. Sometimes, the patients were little kids, who sat on their mothers' laps and screamed. A few were very brave and only looked away. She stashed surprise toys to give them—a tiny plastic horse for a girl, a teensy motorcycle for a boy.

She liked the people she worked with and felt empathy for the sicker patients she saw. Once she had worked in a hospital where she'd made a real effort to cheer the very ill but couldn't seem to cheer herself. The dying who grasped at anything that might give them a few more months of life had brought her to her lowest level. She had seized the opportunity to work in the physicians' office.

Tina was in another building across town. If she hadn't been on duty at Immediate Care the day Meg hurt herself, she would probably not have met her.

When she returned home from work, Nicky was leaning on the brown horse's stall door. A muzzle, leash and choke collar dangled from her hand. A galvanized tub sat in the middle of the aisle with the bottle of shampoo the vet had given Meg. The two women studied the dog, which was backed up in the far corner. A low growl emanated from the matted hair. Like Scrappy, it was hard to tell front from back when in repose.

"Let's do it outside, so the fleas don't run to the other horses." All four horses were looking over their stall doors with ears pricked. Tango nickered and the others joined in. Of course, it was feeding time.

Meg fed and watered them, while Nicky took the tub into the yard to fill it with warm water. Back in the barn, she watched as Meg slipped the choke collar over the dog's head and the muzzle over his nose with almost as much speed as the vet had when he was there. She wore leather welding gloves and her old cowboy boots.

"You're either very brave or very foolish," Nicky said. "Did he bite you?" The cornered animal fought wildly and then gave up, collapsing into a quivering heap.

"Yep. Twice, but not hard." His jaws had trembled when he caught the toe of her boot. She leaned over now and picked him up, although she knew it meant she was in for a flea bath herself. "Let's get this over with before he dies of fright." He weighed very little and his body trembled in her arms. "He's one hungry dog. We'll feed him right after this."

When she put him into the warm water, he let out a pitiful wail. "He's probably never had a bath before."

Nicky cut off the matted hair while Meg gently washed the cowering dog. The water turned dark gray. They replaced it with fresh time after time, till it was free of dirt and suds. Fleas floated on the surface. A few climbed up Nicky's and Meg's arms.

"Yuck," Nicky said, plunging her arms into the water.

Meg lifted the dog out of the tub and wrapped him in a towel. She fluffed him up and tied him on the cement floor in the barn, then removed the muzzle and left the towel on the floor next to him.

"Okay, I'll wash the horse with this soap now. Maybe you can

60

change the bedding." She gave Nicky a tired smile. "Thanks for helping."

"Hey, you don't have to say thank you."

Meg slipped a halter over the brown horse's head and he grunted with pain. She took it off quickly and slid it over his neck instead. He stood quietly, never pulling back, as she shampooed him and hosed him off. Taking him to his freshly bedded stall, she put medicine on the wounds where the vet had cut off the halter. He looked at her out of sorrowful eyes. "Sorry, buddy." The last thing she wanted to do was hurt him.

"Let's call him Brownie," Nicky said, leaning again on the stall door.

"That's original. You want to get the dog?"

"Are you kidding? You took off his muzzle."

Meg put on her welding gloves and led the dog to Brownie's stall. Nicky put down a bowl of dog food and Meg slipped off the choke collar. The dog retreated to the far corner of the stall, ears down, tail tucked.

By then the other horses had finished eating, and Meg turned them out. Nicky let Scrappy out of the house, and he made a straight line to Brownie's stall where he wriggled under the door. She and Meg watched the two dogs touch noses and sniff bottoms as they walked stiff legged around each other.

"They can't play in there," Meg said.

"I know." Nicky grabbed Scrappy and carried him back to the house.

The night was cloudy and humid. Distant thunder rumbled. They had not eaten yet. Meg had had little chance to ride either Tango or Jack. Nor had she called Callie to ask if Lucy could ride. How would they ever be ready to show? She was exhausted.

"What do you want for dinner?"

"Salad and a peanut butter sandwich. Then I'll bring the horses in and go to bed. There has to be a better way to manage, Nicky."

"Today was so long because we had to wash the dog and horse and clean down that stall."

"I think we better wash ourselves." She had an itch on her

back she couldn't reach.

"Good idea."

After bringing in the horses, eating and showering, they collapsed in bed, too tired even for sex. "I used to have more energy," Meg said.

"You've been pushing yourself hard. It's like having two full-time jobs."

"I can't quit the one that pays." She'd thought running her own stable would be a lot more fun. Nicky lay near enough to touch hands and toes.

It rained in the night. Lightning lit the sky and thunder bellowed. Meg closed the windows, and Nicky pulled a sheet over them. Scrappy slunk under the bed. In the morning most of the puddles had soaked into the thirsty ground, and the leaves and grass looked bright again.

On Friday, between patients, Meg considered ways to streamline the chores at home so that she'd have time to get Tango ready to show. Short of hiring someone, she could think of no way.

And then she remembered Lucy, who was afraid of nothing. During her break she called Callie's number and left a message.

Chapter Six

The barn now began to routinely overflow with people around five. Tina was there nearly every day, sometimes with her mother. Tony dropped Lucy off. She groomed and rode Jack and helped clean stalls and fill water buckets. By choice, Brownie had become Nicky's charge. She cleaned his stall and groomed him and felt personally responsible that his coat was beginning to lose its dullness. The black-and-white dog crawled under the stall door when he heard Scrappy bark, but he crept back to his corner when things got busy. Nicky named him Desperado.

Mid-afternoon on Friday, after spending several mornings either tweaking her photos in Photoshop or matting and making frames for those she'd processed and printed, Nicky left Scrappy in the house and went hunting for new photos. Margo had sold several pieces of her work and needed new material. She left the driveway and headed west, passing a rundown farm a few miles down the road. A lone horse leaned on the barbed wire of its small pen, reaching for the grass on the other side. She'd seen him before and thought he might make a good photo with the background of the shed behind him. As she slowed, a girl about Lucy's age went into the pen and led the horse to a small pasture, where he stood knee deep among wild mustard. Patches of the field were worn down to dirt. She snapped a couple of quick photos from the open window before driving to the public land another mile down the road.

There she followed a trout stream into the woods. Although she had drenched herself with insect spray, deer flies buzzed around her head. She put on a hat and doggedly continued walking, knowing ticks were patiently waiting in the long grass for a warm-blooded animal like her to walk by. If she hadn't been looking down, she would have stepped on the fawn. It lay curled in a ball where its mother had left it. She took a few photos and backed away. The fawn never moved.

On the way back to Meg's, she passed the girl riding her horse bareback in the ditch. She stopped and asked if she could photograph her. The girl scowled while the horse took the opportunity to snatch at grass. Her shoulder length hair was straight and stringy, her skin red and splotchy. The horse was a small sorrel with a long back and a thick crest.

"My name is Nicky. I live down the road a few miles. I'll make sure you get copies of the pictures."

"Do you know the horse stable?" the girl asked.

"I live there."

"Those are beautiful horses. Why don't you take pictures of them?"

"I have taken pictures of them."

"My name is Allie and we're going to the stable."

"Are you?" Nicky took a couple of shots of the girl and the horse standing among day lilies and spiderwort.

"I'm looking to work there. My dad says I have to pay for

Rhubarb's keep or he'll shoot him."

God almighty, she thought. "See you there." By the time the girl and her horse got to the stable, Meg should be home.

It was nearly another hour before the girl showed up, riding the tired little horse up the driveway toward the barn. She jumped off onto the grass and stood wide-eyed, holding the horse's reins. Rhubarb bent his head to graze.

Meg was riding Tango in the arena. Tina was on Sam and Lucy was tacking up Midnight Jack. Nicky had told Meg that Allie was coming, and Meg had said she couldn't pay anyone anything, that Lucy was working for riding privileges only. Nicky had turned Brownie out in the smaller pen and was leaning on the fence.

"That's a long ride," she said to Allie, whose gaze was riveted on the horses in the work arena.

"Can I work here? I'll do anything," Allie said. The girl's eyes were the color of her hair. Hope was written all over her.

Nicky hurt for her. "You'll have to ask the lady on the sorrel horse out there. Her name is Meg."

"Oh," the girl said.

"I'll get some water for your horse. He must be thirsty." Rhubarb had not lifted his head from the grass at Allie's feet.

Nicky went into the barn, filled a bucket with water and grabbed a flake of hay to carry out to the small horse.

"Thanks," Allie said as Rhubarb sucked up the water and tore into the hay. "I'll pay you back."

"That's okay," Nicky said.

Meg now sat on her horse in the middle of the arena, calling instructions to Tina and Lucy. Her hair shone in the late afternoon sun. Allie sat on the ground, still holding the reins, still watching the riders in the arena. The hay was nearly gone.

Nicky handed the girl a cup of water and walked into the riding arena and up to Meg. "Allie is waiting to talk to you. It took her more than an hour to get here and she's been here at least a half hour." She heard the edge in her voice.

"Okay. I'm coming," Meg said, sounding annoyed herself.

She dismounted and led Tango inside. She was taking off his tack when Nicky walked in with the girl.

"This is Allie, Meg. She has something to ask you." She stood behind the kid as if to back her up.

"Hi," Meg said, finally looking at the girl. "You rode here on your horse?"

"Yes, ma'am. His name is Rhubarb and my dad is going to shoot him if I don't get a job to pay for his food."

Meg stared at the girl. "Your dad wouldn't do that, would he?"

"Yes, he would. He gave our dog away, but he can't find no place for the horse." Her eyes pleaded with Meg.

"Why did he buy you a horse in the first place?"

"When our neighbors moved away, they left the horse. I been taking care of him. He's a nice horse, but he's not near as big as yours or as pretty."

Meg pulled the saddle and pad off Tango and stood holding them as she looked at Allie. Lines were etched between her eyebrows.

"I'll put that away, ma'am, if you tell me where."

Meg looked at Nicky as if for help. "My name is Meg. I'll put them away. Everyone here takes care of their own tack."

"Yes, ma'am," the girl said.

"I can't pay you anything, but I can feed your horse. Will you brush this one and put him in this stall?"

The girl leaned into Tango, brushing his sweat-dampened coat till his nose wiggled with pleasure.

Nicky followed Meg to the tack room where she slung her saddle on its rack and hung up her work bridle. "That was nice, Meg."

Meg swung toward her. "Damn it all to hell, Nicky. She better be a worker." Her eyes looked like storm clouds. "Do you really believe what she said about her dad?"

"I don't know. It's a pretty poor looking place."

"*This* is a poor looking place."

"I'll pay for the feed," Nicky said.

Meg squeezed her arm. "You don't have to do that."

"Yes, I do, ma'am," she said straight-faced, and Meg laughed. "I thought you'd lost your sense of humor, ma'am."

"Okay, Nicky," Meg said as Lucy came into the tack room, carrying her saddle.

"That's Allie Poole out there. I went to school with her when we lived here. Does she have a horse here?"

"That little horse is hers," Nicky said.

"How well do you know her, Lucy?" Meg asked.

"I thought she was poor. She dressed poor."

"Well, she's working here so she can feed her horse."

"Oh," Lucy said. "Am I still working here?"

"Of course. You're going to ride and show Midnight Jack, if we can get his papers put in your name."

"Maybe Allie can show her horse," Lucy said excitedly.

"I don't think her horse is a quarter horse." When Lucy left, Meg added, "I think Rhubarb is a big pony."

In bed that night when Meg asked Nicky if she was going to the horse show with them, Nicky turned her head and looked into Meg's eyes. "You know, we have almost no time for each other? When we finally go to bed, we're too tired to do anything but sleep."

"I never thought this would take so much time and pay so little," Meg said, her eyes serious.

"Do you miss your life before you started boarding? You had plenty of time to ride and show then."

"Sometimes." Meg shifted her weight onto her elbow, her fingers buried in her hair.

"Have you gotten hold of Jeannette?"

"No." Meg frowned. "We're going into the second month and she hasn't sent any money or called, but you know what? I don't want to sell Jack. I'd rather sell Tango."

"Yeah? You know what? I wish I had more energy for something besides talk."

"Me too." Meg moved in for a kiss. "Think you can rise to the occasion?"

Nicky rolled Meg on her back. "I always do." She buried her fingers in Meg's hair and held her fast as she kissed her.

"Hey, this is supposed to be a joint venture," Meg said when she could talk.

When Meg was ready, her head thrown back, her long neck exposed, Nicky bent to taste the texture of her golden skin, slippery with sweat. She heard their muffled, throaty cries as from a distance, as if they came from others. For her, mingled with the intense pleasure of release was a twinge of regret that they could prolong this only so long. Like a good meal, they were too quickly sated.

After catching their breath, they looked at each other and laughed. It amazed her, this ease she felt with Meg, as if they'd been intimate for years. She thought how she and Beth had lost the fun part of making love and felt the familiar ache whenever she realized Beth was lost to her. With it came a niggling sense of guilt, as if she'd too willingly jumped from Beth's bed to Meg's.

She had no idea how Beth was faring. Was she lonely? Did she ever miss Nicky? Their relationship had gone downhill after they moved in together. Would that happen to her and Meg? Were all relationships doomed by repetition, by compromise and familiarity until making love became a chore? She fell asleep with one hand over Meg's slender wrist. It was too hot for closer contact.

The horses were running, necks stretched, hooves pounding, a stream of color racing past her surprised eyes. Meg ran with them, shouting "Whoa, whoa, whoa," her long legs and cowboy boots flashing between the horses' legs and pounding hooves. Nicky stood frozen in place, screaming, "No, no, no."

She awoke, sweating, to the sound of thunder. Rain was falling. She glanced at the clock on the other side of Meg, who slept with the sheet pulled up to her chin. Five o'clock. Faint light penetrated the gloom. She went to the bathroom before going back to bed, where she snuggled next to Meg, feeling her soft breath bathing her cheek.

Mornings during the week were always a scramble. Nicky filled water buckets while Meg picked up the stalls. Then Nicky threw a couple flakes of hay in the stalls and fed the black-and-white dog while Meg dumped grain in the feed boxes. This done they went inside. While Meg got ready for work, Nicky made coffee and fried a couple of eggs or poured cereal into bowls and popped bread into the toaster.

This morning when they hurried through the rain and threw open the barn door, they saw Allie's little horse tied in the aisle. Manure flew through the air into the partially full wheelbarrow blocking Tango's stall door. The girl hadn't heard them, probably because of the pelting rain on the steel roof. The horses had, though. Their heads swung toward the door and they nickered. Allie's head shot up inside Tango's stall.

"Did you ride here bareback in this weather?" Meg asked with obvious disbelief, even though the evidence was in front of her. The little horse's coat was wet. A poncho hung on the same hook to which Rhubarb was tied.

"We stayed mostly dry because of the poncho." Allie came out of the stall. Her tennis shoes oozed water. "It's a warm rain."

"What time did you get up?" Nicky asked.

"It was getting light. The birds weren't singing, though." The girl looked from one to the other.

Five o'clock, Nicky thought. When she awoke from the dream. "Have you eaten?"

"I don't eat breakfast."

The girl looked so bedraggled that Nicky said before glancing at Meg, "You can eat with us."

"You don't have to come over when it's raining," Meg said.

"I have to feed Rhubarb." She looked down at her wet feet.

"We'll feed your horse," Meg said. "Are you through picking up stalls?"

"Yes," the girl said proudly.

"Then you can water, while I feed. Maybe Nicky will make us breakfast."

"I can cook too," Allie said.

There was little privacy to talk about the girl before Meg left for work. Meg called Nicky into the bedroom as she dressed. "Don't let her ride the pony home in this rain."

"I could pick her up mornings, if Rhubarb stays here."

"I'll call you later when I get a break." Then she was gone.

"I'll wash the dishes," Allie said.

Nicky sat at the table, nursing a cup of coffee. "Don't you have chores at home?"

"My dad's gone today."

"And your mom?"

"Oh, she left last year. She's going to send for me."

"What about Rhubarb?"

"Maybe we can take him with us." She washed faster.

Nicky got up to dry the dishes. She ached for the girl.

Without consulting Meg, Nicky put Rhubarb in the stall next to Brownie. She let Allie give him a little hay and grain. "I'll take you home now. I'll come get you at five. Be waiting out by the road." There was no way they could let Allie stay here alone, even though she was on summer vacation.

"I'm good at cleaning houses too." A desperate look crossed the girl's face.

"There'll be plenty for you to do this afternoon." An all-day steady downpour had settled in. "I'm going right past your place."

"Okay," Allie said in a defeated voice.

Before she dropped Allie off at the small house with the open porch and the huge antenna on the roof, she asked, "What does your dad do?"

"He works for Mr. Heinz down the road. Mr. Heinz has the arthritis and can't take care of nothing anymore." Before she slid off the seat into the grassy ditch, Allie turned and asked, "You'll come back at five?"

"I will. If I'm late, wait on the porch."

She drove back to the farmhouse, where she checked her e-mail and called Margo, who said, "You must be psychic. Doreen called looking for you. She has a wedding scheduled for next Saturday and wanted to know if you'd work it with her." *The day of the horse show*. "Is your phone turned off, Nicky? I tried to reach you."

She checked. When she took nature photos, she turned the cell off. She'd forgotten to turn it back on. "I'll call her."

She hated photographing weddings. They were all alike. She'd rather go to a horse show. For years, she and Doreen had photographed weddings and other events, like the annual quarter horse banquet and awards. When the economy crashed, so had their fledgling business.

"What time and where?"

"St. Paul's Episcopal Church. Be there at three."

"Maybe I can film the reception. What time is that?"

"Have you got another job?" Doreen asked.

"No, I was going to a horse show and try to stir up a little business."

"Okay. The reception is at the Fox Valley Hotel. Think you can make it there by six?"

"Stick around until I get there. Okay?"

At five, Allie sloshed through puddles and jumped into Nicky's car. "How's Rhubarb?" were her first words even before she put an arm around Scrappy, who sat between them.

"Buckle up, kiddo. Rhubarb's fine. He was prancing in his stall when I left."

Allie laughed. "He always does that. He don't like being shut up. Your dog is friendly." Scrappy was leaning against her.

"I don't blame Rhubarb. I wouldn't like it either. Push Scrappy away if he gets too friendly."

She hugged the dog. "I miss my dog. Do you ride the horses?"

"No. I help with them, when I can. They take a lot of work." She could hardly believe how much time their care ate up.

"Will Meg teach me to ride, like she did Lucy and that other woman?"

"I don't know. Looks to me like you're already a pretty good rider, riding bareback all the way to the barn."

"I taught myself," she said proudly.

"Good for you."

"What do you do with your pictures?" Allie asked, looking at Nicky over Scrappy's prone body. His head was in her lap.

"I sell them."

Nicky turned into the driveway and drove slowly through the puddles to the barn. "Here we are."

The barn was crowded. Lucy was riding Jack in the small indoor arena. Tina was grooming Sam. Meg was cleaning equipment in the tack room. "Hey, ma'am, what do you want Allie to do?" Nicky asked, sticking her head in the door.

"Who? Oh, the girl. She can clean stalls and water and sweep the aisle. She needs to exercise her pony. He's rocking back and forth in that stall, pushing on the door."

"She'll have to ride him inside. I'll take her home when she's done with everything."

"Tell her she can walk and trot but not canter. The arena is not big enough."

Chapter Seven

Meg watched the shadows of tree branches move against the bedroom wall. When Nicky's breathing was steady, even, as in sleep, she got up quietly, put on sweat bottoms and went into the kitchen. She was scribbling numbers on the back of an envelope when Nicky found her.

"What are you doing, Meg? It's after one."

"I can't sleep." She looked at Nicky, knowing her worry showed.

Nicky sat down next to her. "How much do you need?"

"The figures don't add up. This is nuts." She leaned back in the chair.

"It'll look better tomorrow, Meg. Come on back to bed. I can help with the money."

"No, Nicky. I don't want to take anyone down with me."

"No one's going down." Nicky took her hand and led her back to bed. "Tomorrow is going to be another long day."

"I need to transfer Jack's papers if Lucy is going to show him in youth. I think I'll call Jeannette and tell her I have an offer on Jack. Maybe she'll call me back then. Besides, Jack and Sam are the only ones ready to show on Saturday and I can't ride them both in the same class."

"Well, then, don't go. I have a wedding to photograph. Something Doreen booked."

"I'd almost rather sell Tango than Jack."

Nicky turned to look at Meg. "You really want to sell Brittle's little brother?"

"He's not the horse Brittle was and I'm the only one who can ride him. And then there is Brownie. What do I do with him?"

"Can we talk about this stuff tomorrow?" Nicky asked.

The radio came on at six a.m., slowly filtering into Meg's consciousness until she made sense of it. She was awakening to news not just of the war in Iraq, but the one in Afghanistan. She wasn't a reader, but she had picked up Callie's copy of *A Thousand Splendid Suns*, and although horrified by the brutality of conditions in Afghanistan, she doubted Afghanis would tolerate American soldiers in their country any more than they had put up with the Soviets.

Over coffee, Nicky said, "You were a chatty one last night."

Meg gave her a sheepish smile as she got up from the table. "I'm sorry. I'll keep my mouth shut tonight." She brushed her teeth and gave Nicky a kiss. "See you later."

She nearly fell asleep during a lull at work. Amelia, one of her co-workers, tapped her on the shoulder as she snoozed off during a break. "Wake up, honey. Did you have a bad night?"

"Yep. My brain wouldn't shut down."

"Don't you hate it when that happens? Why worry at night when you can't do anything about anything? Want to talk about it?"

"Thanks, but I don't think there's enough time."

She remembered to call Jeannette later, when she was standing outside Tango's stall. Tina was grooming Sam nearby as she pulled her cell out of its holder, covered an ear and punched in Jeannette's number. After five rings, she got the usual message, "Leave a name and number. I'll call you back."

"Hey, Jeannette, I may have a buyer for Jack. If this falls through, though, I need a signed transfer form for him to be ridden in youth classes. Give me a call."

"Do you really have a buyer for Jack?" Tina asked.

"No, but she'll call back if she thinks I do." She turned and nearly fell over the wheelbarrow the girl, Allie, was pushing toward Tango's stall. "Hey, watch where you're going, kiddo."

"Sorry, ma'am." The kid looked stricken.

"It's okay. It's better if you take the horse out of the stall when you clean it. Can you do that?"

"Yes, ma'am."

"Meg. My name is Meg, Allie." She wanted there to be fewer people in the barn. Lucy was grooming Jack. Tina's mother had taken a seat on the bench in front of the tack room. Brownie hung his head over his stall door and nickered softly. "When you're done with stalls, would you groom Brownie?"

"Yes, Meg ma'am."

Meg stared at her but said nothing. Her phone rang. She put it to her ear and walked toward the door. "Meg here."

"Hi, Meg." It was Jeannette. "I got your message. Who wants to buy Jack? Anyone I know?"

Meg sat on her anger, thinking about all the messages Jeannette had ignored, all the calls she hadn't answered. "I need a signed transfer."

"Do you have a buyer or don't you?"

"You haven't paid Jack's board. His papers don't have to be in my name for me to show him in regular classes. I have someone to show him in youth, but his papers have to be transferred to her or her family's name. You know that. Maybe I should just deliver him to your doorstep."

"Hey, don't get all testy. I forgot. Okay? I'll have my lawyer send you a paper to sign saying you're transferring Jack for show purposes, that he still belongs to me until money changes hands, and I'll send you a signed transfer."

"Okay, as long as you also send me a signed statement that says I get ten percent of Jack's sale price. As you know, the show season is halfway through."

She gave Nicky's hand a quick squeeze as Nicky walked by with Scrappy. It was raining again and she hadn't noticed. The barn was once her favorite place, a place to escape to, but now she wanted to escape from it.

Nicky found her leaning on the fence, looking at the field the horses had eaten down to nothing. "What's up, sweetie?"

"I thought it would be different."

"Come back inside. It's cold and wet out."

"It's quiet here."

"Did you talk to Jeannette?" Nicky put part of her jacket around Meg.

"She's such a bitch. I threatened to drop Jack on her doorstep. That got her going. The only good thing that's happened since Brittle died is you." She gestured at the pasture. "They've ruined the field. I need more land."

"You could lease some of Dan's."

"How? He farms it all."

"Natalie wants to move into town. Her restaurant is making money. The farm is losing it."

"How could she ask him to give up farming?" She pulled away from Nicky and glared at her as if she were at fault.

"Hey, Natalie is strong-minded. You know that. Besides, she's pregnant and wants to be closer to work."

"When did you find this out?" How could she manage without Dan nearby?

"Today."

"Goddamnit. That's it. If they sell, so will I." But what would she do with Jack and Brownie and Tango? "What will Dan do?" She thought he loved farming.

"I don't know. You're shaking, Meg. Let's go inside. This is what you wanted. Give it a chance."

"Like I have a choice."

Tony's old car splashed through puddles. He got out and sprinted toward the barn as Meg and Nicky opened the door. "Hey, ladies, you like standing in the rain?" Tony worked for Dan. He'd be out of a job too. And who would bring Lucy out and take her home if her brother wasn't around?

As if reading her mind, Nicky said, "Natalie said Tony could bus tables at the restaurant."

"He'll love that," Meg said sarcastically. "He wants to be a farmer."

"Well, you practically have to own a mega farm to make a living nowadays."

Tina and her mother were leaving. Tina's dark eyes searched Meg's, but she only said, "Goodnight." She popped open an umbrella and held out her arm for her mother. "See you in a couple days."

The barn was suddenly quiet. Allie stood alone in the aisle. "Lucy and I watered and gave them all hay."

"Good. I'll do the rest. Nicky will take you home."

"Rhubarb?" the girl said timidly.

"He'll be fine here tonight."

When Nicky left with Scrappy and the girl, Meg filled Desperado's bowl and gave the horses grain. She hadn't felt this sad since Brittle died. It was Dan who had comforted her then, who had climbed on the backhoe and buried the two horses, hers and Lucy's. She sat on the bench and listened to the horses eating. When she felt the dog's nose on her hand, she jumped. He leaned against her leg and she cried.

Jack's papers arrived in time for the three-day quarter show over Labor Day weekend. Meg asked Allie to watch over Brownie and Desperado and asked Dan to see that she did. Dan now had sold most of his dairy herd and put the house and barn up for sale. He had offered to lease the adjoining field to Meg and put a gate in between the two, but Meg knew she couldn't swing the money. However, the hayloft was full. She and Nicky had helped Dan and Tony put up the third cutting. It would get her through the winter.

Lucy rode with Tina, who followed Meg and Nicky. The trailer carried Sam and Jack and Tango. Lucy's mom, Callie, and her partner, Vicki, had reserved a motel room near the fairgrounds, as had Tina. Meg and Nicky would sleep in the trailer.

The tack was polished and in the trailer, as were the show clothes. Meg and Nicky had thrown their bags in the trailer's dressing room, along with Nicky's camera equipment and a cooler filled with soda and beer and peanut butter and apples and oranges. Hay and grain and buckets rode in the back of the truck.

One of Meg's greatest fears was having an accident with horses in the trailer. She was a little nervous when they left the driveway and again when they merged onto Hwy. 41 going south, but by the time they reached the fairgrounds she was worried about other things, like how Lucy would get along in the show ring with Jack when she'd only shown at the county fair. Tina had never shown at all and sometimes appeared nervous and unsure. Midnight Jack and Sienna Sam were push-button horses, but their riders had to push the right buttons.

Meg unloaded the horses and handed Sam's lead to Tina and Jack's lead to Lucy, telling them to tie the horses to the trailer, one on each side. She would tie Tango next to Sam, whose stall was beside his. Sam would keep Tango calm, she hoped. Already he was eyeing the horses around him as she tied him up. She put a hand over his nostrils when he nickered. "Shhh. Behave yourself." It occurred to her that maybe she was the one she should worry about. Tango was an unknown in the show ring. Perhaps she would just ride him in the make-up arena to get him used to being around a lot of horses.

They were there early enough to ride before entering classes. Meg was already dressed in a long-sleeved shirt and jeans and boots. All she needed were a western hat and chaps. Tina was also dressed. Lucy changed in the trailer. Her mom pulled her hair back into a ponytail in front of the truck mirror.

"How are you, Callie?" Meg put a hand on Callie's back.

Callie jumped. "Nervous."

"Parents always are," Meg said with a smile, well aware of the effect she had on Callie. "Are you and Lucy ready for this?"

"I am," Lucy said confidently. "I want Mom and Vicki to buy Jack."

"Well, they can have him for fifteen thousand."

Callie looked stunned. "What horse is worth that kind of money?"

"Jack is, Mom. I'll ask Vicki."

"Don't you dare, Lucy."

Vicki had gone off with Nicky to roam the grounds. Nicky would take photos of the exhibitors and ask if they wanted them printed. The only problem these days, she'd told Meg, was that so many other people had digital cameras. But the good thing was that these people were often so busy they missed the best photo opportunities. Besides, they seldom had the lenses needed for good distance pictures.

Meg rode into the make-up arena behind Lucy and Tina. She had her hands full with Tango. The horse wanted to be next to Sam or Jack and fought Meg when she edged him in between two strange horses on the rail. She pulled his head down and urged him forward with her legs. When he began to respond to her cues, it was as if she were on Brittle again and her heart soared. But she knew he couldn't be trusted. His ears told her she didn't have his full attention. They flicked back and forth.

She walked Tango until she felt him relax under her before asking for more. On cue he picked up a trot and she moved him away from the rail in order to pass. She brought him back to a walk and asked for a canter. When he eased into that too, she considered showing him in Junior Western Pleasure.

Tina had not moved Sam out of a walk. Lucy was cantering Jack on the inside of the ring. When she passed Meg, she said something and Jack slid to a stop. Lucy nearly went over his head.

"Pay attention, Lucy. He wouldn't stop if he hadn't thought you asked for it. Let's get out of here. You don't want him sweating." Tina followed them through the gate onto the grass.

"I was having fun," Lucy said. "People kept asking me if Midnight Jack was my horse. Everyone knows him."

"It's okay to have fun as long as you don't lose focus. You understand, Lucy? You and Jack are a team. You have to be in sync." To Tina she said, "Why didn't you trot or canter, Tina?"

"I don't know if I can do this," Tina said.

"Sure you can. Sam can do it all by himself. I'll be the ringmaster. I'll tell you what to do. Okay?" She found a remote corner of the fairgrounds and asked them to walk, to trot, to walk again, to canter. "See, you did just fine. Just ride that way in the show ring."

Lucy grinned and Tina gave her an uncertain smile. They tied the horses to the trailer, and Tina and Lucy and her mom went with Meg to enter classes. Meg put an arm around Tina's shoulders. "It's always scary the first few times, but Sam will take care of you if you let him."

People had been saying hello to Meg since she got there. She ran into Janet Larson at the entry booth. "It's good to see you back, Meg. You've got Sienna Sam and Midnight Jack with you, I see."

"Good to be here. Midnight Jack is for sale."

"I talked to Jeannette about the time Sam sold. I thought we were losing him. You've got two of the best horses in the state in your stable. Congratulations."

She smiled. "Lucky me," she said, thinking how she was strapped for cash all the time. As soon as her paycheck was deposited in the credit union, she was spending it.

Meg entered Midnight Jack in Senior Western Pleasure and Tango in Junior Western Pleasure. She couldn't ride both Sam and Jack in Senior Pleasure, and it was Jack who was for sale. Tina decided to ride only in Amateur Western Pleasure, but Lucy wanted to show in both pleasure and horsemanship in youth.

"You'll have to do a pattern in horsemanship, Lucy. You sure you want to enter that class?"

"What's a pattern?"

It was posted on the side of the entry booth. *Canter on the right lead. Stop. Canter on the left lead. Stop and back. Proceed to the end of the arena.* There was a diagram along with the instructions.

"It has to be a controlled canter and a clean stop and back. Think you can do it?"

"I'll try."

"Well, don't be the first to go."

Callie paid for Lucy's entries. Tina and Meg paid their own.

Meg was near the gate when Lucy went in on Jack and stood in line with the other entries. She sat Jack like a little pro, back straight, feet under her, reins barely in contact. Jack stood quietly, only his ears twitching when a horse and rider left the line to ride the pattern. When it was Lucy's turn, Jack walked out from the line, his ears perked forward. He picked up the right lead, came to a sliding stop, took the left lead, came to another stop and backed smoothly. Lucy was grinning as he walked to join the other horses at the end of the arena.

Surprised at how tense she was at the beginning of Lucy's pattern, how much it mattered to her that Lucy did well, because if she did well it made her look good and vice versa, Meg clapped Callie on the back with relief. "She looked terrific."

"I can't take much of this," Callie said. "I'll melt into a nervous puddle."

Meg laughed. "Now if she does just as well on the rail, she's sure to place."

"I think she should win," Vicki said from the other side of Callie.

"She's so brave," Tina said softly.

Nicky aimed her camera, ready to shoot.

Lucy took second place and patted Jack on the neck as she rode out of the arena to applause, but she said to Meg and Callie as she waited for her next class, "They don't like me."

"Who doesn't like you?" Callie asked.

"Those kids. They said anyone could ride Jack."

Meg snorted. "Don't pay any attention to them. They're jealous."

"Why? I didn't brag or anything."

"Because you rode in and took second place. They've been showing all season."

"I guess I'd be mad too. He's such a great horse. They're right. Anyone can ride Jack."

"You rode well, Lucy. You deserved what you got. Didn't she, Callie?"

"You did, sweetie. You really did. I'm so proud, but watching made me so nervous."

Meg gave Callie a wry smile and Callie turned red.

When Tina rode into the ring, she looked scared. It was a large class, but Sam carried her around the arena without a flaw, avoiding other horses when he transitioned to another gait, stopping smoothly. Tina looked surprised when she won sixth place.

Meg said nothing, but she thought Sam should have won first place for performing so well despite Tina. She walked to the trailer with Sam and Tina.

"I'm sorry, Meg. I know I spoiled it for Sam."

"All you have to do is relax, Tina. He'll do the rest."

"I never was good at getting up in front of a lot of people."

"I thought this was what you wanted to do." Meg watched her dismount.

"I didn't say I wanted to show. I wanted a good, safe horse."

She said the first thing that came to mind. "I could have found you a horse that fits that description for a lot less than fifteen thousand."

Tina smiled. "Mary needed to sell him and he deserved a good home. Maybe Lucy can show him in youth after Jack sells."

"*If* Jack sells," Meg said, and added, "Sam would have to be in Lucy's name for her to show him and then you couldn't ride him in amateur classes."

When she rode into the arena on Tango for Junior Western Pleasure, Mac, the vet, who was showing his young stallion, said,

"Lucy did a nice job. There's some interest in Jack. I'll talk to you later."

She kept Tango on the rail, feeling his tenseness between her legs. His long neck and head were level as he walked and his ears moved as she spoke softly to him. "Easy. Don't embarrass us." He was walking fast and rather than pull on the reins she let him pass the horse in front of her. When the ringmaster asked for a trot, she squeezed him lightly and clucked and he picked up a trot. She felt him relax a little now that he could move. When they dropped back to a walk and she asked for a canter, his head and neck rose a little and he picked up the right lead. She could have kissed him.

Tango didn't place, but she was thrilled by his performance. It was his first show, and she knew the judge could see his nervousness. The ringmaster said, "Pretty horse. Pretty lady," as she filed out with the others.

Lucy in Youth Pleasure and Meg in Senior Western Pleasure placed second on Jack. As Meg tied him to the trailer, Mac walked over with a couple and one of the kids who had been in Lucy's classes.

"Meg, this is Laura and Tom Healey and their daughter, Chelsea. They're interested in Jack."

Meg smiled and shook their hands and said hello to Chelsea. She remembered how the girl had sawed on her horse's mouth in anger when she didn't place. She saw their looks of surprise when they saw her truck and trailer and the horses tied to the trailer.

"Nice horses," Tom Healey said. "We're wondering if we could ride the gray horse. Mac says he's for sale."

"Of course," she said. "Have you got a saddle you'd like to put on him?"

"Chelsea has her own saddle." He gestured. "It's in the trailer."

Meg untied Jack. "We'll go there. It's easier than bringing the saddle here." She felt sick. Losing Jack was bad enough. Losing him to a girl who would ruin his tender mouth was something she couldn't do.

The Healeys owned a steel gray matching truck and trailer, and Tom joked, "He matches the trailer," as he saddled the horse and gave his daughter a leg up.

"He works best on a loose rein, Chelsea," Meg said.

The girl wasn't listening. She held the reins taut and prodded Jack with her heels. He stood still, obviously confused. Meg stepped forward and loosened the reins from her grip. "Now squeeze him a little."

Chelsea looked Meg in the eyes and pounded Jack hard with her feet. He broke into a fast trot, then skidded to a stop when she said, "Whoa."

"Okay. That's enough." Meg took the reins out of her hands. Her mother said, "Get off, Chelsea."

"I haven't ridden him yet," the girl said with a stubborn set to her mouth.

Meg looked at the girl's horse tied to their fancy trailer. He was a nice little palomino gelding. His pretty head was twisted their way. He'd probably once been a good youth horse. She nodded at him. "You've already got a good horse. I noticed him in the youth classes."

"He's for sale. We're looking for something bigger, something to ride when Chelsea turns fourteen."

She turned her attention back to the girl. "You have to ride Jack his way. He wants to work for you, but you have to cue him right."

Chelsea took her feet out of the stirrups and slid off Jack, who stood perfectly still. She smacked him hard on the rump as she walked around him, and he jumped. Meg was furious. She turned and walked Jack back to her trailer, knowing that Jeannette's anger might exceed her own if she ever found out that Meg had turned away potential buyers.

Tom Healey came over to her trailer as she fed the horses. "Would it make a difference if I said I was sorry?"

"You didn't do anything," she said, getting mad all over again. "Mr. Healey…"

"Call me Tom," he interrupted.

"Your daughter will never win or place unless she changes her attitude. You ought to take that nice little palomino away from her until she changes her behavior. Midnight Jack should be appreciated, not abused."

Healey said, "I know. I was just going to ask if you'd give her lessons. Chelsea is in remission. She was diagnosed with childhood leukemia five years ago. She's undergone chemo and a bone marrow transplant. She gets frustrated easily."

He'd gotten to her, but she doubted the girl would learn anything from her. "I don't have a matching truck and trailer or a fancy barn. My facilities are very basic."

He lifted his brows. "But you're good with horses. The girl who rode Jack did well. You should have won."

"Well, I didn't." The anger was gone, leaving her feeling flat. "I'm sorry about Chelsea, but I don't think we hit it off. She needs someone more patient than I am."

"She needs someone who'll keep her in her place. My wife and I agree on this. She needs to be reined in. Pardon the pun." He actually smiled.

She tried to smile back but could only grimace. She'd be fifteen hundred dollars richer and out from under the cost of feeding Jack. Could she give the girl lessons and pay for Jack's keep that way? "Why don't we sleep on this?"

As soon as Healey left, Lucy appeared. "Don't sell Jack," she pleaded. "That girl is a brat."

"He's not mine to keep, and you shouldn't be listening in on other people's conversations."

"I'll ask Vicki. She'll buy him."

She put a hand on Lucy's flyaway hair, which was coming out of the ponytail. "Sam is a good horse too. Tina says you can ride him when she can't."

"That girl will be mean to Jack."

"That girl may be taking lessons from me."

Lucy whirled away. "I hate her."

Meg and Nicky made peanut butter sandwiches and ate chips Nicky had thrown in at the last moment. Meg wouldn't leave the horses, and Nicky wouldn't leave her. Later, she and Nicky took turns showering at Tina's motel room.

The next day Healey approached Meg as she sat on Jack, waiting to enter the arena. Lucy and Jack had won the Thirteen and Under Western Pleasure Class. "We talked to Chelsea last night. She's willing to come to your place for lessons on Jack."

"Okay. I'm available Tuesday at five thirty. That'll give Jack one day to rest. I'll give you directions later." Jack shifted his weight under her, resting a hind leg.

"I got directions from Mac. Good luck." He put a hand on Jack's rump and disappeared into the crowd of horses.

Then her class was called and she and Jack entered the arena.

On the way home, Nicky said, "You had a good weekend." She'd won Senior Western Pleasure, beating the trainer who'd won on Saturday. Tango had performed well, although he hadn't placed. After much persuasion, Tina had shown Sam again and came in third. She had looked astounded when the announcer said, "In third place, Christina Rodriguez on Sienna Sam." And, besides winning the Thirteen and Under Western Pleasure class, Lucy had placed fourth in horsemanship.

"Did you too?" Meg asked.

"I got quite a few orders. It was sort of like the first time I went to a show with you, only it was Vicki helping me out this time."

"I like Vicki." Meg smiled. Riding Tango made her sweat, because he was unpredictable, but she loved being in the arena with a good working horse. It made all the preparatory work worthwhile, and it *was* a lot of work—clipping and washing horses, cleaning tack, loading the trailer before a show, then the last-minute grooming and riding before going into the arena.

Chapter Eight

Allie was standing in the aisle, as she had been when they left. Brownie and Rhubarb nickered as the horses were led into the barn, and Desperado wriggled under the stall door.

"How did it go, Allie?" Meg asked, turning Tango loose in his stall.

"Good, ma'am." And Meg rolled her eyes.

Allie hurried to take Jack's lead, but Nicky waved her away. "Even I can handle Gentleman Jack. Meet the star of the show."

"What did he do?" Allie asked, eyes wide.

"He won or placed in all his classes."

Allie opened Jack's stall door and Nicky took his halter off. He dropped to his knees with a grunt and rolled.

"What classes?" And when Nicky told her, she said, "I want to be just like Lucy." Lucy had gone home with her mother and Vicki.

"Maybe one day you can show too." Nicky caught Meg's

warning glance and shrugged. What was wrong with giving the girl a goal?

When Meg brushed past her on her way to unload the trailer, she murmured, "Don't make promises."

Allie was right behind her to help carry in the saddles and bridles and halters and leftover grain and hay. Late in the afternoon, the girl took Rhubarb out of his stall and started to lead him out of the barn.

"Where are you going?" Meg asked. "He hasn't finished eating."

"He can finish eating in the morning. My dad gets mad if I'm not home before he gets there."

"It's getting dark out. Leave Rhubarb. He's not taking up anyone's space. Nicky will drive you home."

Tina said, "I'll take her home and bring her back tomorrow. I'm going that way anyway."

"Thank you, ma'am."

Tina laughed merrily. "Come on, Allie."

Meg was inside changing her clothes when Laura Healey parked next to Tina's BMW. Nicky saw the Prius through the window of her upstairs computer room, grabbed the photos she had taken of Chelsea on the palomino and clambered down the stairs. She hadn't been around when Chelsea had ridden Jack but had heard an abbreviated account from Meg.

She handed the three photos she'd printed of Chelsea showing the palomino to Laura Healey, who opened the folder and looked through the pictures. "What good likenesses. These are wonderful." She handed them one by one to Chelsea, who gave them back with only a cursory glance. "Aren't they marvelous, Chelsea?"

The girl shrugged. She looked a lot like her mother with reddish hair and freckles. "If you say so." Her gaze traveled over the house and pasture and barn. Her upper lip lifted on one side. "Nice place."

Nicky was reminded of Natalie when her younger sister

first came to live with her at the insistence of their parents. She ignored the sneer. "I'll show you the barn. Meg will be out in a minute. She just got home from work."

Chelsea glanced at her watch. "It's five thirty. Didn't she tell us to be here at five thirty, Mom?"

Laura Healey reddened. "We'd love to see the barn." She put the prints in the Prius. "I'll write a check for these before we leave. Okay?"

Nicky said, "Thanks," and led them into the barn.

"What a dump," Chelsea mumbled, and Nicky thought Meg had been right in her assessment of the girl. She was a hard case.

Tina was saddling Sam, Lucy was grooming Jack, and Allie was cleaning stalls. They looked at Chelsea and her mother. Tina stepped forward with a welcoming smile and introduced herself. Allie stared with curiosity. Lucy scowled fiercely. Nicky introduced them all.

"How nice to meet you." Laura smiled, shaking Tina's hand. "I watched you ride. Congratulations. I'm envious. What a busy place." Nicky thought she was much too nice to have produced this surly child.

"We didn't see this brown horse at the show. Isn't he pretty!" Laura exclaimed.

Nicky looked at Brownie with new eyes. He had filled out. His coat shone. His mane, no longer shaggy and burr-filled, lay flat with a little flip on his long neck. The changes had been so slow that she'd hardly noticed them. He nodded his head, impatient to be out of his stall.

Desperado shot out from under the door where Brownie was standing, startling them all but especially Chelsea and her mother, who took a few steps backward. At the same time, Nicky noticed Scrappy running their way. She had left him in the house. She said quickly, "The dogs won't hurt you. Desperado here sleeps in Brownie's stall. They're sort of inseparable."

Laura put a hand on her chest. "I love dogs. We have a miniature schnauzer. He's really Chelsea's dog." She smiled at her daughter, who looked away.

Meg was striding toward them, wearing an old pair of jeans, a wrinkled T-shirt and cowboy boots. As usual, her hair was tied in a high ponytail. "The dog escaped when I opened the door, Nicky." And to Chelsea and her mother, "Sorry you had to wait. One of those long trains stopped me on my way home from work. Did you have any trouble finding the place?"

"No. Mac gave good directions," Laura said.

"Good." Meg eyed Laura's daughter. "Are you ready to ride, Chelsea?"

"I brushed Jack," Lucy said.

"Thanks, Lucy, but from now on we'll let Chelsea get him ready when she's here." Meg's arms were crossed. "Did you bring your saddle?"

"It's in the car," Laura said.

"I'll get it," Allie offered.

"Thank you, Allie, but Chelsea can carry her own saddle." Meg uncrossed her arms and put her hands in her back pockets. "Would you brush Tango for me, Lucy?"

Nicky saw the hurt expressions on the girls' faces. They worshipped Meg and thrived on her approval. Meg said to Laura, "Did you see the pictures Nicky took of Chelsea and her horse?"

"We did. I ordered some at the show. They're in my car."

Allie hurried to open the door for Chelsea, who was lugging the saddle. It wasn't the same one she used for show, Nicky noted. There was no silver on this one. She dumped it on its horn on the aisle floor near Jack, who was still tied in front of his stall. He turned his long neck to look at her.

"You want to get him ready, Chelsea?" Meg said. "Allie will show you the grooming equipment and his pad. We won't need the bridle this time."

Chelsea stomped toward the tack room behind Allie, who seemed clueless to Chelsea's anger. "That's my horse down there at the end." She pointed. "His name is Rhubarb. That's because he's a sorrel, like Tango."

Chelsea stopped and glared at Allie, who said, "Jack's a star.

I haven't ridden him yet. I rode Brownie, though. He's a good horse too. Somebody left him and the dog tied to the fence. They were starving."

Chelsea showed some interest. "Are you for real?" she asked as they disappeared in the tack room.

Allie was still talking when they came out. "I work here so that Rhubarb can stay. My dad was going to shoot him."

A flicker of shock crossed Chelsea's face. Her mother gasped.

Meg said, "Okay, Allie. Let Chelsea tack up Jack."

"Can't I help?" Allie asked.

"I don't need help," Chelsea said crossly.

Nicky put an arm around Lucy, who looked like she was going to cry. "I hate her," Lucy said under her breath. "She's a spoiled brat."

Nicky sighed. "Why don't you go help Allie? I'll be outside with Mrs. Healey."

"I want to see her ride. I'll bet she's not as good as me."

"Not this time, Lucy," Nicky said, guessing this was going to be hard enough for Chelsea and her mother without everyone watching. "You and Allie groom the horses and clean the stalls."

Tina was already in the riding arena, working Sam. Chelsea had plodded out to the center of the arena slightly behind Meg, who had attached the longe line, a long lead, to Jack's halter. Meg checked the girth for tightness. "Okay, Chelsea, you can get on now."

Chelsea grabbed the saddle front and back—she couldn't reach the horn—hopped three times and pulled herself up far enough to throw a leg over Jack's back. When she sat upright, Meg adjusted the stirrups and told her to put her feet in them and to put her arms straight out from her shoulders, like she was flying.

Nicky and Laura had stopped talking. Laura said, "What if she falls off?"

"She won't," Nicky assured her, although she was thinking the same.

"Heels down a little, sit deep in the saddle and keep your eyes on where you're going," Meg said.

"Should I leave?" Tina asked.

"Nope. Keep riding. Are you ready, Chelsea?" The girl was looking straight ahead. She gave a slight nod.

Meg clucked once. Jack started walking. Meg fed out the lead line till the horse was on the rail, walking behind Sam. Tina asked Sam for a canter. Jack continued his flat-footed walk, head down and neck level with his withers until Meg said, "Squeeze him gently. No, don't put your arms down and don't look at me."

Meg made the kissing noise, and Jack picked up a soft trot. His head and neck bobbed a little. "Sit deeper, Chelsea. Move with him."

"Wow," Laura said. "I never would have believed this had I not seen it."

It was the first time Nicky had seen Meg give a lesson this way—no reins, arms out, like a cross.

Tina and Sam were in sync with Jack. They were trotting too. Tina's reins hung loose. She looked relaxed. Nicky said, "Way to go," when she passed.

"Sit tight, Chelsea. You're going to ask for a canter now. Touch him with the outside foot, so that he picks up the inside lead." When Jack didn't immediately canter, Meg said, "Normally, you'd lift the reins a little when you tap him. Tap him a little harder." Jack's ears twitched and he lifted himself into a rocking horse canter, following Sam around the rail. A hint of a smile crossed Chelsea's face.

Her mother clapped her hands. "Look at her. No hands. Doesn't she look great?"

"Cool, Mom," Chelsea said as she and Jack flowed past.

"Good," Meg said, looking pleased. "Sit tighter, Chelsea. Keep your heels down. You're going to ask him to stop. You know the word. You say it."

"Whoa," Chelsea and Tina said in unison, and both horses put their hindquarters under them and stopped.

"Good. Both of you. You can put your arms down now,

Chelsea. I think that's enough for today. We'll put a bridle on him, if you decide to come again."

Chelsea dismounted, jumping the last foot or so to the ground. Meg walked up to her, unsnapped the longe line and replaced it with a lead rope. "Now you can take him inside, remove his tack and brush the sweat off him."

Nicky saw the exchange up close. Meg smiled at the girl, and Chelsea ducked her head and led Jack away.

"Why no bridle?" Laura asked.

"I wanted to show her that Jack works best with no pressure on his mouth." Meg gave them a pleased smile. When Laura turned away to go into the barn, she winked at Nicky and held the gate open for Tina and Sam.

"Thanks, Tina. You were just what we needed."

"Thank you. It was a good lesson. Add it to the tab."

Meg threw back her head and laughed, and Nicky longed to kiss her neck. When Tina was out of earshot, she said, "You're sexy when you take charge."

"Well, you're pretty hot yourself. What are you doing tonight?"

"What do you have in mind, boss lady?"

"A little orgy maybe."

However, Dan knocked on the door when they were cleaning up the dishes. It was dark out. "Come on in," Meg said, a dishtowel in hand. "Can I get you a beer?"

"Sure." He sat at the table, took off his ball cap and ran his fingers through his dark hair. "We found a place to live near the restaurant. We have an offer on the farm, but I guess you know that." He twisted off the cap and took a swig of the beer. "I've got a job in construction. I'm a pretty good welder. What I want to say is if you ever need help out here, all you have to do is ask. And if Meg won't ask, you ask, Nicky. You hear?"

"I hear," she said. She didn't know he had an offer. "Why would I know about any offer? Natalie never tells me anything."

Meg wiped her eyes on the dishtowel. "Goddamnit, Dan.

Why can't you raise your kid here?"

Dan smiled sadly. "Hardest thing I ever did was sell the cows. Probably the smartest thing too." He looked as gloomy as they did, slouched back in the chair with his long legs stretched out under the table. "Tina made the offer. It's contingent on someone buying her place."

Nicky said as if she'd misheard. "Tina?"

"Yeah. Surprised the hell out of me. She said she'd make the barn into a stable like yours and help you out."

Meg looked stunned. "How? By taking boarders away from me?" Like herself and Sam?

"I don't know, but that's what she said. She wanted to help you out. I'm sorry, Meg."

"Yeah. Me too."

"The market's bad. So you probably don't have to worry about her selling her place." He drained the bottle and got up. "Thanks. I mean it about letting me know if you need anything. I feel like I'm letting a lot of people down. Tony is going to work for Herman Heinz, so he can still bring Lucy out."

"That's where Allie Poole's father works," Nicky said. "Allie's dad was going to shoot her horse, rather than feed it. That might not be a good place for Tony to work."

Dan frowned. "I know Dennis Poole. I like him. He and his daughter live in that little house on Heinz's property. It's free and it's just the two of them. Dennis bought her that pony after her mother died of cancer. Why would he shoot it?"

Meg looked at Nicky. "You said her mother left them, that she was coming back to get Allie."

"That's what Allie told me."

"I think that's one troubled little girl," Dan said. "It's a shame she goes around telling people her dad would shoot her horse."

"And gave away her dog," Nicky added.

"They didn't have a dog as far as I know. Heinz has a dog, though." He put on his ball cap, looking more like the Dan they knew. "I have to go home. We won't be leaving till the crops are in."

After he left, Meg put her face in her hands and mumbled,

"I thought maybe he would change his mind. Damn your sister, Nicky. She's behind all this."

"I don't understand how she could do this to Dan and you." Nicky took one of Meg's hands, forcing her to raise her head. "Dan will come if we need him," she said, knowing Meg would never ask.

"I guess you can't count on anyone," Meg said. She wiped angrily at the tears on her face.

"Don't cry, sweetie. You can count on me." Nicky seldom used the same endearments with Meg that she had with Beth. The switch in allegiances had been maybe too abrupt, even though she'd always had a thing for Meg.

"And if Beth wants you back?" The tears were gone. Meg's gray eyes were clear.

It was as if Meg could read her mind. "She doesn't want me back, and I wouldn't go anyway." She was ninety-nine percent certain of that.

Meg said, "We've been taken in by a thirteen-year-old kid."

"I know, and I felt sorry for her. I think she and Lucy were hurt when you were so dismissive."

"Lucy will be riding Sam if Jack sells. I can't be worrying about hurting someone's feelings all the time. They'll get over it."

"Lucy hates Chelsea."

"Does anyone like Chelsea except her parents?"

After Meg fell asleep, Nicky lay awake a long time. She had seen Beth around noon when she'd met Margo and a client for lunch. Beth was in a booth with Mark and Patricia, and Nicky thought her heart stopped for a moment.

"Want to go somewhere else, Nicky?" Margo asked.

She'd stood rooted to the floor. Margo took her arm, but before she could respond, Beth looked up and saw her. She gave Nicky a small smile and a nod of acknowledgment. Nicky let Margo lead her out of the restaurant.

"I never saw that suit before," she said to Margo as if that was important. The Beth Nicky knew would have come over to say hello. She wouldn't have dismissed her as if Nicky had never meant anything to her.

"Let's try the restaurant down the street," Margo had suggested to the client, a woman who was interested in Nicky's photography.

She went to sleep, wondering why Beth's new suit, one she had never seen, was important to her.

The next day was cool, windy and cloudy. It suited their moods. Meg hardly said a word, as if there were nothing more to talk about, when there was everything. What to do about Allie, for instance, and more importantly, how to behave around Tina.

Nicky was taking shots that day of the woman who had gone to lunch with Margo and her. She was writing a book, which was all she'd talked about while eating her sandwich. Nicky remembered nothing of what she said, nor had she eaten her own lunch, but she knew the woman wrote a column in the local newspaper and wanted a professional photo to go with the byline and a photo to send with her manuscript.

She drove to Margo's, where a backdrop had been set up for the photos. The shoot took about forty-five minutes, which included loading the photos on the camera's memory card onto Margo's computer and the journalist choosing the one she wanted. After the writer left, Margo asked Nicky if she was all right.

"Of course," Nicky said and asked, "What was her name again?"

Margo said flatly, "You're not over Beth."

"I was just surprised to see her."

"Wearing a new suit," Margo said, hands on hips.

"Stupid, huh?"

"No. It means your relationship with Beth is unresolved."

Was it? Nicky wondered. "She resolved it for both of us."

She left Margo and went in search of Natalie. It wasn't a good time of the day to confront her sister—the staff was getting ready for lunch—but she was still fuming. She walked through the front door and into the kitchen, where the chef and wait staff stared at her in varying degrees of horror. "Where is Natalie?" she asked, as her sister came out of the walk-in refrigerator with her arms full of lettuce.

Natalie did not appear surprised. "Hi, Nicky. Let's go sit at a table."

She studied her sister carefully, but saw no telltale bulge of pregnancy under her white apron. "Congratulations," she said grimly as they sat at a small corner table near the kitchen's swing-through doors.

"Thanks, but that's not why you're here, is it?" Natalie's eyes, so like her own, never wavered.

"I'm happy for you and Dan about the baby." She leaned on the table. "It seems to me a farm would be an ideal place to raise a kid."

"Dan is ready to call farming quits. He's hung on financially because of people like Meg who depend on him."

"He didn't sound very happy about it when he came over and told us."

Natalie looked away. "Yeah, I know. When I said I wanted to be closer to work, because of the baby, he seemed to think it was a good idea. But the closer we got to selling out the sadder he seemed."

The anger that had propelled Nicky here all but vanished. "Then why sell?"

Natalie shrugged one shoulder and avoided Nicky's eyes. "The cows are sold, the farm is on the market, there is an offer on it."

"Yeah, from Tina, who wants to turn the barn into a stable. She's Meg's only paying boarder."

"I know." Natalie met Nicky's gaze again. "It's too late, Nicky. We can't buy more cows and start over. Tell Meg I'm sorry."

Nicky got up. "You tell her, Natalie."

Natalie was chewing on her upper lip. She said nothing when Nicky walked away.

Chapter Nine

Tina's car was parked in the driveway when Meg got home from work. Meg changed clothes and threw herself on the bed. The thought of talking to Tina as if everything were the same made her feel slightly nauseous, but she had scheduled a riding lesson for this afternoon. It was a cool, windy day, and the last thing she wanted to do—no, not quite the last thing, which would be giving Chelsea a lesson—was stand in the riding arena and shout words of encouragement to Tina as the wind snatched her voice away.

She was hoping Nicky would come home, so she wouldn't have to face Tina alone, but the house was silent, except for the humming of the fridge. Tina's move to buy Dan's property had been so unexpected. To lose Tina might signal financial disaster, but to lose Dan was like having a safety net snatched out from under her when she was falling from a great height. She fell asleep, curled on the bed like a prawn.

The knock woke her with a start. Tina was standing in the open doorway, dressed in jeans and jacket. "I thought something had happened to you."

Meg put her feet on the floor. "I'll be right out."

"Is it okay if Lucy rides Jack?"

"When I get there," she said curtly.

Tina disappeared from the doorway and Meg pulled on her boots, grabbed her jacket off the hook by the back door and went outside. The wind caught her hair and she tightened the elastic band that held it off her neck and face. There was still no sign of Nicky.

The barn was warm and redolent with hay and horses, smells she loved. She thanked Allie who had brushed Tango and got his saddle and pad out of the tack room.

"Can I ride Jack?" Lucy asked. Her flyaway hair was also tied back in a ponytail.

"Sure," she said. She'd meant to tell Allie to ride her horse home, but it was cold out and Rhubarb's only shelter was the open fronted shed. She wouldn't take her annoyance out on the pony. She told Allie instead to turn him out in the riding arena with Brownie when they were through riding. She hadn't asked Allie if she had ridden Brownie as she'd told Chelsea. She figured it was just another lie.

Tango was antsy, having been cooped up in his stall all day. He pranced sideways beside her as she led him out to the arena. She felt him arch his back when she threw a leg over the saddle. She pulled his head up from his knees and squeezed him into a trot to burn off energy.

Sam and Jack were not their usual well-behaved selves either. They wouldn't settle down and work till they'd had a chance to move. A scared look appeared on Tina's face when she felt her control slipping. Nastily, Meg hoped she was having second thoughts as to how she was going to manage Sam on her own.

After she worked the kinks out of Tango, she sat on him in the middle of the arena. She told Tina and Lucy to tie their reins to the saddle horn and assume flying positions with their arms as she'd made Chelsea do. Even though she could see Tina's fear, she made them walk, trot and canter in this position. Tina grabbed the saddle horn several times but gamely put her arms out again as if she were on a cross.

"This way you learn to trust your horse and maintain your balance," she said at the finish. "Good job, Lucy," and then because Tina smiled bravely, "You did well, Tina."

Instead of going into the barn, she took Tango out in the field and rode around the fence line, working off some of her frustration and anger. When she led Tango into the barn, it was almost dark. Tina was gone, having apparently taken Allie with her. Lucy had also left. She'd heard the unmistakable sound of Tony's car roaring up the driveway.

She put Tango in his stall and went to get Brownie and Rhubarb out of the riding arena. The horses were shadows at the far end of the ring. Desperado slithered under the gate and streaked across the pen, startling her. He nipped at the horses's heels, dodging their kicks, herding them across the space toward where she was standing. Amazed, she looked down at him as he sat on his haunches, panting, looking pleased.

"You're part border collie, aren't you?" she said, bending to pat him. He moved away from her touch, but later, after she'd finished feeding, he leaned on her leg as she studied Brownie over the stall door. She was thinking that she should ride him. She'd guessed he was a thoroughbred, maybe taken off the track, no longer making any money for his owner. Neither he nor the dog resembled the animals that had been tied to her fence. Both had shiny coats and bright eyes and just the right amount of meat on their bones.

"What do you think, Desperado? Think he'll make a good hunter jumper?"

The dog's tail brushed the aisle floor. She made no move to touch him.

She was eating when Nicky came in the door. "Where have you been?" she asked with some heat. She'd started to worry when it turned dark.

"Driving around, taking pictures." Nicky's hair looked as if she'd been raking her fingers through it. It was what she did when she was upset.

"After dark?" she asked, certain that it had something to do with Beth. It had all been too easy, the transition from Beth to her.

Nicky looked in the fridge.

"Finish up the leftover chicken. I made a salad too."

Nicky leaned against the counter, eating. "Was Tina here?"

"Yep. She brought Allie."

"You can look her in the eye, knowing what she's doing?"

Meg leaned back in her chair and crossed her arms. "I made Tina and Lucy ride without reins, arms out, like Chelsea. It scared her, but Lucy thought it was fun."

"Yeah? I hope it scared the shit out of her."

"I wanted to make her wonder if she'd be able to control Sam on her own. Of course, Sam will take care of her. She doesn't trust that yet." She had this ache in her chest that wouldn't go away. It hurt to breathe. To her the betrayal was huge. She didn't know what to do with it. "Did you get some good photos?"

"I took this woman journalist's picture today at Margo's. She writes the business column for the paper, and now she's writing a book about how to start a company. What a talker. The three of us went to lunch yesterday. I thought she'd never shut her mouth."

When Meg said nothing, Nicky asked, "What?"

Meg shrugged. "Nothing, Nicky. I'm tired. I think I'll shower and go to bed. You can clean up."

As she turned the water on and closed the curtain, Nicky climbed into the tub with her. "I'll wash your hair."

"Okay." Meg put her hands on Nicky's waist. "I'll do yours when you're done with mine."

Meg closed her eyes against the soap and let Nicky's fingers massage her scalp. Nicky's hands were still buried in Meg's hair when their mouths met in a gentle kiss. Meg was glad her tears would go down the drain unnoticed, when she realized that Nicky was crying too. She slid her arms around Nicky's slippery body and pulled her close. When the water began to cool, they washed each other and stepped out of the tub, dry-eyed.

In the dark bedroom, Nicky said, "I saw Beth in the restaurant yesterday. She was wearing a new suit."

"How is she?" Meg asked, wondering about the significance of the suit but too tired and disheartened to ask or even try to figure it out.

"I didn't talk to her. Margo dragged me out the door, but Beth saw me. She nodded as if we were mere acquaintances."

Meg said nothing at first. Scrappy's quiet snores filled the silence as she turned her back. She failed to understand how anyone managed to be friends with an ex. After the passion and the fighting ended, what was left besides bad feelings? She never wanted to see Denise again. In fact, she had no good memories of Denise and shuddered at the thought of ever having had sex with her. She said, "Sorry, Nicky," although she wasn't sorry.

Nicky tucked herself up against Meg and Meg scooted backward into her embrace. She was almost asleep when she felt Nicky's hand between her legs. "Not tonight," she mumbled.

"Yes, tonight." Nicky turned her on her back and attempted to coax her into passion.

"I want to sleep, Nicky." But, of course, Nicky's gentle stroking roused her to respond. It wasn't the roll-around-the-bed romp that they often had, but a tender teasing touch that brought them both to a healing climax. At least, Meg was soothed by it. She just hoped she wasn't a surrogate Beth.

The next afternoon the sun came out and the winds died down. Chelsea's second riding lesson was that day. Meg thought about what she would do with the girl and Jack. Maybe fifteen minutes of riding without reins. If Chelsea used the reins as told, Meg would let her have them.

Chelsea was in a mood almost as foul as Meg's. Meg didn't know what to do with her anger at Tina, her dismay with Dan, her impatience with Allie, all of which nearly overwhelmed her whenever she came home. She directed it at Chelsea, who snapped back.

"I didn't pull on his mouth. I just asked him to stop and he kept trotting."

This was true, but Meg suspected the girl was squeezing Jack when she'd said whoa. "Try it again. Trot around the ring and ask him to stop." When the same thing happened, Meg took the reins away. "You're giving him conflicting cues."

"I'm not and I'm not riding without the reins."

"Okay then. Get off and put him away. I don't have time for this." She turned her back on Chelsea and caught sight of Laura Healey standing at the fence. The look on her face made Meg swing around. Chelsea was jerking on the reins.

Meg pulled her off the horse and handed her the reins. "Put him away and if I catch you hurting him again, I won't give you lessons."

"I don't want your stupid lessons. What do you know? Your barn and trailer look like they're for cows."

Her anger turned to surprise. She almost laughed. She snatched Jack's reins from Chelsea and led him away. That Jack might go to this spoiled brat—Lucy was right—made her feel even worse than she had before.

Chelsea's mother followed Meg into the barn. "I'm sorry. Her best friend moved away. Not only her best friend, but her only friend."

Meg was surprised she had any friends. "I can't help her if she doesn't want me to."

"I know. I won't bring her back until she's ready to apologize and to listen." Laura Healey sighed. "She was such a nice little girl."

Meg shot a look at Chelsea's mother. "She's thirteen."

"And she knows every day that the cancer might come back."

"I'll try to be more patient." Meg remembered some of the patients she'd worked with and wondered how she'd react if she feared a return of some life-threatening illness.

"We want you to treat her like you would any other kid."

Meg nodded. "Fair enough."

Laura left and Meg got Brownie out. She brushed off Allie's offers to groom him, telling her to ride Rhubarb, who was rocking back and forth in his stall. "He needs exercise. Take him out in the ring."

"I don't have a saddle."

"Use Lucy's. She won't be here today." She knew she was avoiding talking to Allie about her lies. She didn't know how to confront her or even if she should. She also couldn't afford to feed Rhubarb all winter. Even if he didn't eat as much as the horses, he took up space. But every time she decided to tell Allie to take him home, she found a reason not to. It was cold or rainy or hot. Today would be a good day, but she was unable to tackle any more unpleasantness at the moment.

Curious about Brownie, she saddled him. She had to stretch to put her foot in the stirrup when she mounted him out in the arena, where Tina and Allie were riding. He trotted sideways and chewed on the bit, and she felt his power between her legs. She asked Allie to open the gate to the pasture. Holding her breath, she let him trot once around the field, a jolting trot as he fought the bit, before she let him go. He bolted as if out of a starting gate. Her eyes watered at the speed. He jumped the creek and never broke stride, and she wondered if he would stop when asked. As he was about to pass the gate the third time, she tightened the reins. "Whoa," she said, realizing by then that Brownie had only been taught go. Desperado shot out from under the gate and nipped at the horse. The dog somehow avoided being trampled. Brownie turned and slowed before breaking into a trot. He was blowing hard, and she trotted him out with Desperado running beside them.

When she dismounted, her legs were shaking. She had felt as if she were on an unstoppable force. She led Brownie through the arena into the barn, sensing Tina's and Allie's eyes on her.

"I was frightened for you," Tina said when she tied Sam outside his stall.

Meg's heart was still thudding. "Me too." She turned to Allie. "I heard you tell Chelsea you rode Brownie."

The girl had her back turned. "I did," she said, "without a saddle."

"Where did you ride him?" Meg asked.

"Over there." Allie pointed at the small indoor arena. "He didn't run."

"Don't get on him again or any of the horses when I'm not around."

"I won't," Allie said in a small voice.

"You won't what?" Meg insisted.

"I won't get on any of the horses when you're not here."

Meg was tired of being angry, tired of facing people who made her feel that way day after day. She was beginning to hate the barn, which had been her favorite place to be. "You don't have to come over every day, Allie. School's started again now, hasn't it? You must have homework."

"I do it at school," Allie said, finally looking at Meg. Her face was contorted as if she might cry. "Why do you hate me?"

Shocked, Meg said, "I don't hate you, but I do know some of the things you told us weren't true."

"I didn't lie. My mother went away, and she's going to send for me."

Did that make Allie's mother's death bearable for the girl? Meg wished she'd never started this conversation. "And Rhubarb? Where did he come from?"

"My dad bought him at an auction." Allie looked sullen. Her eyes shifted away from Meg's.

"Why would your dad shoot him if he bought him for you, Allie?" She spoke gently.

"'Cause he eats more than he cost." The girl leaned against Rhubarb and began to sob.

Meg wondered if the tears were an act. Even when Tina went

over and put her arms around the girl, Meg persisted, "I've heard otherwise, Allie. You can continue working here if you tell the truth. Otherwise, I'm going to have to let you go." As if she'd ever hired the girl. She did feed her horse, though.

"I'm not lying," the girl wailed, burying her face in Tina's chest.

"I can't trust you if you tell stories."

The sobs turned into hiccups and stopped. "I just want to work here, that's all."

"Okay. Did your dad say he would shoot your horse?"

"No," Allie said almost inaudibly.

"All right. You can keep Rhubarb here till someone else needs his stall."

"Can I come and help?"

Meg felt like a shit. "Yes." She refused to look at Tina, who said, "I'll take you home, Allie."

When they left, Meg fed the animals and sat on the bench. She didn't want to go inside till Nicky came home. Desperado crept out from Brownie's stall and leaned against her, looking at her with soft brown eyes. She put a hand on his head. He flinched but stayed put, and she felt ridiculously honored. "You're quite a dog, you know that?"

She tried to coax him out of the barn into the now dark night, but he scrambled on his belly back in with Brownie. In the so-called yard—Meg seldom mowed—she paused to listen to the insect serenade and look up at the dizzying array of stars.

It was cooler now. She was blanketing the show horses, keeping them as sleek as possible. There was an open show on the weekend, where she planned to show Tango. He needed the exposure, not Jack or Sam. She considered asking Allie's dad if she could show Rhubarb in youth horsemanship and the pony western pleasure class as sort of a reward for coming clean. Besides, she needed written permission from him for Allie to even be helping around the place. Callie had long ago sent a note thanking Meg and giving her the right to decide what and when Lucy rode.

On a whim she jumped in the truck and drove to Allie's. The lights were on in the small house. She stood on the open porch and knocked. A deep voice from inside told Allie to get the door. Allie pushed it open and stared at Meg with widened eyes. She looked as if she were caught in a trap. "Please don't tell my dad. He'll take Rhubarb away."

Meg understood. Allie thought she was going to tell her dad his daughter was a liar. She said, "Ah, but you're doing it again."

"I won't do it no more. I promise."

"Would you like to show Rhubarb on the weekend?"

"What?" the girl stammered.

"Who is it, Allie?" The man coming up behind Allie with a hot pad in his hand was not much taller than Meg. He was balding and thin with smallish features, like Allie's.

"It's Meg. She owns the stable where I work." Allie looked from Meg to her father, the worry apparent on her face.

"Well, ask her in. Where are your manners, Al? Come in, ma'am. It's a cool wind blowing out there."

Meg smiled and stepped inside. "I don't want to interrupt your meal. It looks like you're cooking."

"I am. Would you like to sit down with us? We've got leftover stew and beets, lots of it. Allie here fixed the beets, didn't you, Al?"

Meg loved it, him calling her Al. She could see the entire living room without turning her head. It was small, with a worn rug and well-used furniture. A television stood in one corner. In the other was a bookcase with paperbacks on the bottom two shelves and photographs on the others. Beyond the living room she saw part of the kitchen.

"She's got the horses to take care of, Dad."

"Do you like beer, ma'am?" Allie's dad asked.

"Yes, and call me Meg." The smells from the stew made her hungry. Her stomach growled.

"I'm Dennis," he said, shaking her hand. "I appreciate what you done for my daughter. Come in the kitchen. It's coziest in there."

It was surprisingly so, she thought, as she sat down where there was no plate and poured her beer into the glass he gave her, although she usually drank out of the bottle. The bright overhead light and white walls and cupboards lit the room up like daylight.

"I'm here, Dennis, because I need written permission for Allie to work at the barn. I'm not paying her. I'm just feeding Rhubarb."

"You don't have to feed Rhubarb," he broke in earnestly. "I have hay and oats to burn."

"Really?" she said, eyeing Allie, who ducked her head. "There's an open horse show this weekend. I wondered if Allie might want to show Rhubarb in a couple of classes. I'm taking my young horse."

"What about Jack and Sam? Aren't they going?" Allie broke in.

"Nope. They don't need to go to an open show. Tango does, and quarter horse shows don't have classes for ponies."

"I want to ride Jack or Sam."

"Do you know how rare a good pleasure pony is?" she said.

"Rhubarb is a horse," the girl said stubbornly

Meg sighed inwardly. "I measured him. He's almost a horse, but he's much more valuable as a pony." Seeing the girl's longing, she said, "Maybe you can ride Sam at the barn. You'll have to talk to Tina about that."

"Who's Tina?" Dennis Poole asked, putting a plate of stew and beets in front of Meg. "You've got to eat, Meg, or we can't." His cheeks creased upward with his smile. "It wouldn't be polite, would it, Al?"

He was an easy man to talk to. He told her he always wanted to be a farmer but had never had the capital to buy his own land and equipment. He was buying Herman Heinz's farm on a land contract that allowed Herman to stay in the house.

When she mentioned Dan's place being for sale, he said Heinz was interested in some of the land. When he said the crop was poor because of the long drought, he looked at Allie. "Allie here is not going to have to worry about the weather. She's going to college, aren't you Al?"

"Maybe I'll ride horses instead."

"Have you got homework?"

"No. I done it at school."

"You can clean up then."

"I'll help," Meg said.

"No need. I'll write you that note now."

She was trying to figure Allie out on the short drive home. She'd lost her mother. She lived in near isolation and poverty. Maybe the girl had convinced herself that her mother was alive and going to send for her. And would Meg have let Allie work at the stable if she hadn't thought she was saving Rhubarb?

Nicky stormed out of the house when the truck bounced up the driveway. Surprised to see the house, the yard and the barn lit up, Meg was sure something bad had happened.

"Where have you been?" Nicky asked, hands on hips. "I nearly called the police."

"I go away for a few hours and you're ready to call the cops?" she asked, slightly amused. "I'm usually the one who's here when you get home, not the other way around. Come on, Nicky. My truck was gone. So I was gone. Why would you be alarmed?"

"You should leave a note or call me."

"Like you call me when you stay out late? Where were you when I left? It was dark out." Why were they arguing about something so silly?

"I don't know where I was. I'm used to coming home to you. I sort of panicked. Stupid, huh?"

She put an arm around Nicky. "No. It's sweet. Let's turn out all these lights and go inside."

In bed, after telling Nicky about Allie's dad, she murmured, "Why don't you know where you were?"

"I went to the condo. Beth changed the locks."

Meg had been sleepy, till then. "Did you forget something?"

"We never had a burglar alarm. The police stopped me two blocks away from the place. Someone must have given a description of my car. Probably that bitch of a neighbor. She was always asking who you were when you stayed with us."

Meg asked, her alarm growing, "Did they arrest you?"

"I told them I just moved away and went back to get some of my stuff. They called Beth. They knew her, of course. She said it was all right, that she forgot to give me a key. Then she asked me to come to her office."

She could hardly believe that Nicky had done this. "What did she say?"

"That if I pulled that stunt again, she was going to file charges."

"I'm sleeping in the other room." Meg snatched her pillow and headed for the guest bedroom.

Nicky followed her. "I thought I could talk to you about anything. Do I have to lie?"

Meg hurled the pillow onto the double bed and turned on Nicky. "Yes, please lie. Are you nuts, Nicky? Breaking and entering is a crime. Why would you do such a fucking stupid thing?" She climbed between the sheets and put the pillow over her head.

Nicky slid in next to her. "I didn't really break in. I just tried to open the door with my charge card, like they do on TV. It doesn't work. Twenty-five years and she dumps me because it's a good political move. I should have spent the last ten years with you."

She heard Nicky through the layers of pillow. The last sentence made her feel less like a booby prize. "You're going to spend the next ten years in jail if you do that again."

"You know how many times I wanted to fuck you and didn't because I wasn't going to risk my stupid relationship with Beth?"

"How many times, Nicky?" She put the pillow under her head and noticed how musty the room was. She should air out the house. She should clean it, but she'd rather clean the barn.

"Practically every time we were together. Do you just cast somebody off like a dead layer of skin? I didn't do that to her. I should have told her to stay with Mark."

"What is it about Beth that you can't let go of? Do you want to be her friend or what?"

"Yes. No. She cut me off like I was a turd or something."

The visuals were too much for Meg. She laughed. "And I'm going to cut you off too if you keep this up. Let's go back to bed number one." And she laughed again. "Get it?"

"I get it, potty mouth," Nicky said, pouncing on her, so that she was pinned face down on the bed.

"Not tonight, honey, and I mean it." The "honey" was not an endearment.

Chapter Ten

Nicky went along to the open show because she had nothing else planned for Saturday, and she had to stop following Beth around like some kind of pervert. After she'd seen her in the restaurant, she had become sort of obsessed with what Beth was doing, who she was seeing. It wasn't as if she would go back to her even if Beth asked her to. Yet she had sat in her car one night after dark watching Patricia Robson and Mark Forrester and other people meet in Beth's living room. She hadn't told Meg about any of this, especially after Meg's anger about her being stopped by the police after trying to get into the condo.

Meg wanted nothing to do with Denise, her ex, she knew, but Denise had been and still was a crazy woman. Nicky recalled how Denise had parked at the end of the road, spying on Meg.

How was that different than what she had been doing?

It was a warm, dusty fall-like day. Tina was working her one Saturday a month at the clinic for the uninsured. Lucy was with her dad. Dry leaves scuttled across the ground in front of a slight breeze. The grass was brittle underfoot. She wandered the fairgrounds while Meg and Allie got their animals ready to show.

Allie was so nervous she kept running to the Porta Potti. Meg had told the girl she'd done that at her first show too, that everyone did. Right now Meg was riding Tango in the make-up arena while she coached Allie on Rhubarb. It looked to Nicky like Rhubarb had been shown before. He was working a lot better than Tango.

She snapped photos of Rhubarb and Allie, dressed in jeans and a long-sleeved shirt and Lucy's hat and boots. The girls were the same size, and Lucy had eagerly lent her show clothes and saddle. When Allie rode out of the show ring, looking dazed, clutching a second-place ribbon, Nicky photographed her again.

"You know, you're really a nice person, Meg," Nicky said.

"Don't go telling people that." Meg was sitting on Tango, waiting to go into the Junior Western Pleasure Class. "I think Tango is about to make a fool of me." The horse moved nervously sideways, looking at the animals around him like he'd never seen another horse.

Meg was all business in the show ring. It was amazing to watch her control something so big with a touch of her leg. Her hands were light on the reins, her voice always soft. Tango seemed to know who was in command and except for a little flare-up when he first went into the ring, he responded well. When she made the cut, Meg patted Tango on the neck.

They stopped at Allie's on the way home. "Do you want me to unload Rhubarb?"

Allie, who was sandwiched between them, shook her head. "He's lonely here. Can't I go back to the barn with you and clean stalls and stuff?"

"Nope," Meg said. "We'll take Rhubarb, though. Your dad will want to hear about the show. You rode well, Allie."

Allie looked miserable. "Thanks, but Dad doesn't care if I go to the barn."

"We'll see you tomorrow." The school bus dropped her off at the end of Meg's driveway now. Lucy usually rode the bus with her.

The girl slid out of the truck and crossed the road, shoulders hunched.

"You sure her dad is a nice guy?" Nicky asked.

"Yep. She can't live with us, Nicky. I get tired of having people around all the time."

As Meg unloaded Tango and Rhubarb and handed the pony's lead to Nicky, the horse and pony nickered loudly, which almost made Nicky drop the rope.

In the arena a swaybacked, nearly white horse was leaning on the fence. Except for looking old, he was in pretty good shape. Tacked to the fence post was a note. When Meg ripped it off, a plastic bag fell to the ground. Meg read the note and thrust it at Nicky.

This is Champion. He's a good horse. We're moving and can't take him with us. Thank you. In the bag was a hundred dollars.

"Does this place look like a home for old horses?" Meg said angrily. "Why are people dropping off their unwanted animals at my barn?"

"I don't know, Meg. Maybe word has gotten around that you take in horses."

"I can't afford to feed them. There's no room in the barn for this animal." Champion was trying to nose Tango and Rhubarb.

"Maybe he was a champion once." Nicky looked at the old horse. *What must it be like to be given away?*

"Well, that does it. Rhubarb has to go home. We've just run out of stalls."

"Why don't you put them in the field?"

"So it will never recover?" The grass had been eaten to the ground in places.

It was dark before they were able to go inside. Nicky got a beer out of the fridge. "Want one?"

114

"No. I'm beginning to hate this place, Nicky." Meg slumped in a chair.

"Me too." She took a swig of beer. "Why not sell Jack to the Healeys?"

"And let Chelsea destroy a great pleasure horse?"

Nicky shrugged. "You're the one being destroyed." She sighed and sat down across from Meg. "Look. There's more to life than horses and horse shows."

A glare from Meg shut her up. "Go, if you don't like it here. I knew you wouldn't stay."

Stunned, Nicky stared at her. "Where would I go?"

"I don't know, Nicky." Meg looked deflated. "Back to Beth? Then you wouldn't have to spy on her."

"She doesn't want me and I don't want her." A headache was gathering at the back of her neck. "I should never have told you about the condo thing."

"You're right. I didn't want to know." Meg stood up. "I'm going to bed. It might be better if you sleep in the other room."

Nicky made a peanut butter sandwich and ate it while waiting for Meg to finish showering. Only when Meg's bedroom door shut did she step into the tub. She went to the extra bedroom with Scrappy on her heels. She continued their argument in her head till she was dreaming it.

The sound of Scrappy's tail thudding on the floor awakened her. Meg whispered "Shhh" to the dog, and climbed in with Nicky, who said, "Having second thoughts?"

"I brought the dog his bed. The floors are so hard and cold."

Nicky put an arm over her. "Scrappy says thanks." Again, the tail swept the floor.

"I'm sorry, Nicky."

"Does that mean you want me to stay?"

"You're the only one I trust."

"Is this okay, or should we move to bed number one?"

"This is good."

Nicky lay awake a long time, staring at the ceiling, thinking about ways to make it better for Meg.

The next morning she set out for Dan's, hoping he would be there. He was showing Dennis Poole the combine, which was parked near the road with a FOR SALE sign on it. He introduced Nicky to Poole, and Poole said, "My daughter hasn't shut up about the ribbons she won yesterday. Thanks for taking her along."

"Thank Meg," Nicky said. It wasn't her doing. She leaned against the big tire of the Massey Ferguson she had mowed roadsides with years ago, noticing the rank odor of weeds still emanating from the six-foot mower behind it. Maybe tractors didn't wear out like cars, she thought. When Poole left, saying he'd get back to Dan about the combine, she said, "Have you sold the land yet, Dan?"

"I'm not going to sell it. I'm going to lease it to Herman Heinz. Poole is moving into the house. They'll be using the barn for storage."

"So you're not selling to Tina?" Meg would be thrilled, she thought.

"My great-grandfather homesteaded this land. I can't sell it. You're wrong about Tina, though. She wanted to take in the freeloaders."

Nicky stared at him. "We thought she was going to take Sam away. Why the hell didn't she tell Meg?"

"It was supposed to be a surprise," he grunted. "Besides, I said she wanted to help, didn't I?"

"Someone dumped another horse yesterday while we were gone—an old, white gelding."

"I'll lease Meg the twenty acres next to her field for ten bucks a month. There's already a shed there. I'll even put in a gate."

She smiled. "I think I like you better than my sister."

"The cows were losing money every month, Nicky. I didn't have a choice." He looked away. "Heinz took some of them."

She wouldn't ask where the others went.

"You want to help put that gate in?"

She rode on the running board of the tractor out to the fence. Dan cut the wires to make space for a gate, and the posthole digger drilled the holes. She held the posts while he tamped the dirt in around them. He hung the gate, and she handed him the tools. "You tell her, Dan. Okay? It's better that way."

"I'll stop by on my way to the restaurant this afternoon." He kicked some more dirt around a post. "Funny, isn't it? How the restaurant at the end of the food chain makes more money than the person who grows the food?"

"It's not funny, Dan. It's wrong," she said.

"Yep," he said, climbing on the tractor, waiting for her to hop on the running board. "Where's the dog?" he asked over the roar of the diesel engine.

"Home. He sleeps a lot more than he used to. He's at least eleven."

He parked the tractor out front with the rest of the machinery.

Meg was thinking about Tina when Dan showed up. How Tina acted as if nothing had happened. How she looked hurt when Meg walked by without speaking or answered a question curtly. It was hard for Meg to be civil around the woman, but she needed the checks for the board and lessons.

Figures ran constantly through her head. Grain costs, vet costs, blacksmith costs and those were only the horse expenses. When she added on the mortgage and taxes and gas and food and insurance, it never equaled her income, even with the extra money for board and lessons. At the end of the month she always withdrew from savings. Bankruptcy was where she was headed, especially once Tina pulled out.

"Hey, Meg, you got a minute?"

She was mad at Dan too, but she owed him too much to be anything but civil. "Sure."

"Can we go inside?" he asked.

She thought he must have more bad news but couldn't imagine what it might be. Her dream had become a nightmare, making her wonder why she'd wanted a stable in the first place. She walked into the kitchen ahead of him. There was no sign of Nicky, but the dog was there. He surprised her when he jumped all over her. Nicky was probably out taking photographs or at Margo's. Nicky was keeping her nose above the financial waters—just—but then she had a twenty-five thousand dollar safety net.

"Want a beer?" she asked.

"No, thanks. I want to talk to you about the twenty acres adjacent to your property. I thought maybe you'd like to lease it. I'm not going to sell it."

She stood with hands on hips, studying his face. "I can't afford it."

"For ten dollars a month you can. Your pasture can regenerate. There's a shed in that field. The stream runs through one corner."

Meg's mind raced. She desperately needed pasture. She'd even thought of asking Allie to take Champion home with Rhubarb. "That's nice, Dan, but there's no temporary fix."

His eyes bore into hers until her gaze wavered. "Don't be a goddamn fool, Meg. I already put a gate in."

"I don't care about having a stable anymore. Tina can board the horses."

"I don't think so, and you'll care when you have to take them to auction. I know."

"I'm sorry about the cows."

"Yeah well, that's what happens to old cows. There's something else you need to know."

His words rattled around in her head, as she tried to digest them. She said nothing for a few moments. "What?"

"Tina was going to leave Sam here and turn the ones who don't bring in any money out on pasture."

She frowned, angry that Tina hadn't let her in on her plans, upset because of all the nights she hadn't slept and the days she'd gone around with Tina's betrayal eating her up. "Why didn't you tell me?"

"She only told me when I said I was leasing the land to Heinz." Dan stood up. "So, where's my ten dollars?"

"At least twenty a month," she said, trying to look serious but unable to squelch a smile.

"Fifteen," he said, putting out a hand. When she took it, he said, "Done," and looked pleased. "It includes the goats."

"I knew there was a catch. Randy?"

"Yep. And Pete."

She couldn't wait to tell Nicky. "How are we going to get along without you, Dan? Who's going to help fix fence or put up hay?"

"You and Nicky and me. Just give a call." He smiled. "I gotta go. Natalie is expecting me."

"She's expecting, period," Meg said as a sort of stupid joke and laughed at his sheepish smile.

He left and she changed out of her work clothes and went to the barn. She would try to find Brownie a home, maybe with the hunter jumper people. She would turn Rhubarb out in Dan's field, and Champion could keep him company. She was saved, at least temporarily, as long as no one else dumped any more horses on her property. She thought she should feel a lot better than she did, though. The sick feeling she'd been carrying around was gone, but so was her enthusiasm. She longed to be back at the beginning, when it was just Tango, before the stable became a second job. Whatever made her think she'd like a barn full of people and horses?

Tina's mom was sitting on the bench. "How are you, Rosita?" Meg asked.

"Good, Meg. I'm leaving for my son's home in Minneapolis, so I thought I'd come say goodbye."

"Are you coming back?"

"Oh, yes, but probably not till spring. Tina has a boyfriend now."

"Oh, Ma. He's just a good friend."

Meg stared at Tina, who was saddling Sam. She was full of surprises. For the first time since she'd heard about Tina's offer on the land, she spoke to her in a friendly way. "I talked to Dan today. He's leasing his property, not selling it," she said quietly, so that no one else heard.

Tina flushed. "Yes, I know." She shot a look at Meg, who

rested one hand on Sam's rump.

"Why didn't you tell me what you had in mind? I would have slept better. It's bad for my health to be so angry."

"I know. I was going to tell you when I bought the land."

"What would you do with a barn full of horses?"

"I was going to turn them out—Brownie and Rhubarb and now Champion. I thought it would make room for more horses here."

"I'm leasing the twenty-acre field next to ours. We can turn them out there."

Tina's face lit up. "That's great, Meg, isn't it?"

"It is." She ran her hand down Sam's rump. "Your board and lessons help, Tina. That's all I need."

Tina nodded. "I'm ready for a lesson right now."

"Why don't you just ride, you and Lucy and maybe Allie. I'm going to take my horse down the road." She was tired of giving lessons.

She was leading Tango out of the barn when the Prius carrying Tom and Laura Healey and Chelsea arrived. She waited impatiently for whatever they had to say. When only Chelsea got out of the backseat, she said nothing. The girl flinched when her eyes met Meg's.

Chelsea spoke so fast that she hardly understood. "I was rude and I apologize."

"Okay," Meg replied after she pieced it together.

"Where are you going?" Chelsea asked.

"Down the road."

"Can I go too?"

"Lucy's riding Jack."

Chelsea looked at the riding arena. "I want to ride like her."

The kid had guts, Meg thought, to eat crow like that. "Okay, but not today. May I talk to your parents?"

"Sure." She stepped aside. "She wants to talk to you and Dad, Mum."

Laura and Tom got out of the car. "Can you bring her out tomorrow?"

When Laura thanked her and said she would, Meg threw a leg over Tango and rode down the road toward Dan's. It was almost October. The leaves were turning and yellow cornstalks rustled in the field. She breathed in the smells. Tango saw a rock and shied, and she calmed him with her voice and legs.

Tina's BMW with Rosita in the passenger seat and Allie in the back passed her, all of them waving. Again Tango came undone. Tony had already gone by to pick up Lucy. He'd lifted a hand as he roared past and Tango jumped into the ditch. It was near dark when she put her horse away. Desperado wriggled out of Brownie's stall, and she bent to pat him while she read the note Tina had left on the tack room door. *Horses have fresh water and hay. The dog is fed. See you soon.*

Nicky was sitting on the porch in the dark. "Hungry?" she asked when Meg came looking for her.

"For you."

"Yeah? Want to eat in bed?"

"Depends on what we're eating." She took Nicky's hand and led her inside.

"What happened?" Nicky asked.

"Later." Meg pulled her T-shirt over her head and wiggled out of her jeans. "Come on. Get those things off."

"You used to do that for me. Does this mean the honeymoon is over?" Nicky jerked off her shirt and shorts and dropped them on the floor.

Meg looked at Nicky for a moment as she sat naked on the bed. "Lie down," she said. When Nicky did, Meg sat next to her. "Look at me," she commanded, her eyes on Nicky's. With light fingers she traced Nicky's collarbones and her upper chest before cupping her breast. She caressed the other breast and slowly worked her way down the ribcage to the navel. She paused there before sweeping her palm gently across Nicky's belly to her pubic mound, where she lingered a moment before plunging her fingers into Nicky's depths.

Nicky maintained eye contact as she lifted her hips toward Meg's touch. With an indecipherable sound, she reached for Meg and pulled her close.

"What the hell, Meg?"

"Are you complaining?" Meg said into her mouth, her fingers moving.

"Let me enjoy it. Don't make me come right away."

"Can't you come more than once?"

"I don't know. Wait, Meg." But it was too late.

Nicky put her hand over Meg's, stilling her fingers. "Damn. I think you've just ravished me. Now it's my turn."

"You know what happened today?" Meg asked and began to tell her.

Nicky kissed her nose and chin and the soft place between her clavicle and neck. Her mouth moved over Meg's breasts, her belly, lingering over her navel.

Meg pulled her up so they were face to face again. "You aren't listening."

"I am. I think it's all wonderful." She buried her fingers in Meg's hair and kissed her mouth.

"You already know, don't you?" Meg said, taking Nicky's face between her hands and looking into her eyes.

"What do I know?" Nicky asked.

"Did you have something to do with this?"

"With what?" Nicky grasped Meg's wrists, trying to free herself.

"Dan told you, didn't he?"

"Yes. I helped him with the gate. Was that so awful? He told me about Tina's plans for the farm. I thought it was better for you to hear it from him. It was his idea to lease the field to you, though. It wasn't mine."

Meg rolled away. "He'd make more money leasing the field to Heinz."

"Just once can't you be grateful? It's his way of making himself feel less guilty." She massaged Meg's shoulders and back, her tightly muscled bottom and thighs. When there was no resistance, she rolled her over and did to Meg what Meg had just done to her. "Now we're even," she said.

122

The next afternoon Meg heard the car coming down the driveway as she was changing clothes. Laura Healey and Chelsea were waiting by their car when she went out into the October day. Everything that still had leaves had turned golden—trees, crops, bushes—under a blue, blue sky. A bit of chill rode on the breeze. "Hi, Laura," she said with a smile. She genuinely liked Chelsea's parents. How could she not? "Ready, Chelsea?"

Chelsea dragged her saddle out of the backseat. "Can't wait." She was a fragile-looking girl with pale skin and high cheekbones like her mother. Her reddish hair was tied back in a sloppy ponytail. She and Laura trailed Meg into the barn. Lucy and Allie looked up from what they were doing. The horses nickered. The barn smelled like fresh-cut hay and horses. Meg breathed in the odors.

Chelsea plunked the saddle down near the tack room and tied Jack in the aisle. Allie ran over to her with a currycomb and brush, and Chelsea thanked her.

"I won second place at the horse show last weekend," Allie said. "Rhubarb is the best pleasure pony in the world."

Chelsea said, "Yeah? Are you going to ride this afternoon?" Jack grunted with pleasure as she leaned into the currycomb.

"I've got to clean stalls. Besides, I don't have a saddle yet. Lucy let me borrow hers for the show. She's riding Sam today, because Tina can't come. She was going to be here, but she had to go somewhere else."

Sure enough Lucy was putting her saddle on Sam. "Did you talk to Tina, Allie?" Meg asked.

"She said I could ride Sam too. Lucy and I are taking turns."

Meg decided to ride Tango later or to just turn him out for a while. She followed the girls to the riding arena. It was as if Chelsea had morphed into someone else—a polite teenager, eager to learn. Allie jumped on Rhubarb, and all three girls rode without reins, practicing their balance. When they took up the reins, Meg put them through their gaits. She stood in the middle of the ring in a haze of dust.

She noticed Nicky standing at the fence, talking to Laura. "Stop," she yelled. "Okay, now back a few feet." When the horses stood still, the girls looking at her for the next command, she said, "Why don't you walk around the field, show the horses something else besides this dusty arena?" She opened the gate for them.

As Chelsea rode out, she asked, "Does this mean I passed the test?"

"You've got a nice seat. We just have to work on the hands," Meg said. She didn't trust the sudden change in Chelsea, *not for one goddamn minute*, she thought.

She walked through the dust to the fence, and Laura asked, "How did she do?"

"Pretty good. Is this new attitude for real?"

"I think so. She was practicing riding without reins at home on Sunny. That's her horse."

"The palomino," Meg said.

"She wanted to come back. She said it was fun here."

"No kidding," she said doubtfully, watching the girls. They were riding side by side with Rhubarb in the middle. She'd love to listen in on their conversation.

Nicky was about to flip the hamburgers sizzling in the frying pan when Scrappy whined. "Will you let him out, Meg?"

"Sure." Meg opened the door and stared with disbelief. Desperado was sitting on the stoop, his tongue hanging out. "Come on in," she said opening the screen wide. The black-and-white dog slunk inside, trying to get past Scrappy, who was jumping around him, letting out little barks of excitement. "Hey, look who's here."

Nicky put a treat under Desperado's nose, handing Scrappy one at the same time.

When they ate supper, Desperado sat by the door. Before they went to bed, he wanted out and Meg walked with him out to the barn. A nearly full moon lit their way. She turned on the lights and the horses nickered. Champion was lying down.

Meg wondered briefly what she would do with him. Desperado slithered under Brownie's door and the brown horse nosed him in greeting. When Brownie went on pasture tomorrow, would the dog go with him? She hoped he'd stay with her.

On her way back to the house, she paused to look at the sky. This was the harvest moon. Combines were crisscrossing fields, their lights on. She was shuffling through fallen leaves. The maple near the house clung to a few bright orange ones that rattled in the slight breeze. She wondered if she'd still have the property next spring. It was doubtful. When her savings were gone, she would lose it. And the horses? She'd already decided she would transfer Tango to Nicky so he couldn't be sold as an asset.

Chapter Eleven

Nicky was framing prints, when her cell rang. "Hey," she said without looking to see who was calling.

"Hello, Nicole. It's your mother." As if her mother had to identify herself. Nicky would never mistake her for someone else. No one else called her Nicole. "Your dad's in the hospital. He had a heart attack on the golf course."

"Oh, God." Her dad had always seemed indestructible. When her mother was in a rage at something stupid she'd done, he would say, "Bad things happen, Nicky," and pat her on the back. Then he'd calm her mother down by saying, "Now, Cleo, it was an accident." It wasn't always an accident, like when she got caught smoking in the school john. Her mother had been livid, not because she had been smoking, but because Cleo had been called into the principle's office and scolded. Cleo did not take kindly to humiliation.

"Can you come see your dad? He asked for you and Natalie."

"Of course, Mom. I'll call Natalie. Will you pick us up at the airport?"

"Rent a car."

"Okay, Mom. Is Dad real bad?"

"He's in ICU at Leesburg Regional Medical Center." Her mother's voice broke, which was so unlike Cleo that Nicky thought her dad was dying. "Mom?" But she couldn't think of anything comforting to say, except, "I'm sorry, Mom."

"So am I, Nicole."

When she called the restaurant and asked for Natalie, the person who answered said, "She can't come to the phone right now. Can I help you?"

"This is her sister, Nicky. Our father has had a heart attack. Please put her on." She sounded calm, but she was actually in turmoil. There was so much to do—call the airlines, pack. What should she pack? She had few good clothes anymore, because she seldom wore anything besides jeans or shorts. Her mother would be distressed if she wore either.

Natalie, who took most things in stride, sounded panicky. "Dad had a heart attack, Nicky?"

Nicky told her what their mother had said. "I'm going to book a flight now. I'll call you back."

"Okay. Nicky, is he going to be all right?"

"Of course, Nattie," she said, not just to comfort Natalie, but herself. "Talk to you soon."

She looked up the airlines on the Web, booked a flight with Delta and called Natalie back. This time her sister answered the phone. "Tomorrow morning at seven. Can Dan take us to the airport at five?"

Then she clambered downstairs and threw clothes into a suitcase. In the very back of the closet in the guest bedroom was a dark blue skirt, white blouse and a navy blazer she'd bought to wear to the interview at the Tech for the job she didn't get. She

127

would wear the blazer over her one pair of dress slacks on the plane. The skirt was in case something unthinkable happened.

When Meg came home, Nicky was putting her toothbrush and shampoo in a plastic bag. Meg stood in the bathroom door in her work clothes. "Are you going somewhere?"

"My mother called. My dad is in the hospital, in ICU, Meg. He collapsed on the golf course." She still couldn't quite believe it. She'd never given much thought about her parents being mortal. How old was her dad? Seventy-two?

"Oh, Nicky. I'm so sorry. When are you leaving?"

"Five tomorrow morning. Dan is taking Natalie and me to the airport." She was crying. Meg rocked her back and forth in her arms.

"What can I do?"

"You're doing it." She turned in Meg's arms and pressed her wet cheek against Meg's warm skin.

She pulled her seatbelt tight and looked out the window as the Boeing 737's engines revved at the end of the Outagamie County Regional Airport runway before take off. Her eyes were streaked with red as much from lack of sleep as from crying. Natalie looked even worse, if that was possible. Her hair was disheveled, her clothes wrinkled. Nicky knew her mother would notice these things and be displeased.

As the jet lifted in the air, she turned to Natalie. "Do Mom and Dad know you're pregnant?"

Natalie shook her head. "They'll know when they see me." It was obvious now, and Natalie was doing nothing to hide her condition. She wore a shirt that stretched across her belly.

Last night Meg had curled around Nicky, holding her tight whenever she gave voice to her fears, till they both finally fell into an exhausted sleep. Meg had dropped her off at the restaurant before five. "Call me when you get there," she'd said, leaning across the truck seat to kiss Nicky on the cheek.

Natalie fell asleep after they changed planes in Chicago. Although so tired that she felt as if she had no strength, Nicky stayed awake till they landed in Orlando. They gathered their luggage at the carousel and rolled it to the National Car Rental desk. Nicky had gone to MapQuest and printed a map with written directions to The Villages the day before. Was it only yesterday that their mother had called? It seemed much longer.

With their luggage stored in the back of the rental, Nicky drove in a daze. Once she was out of town and heading toward The Villages, she turned the wheel over to Natalie. Still, she couldn't sleep and stared out the window, not really seeing anything. When Natalie stepped on the brakes, Nicky's heartbeat soared painfully. "What happened?" she said.

"Goddamn. This old guy has been on my tail for miles. He passed, cut in front of me and slowed down so that I nearly rear-ended him." The vehicle, a Lincoln Town Car, sped up as Natalie tried to pass.

"Let him go, Nattie. We don't want to be anywhere near him."

When she fell asleep, Natalie shook her arm. "Hey, you've got the directions."

They arrived at the medical center in one piece, which Nicky considered a lucky feat, surrounded as they were by tailgaters who failed to signal or use their cruise controls. They were both edgy from the drive and lack of sleep.

Their mother hugged them and said, "Your father had emergency bypass surgery last night. Your brother and sister are with him now." She frowned at Natalie's belly and said, "When did this happen?" as if this were an inconvenience.

"That's why I didn't tell her," Natalie muttered to Nicky as their mother sat down.

"Coffee," Nicky said, filling a Styrofoam cup. "Can you drink it?"

"Of course not. I can't drink anything that's good anymore."

Nicky took a sip and sat down. "Believe me, it's not good."

When they finally saw their father, neither was soothed by his appearance. With tubes connecting him to morphine and electrolytes, oxygen tubes up his nose, wires monitoring his heart on a screen, a catheter leading to a bag of urine hanging from the side of the bed, he looked like a frail impersonation of himself. The rails were up, lest he fall out, although he appeared to be unconscious.

Nicky stood next to the bed, feeling helpless. She put an arm around Natalie, who had tears on her cheeks. "He just had surgery. He'll be better tomorrow," she said, not sure at all that he would ever be better.

At their parents' house that night, Nicky fell into a stupor. The one-story structure, curled around an inner patio, had tile floors and white walls and ceilings. The many windows, black with night, were closed and recycled air circulated through the air conditioning.

"Are you coming to eat, Nicole?" her mother asked.

She dragged herself to the kitchen where everyone crowded around a table in an alcove. The conversation droned around her. She took a few bites of a pizza slice and said, "Mom, where am I sleeping?"

"You and Natalie are in the second bedroom down the hall from the living room."

She cracked a window over her bed before lying down. The night sounds—unidentified insects and birds—obliterated all other sound. They comforted her. Inside, it was all about death. Outside, the noisy sounds of life were in full swing.

The phone rang three times before Meg answered in a sleepy voice. "I woke you up?" Nicky said.

"How is he?"

"Alive. He just looks like he's on his way out. Tomorrow he'll be better."

"Good," Meg said as if she believed her. "I miss you."

"Me too. I have to share a bed with Natalie, who just opened the door. I'll talk to you tomorrow. Sleep tight."

In the morning, sunlight filtered through pale blinds, streaking the cool floors. Cleo sat in the inner patio, drinking coffee with Nicky's sister, Nancy. She poured Nicky a cup. Nicky admired the landscaping, especially what she thought was bougainvillea climbing the brick walls. "Have you called the hospital this morning?"

"Of course," Cleo said. "Your father is conscious and taking food."

She wasn't sure whether she liked better the cool, controlled mother she was accustomed to or the slightly frazzled version of yesterday. The cool mother reassured her. The other seemed more human, more approachable. Would her mother come apart if her father died? "That's a relief."

She looked at her sister, who resembled Cleo. "How are the kids, Nancy?" She had spent little time with her niece and nephew, because they were so busy taking dance or playing sports. Now Jordan was a senior in high school and Jody a sophomore. It was kind of late to bond.

"They're good. Jordan loves sports. Actually, he's the quarterback. And Jody loves people. She was on the homecoming court. You should come to one of the football games."

"I should." She looked over her steaming cup as Neil and Natalie entered the room.

"We organized a search and here you are," Neil said.

Natalie just smiled and sat down, crossing her hands on her belly. She looked bushed. "How is Dad?"

Their mother gave their father's health status and said she was leaving for the hospital in an hour. Nicky and Natalie were sharing a bathroom and were ready in a half hour. Nicky took the book she'd brought along, knowing it would be a long day.

Her dad was still in ICU. His skin was a little less gray. He smiled and squeezed Nicky's hand and congratulated Natalie on the impending birth. They had five minutes with him every few hours.

Lost in her book, Nicky was living the life of the characters when her mother asked her how Beth was. "Who?"

Cleo, whose eyes were the same shade of blue as Nicky's, the only likeness they shared, asked again, "How is Beth?"

"She's running for county judge."

"I think her mother told me that."

"Then you know how she is," Nicky said.

"Touché," Natalie whispered.

"I understand that you're living in that old farmhouse again." Her mother sighed.

"Yep." She looked down at her book. Her eyes moved across the page, registering nothing. Being the focus of Cleo's disapproval was intimidating, even now.

"We're moving into town," Natalie said. "The restaurant is finally successful."

"It's a great place to eat," Neil put in. "Have you been there, Nance?"

"As a matter of fact, we have. Even the kids loved it."

"What is Dan going to do?" Cleo asked.

"He's one of the best welders around." Natalie looked her mother in the eyes.

Cleo flinched. "I'm not your enemy," she said. "Like any other mother, I had expectations for my children."

"Well, that's the thing about having kids. They have their own expectations."

Nicky leaned close. "Let it go, Natalie. This is about Dad. Remember?"

One of the ICU nurses came for Cleo, leaving the four of them alone. Nancy sat next to Natalie and talked avidly about her pregnancies and births. Neil paged through a magazine, jiggling one foot. Nicky went back to her book.

On Saturday, four days after their arrival, Neil, Natalie and Nicky flew home. Nancy stayed behind. She would leave in two more days, after their father was released from the hospital. Nicky could have stayed. She didn't have kids at home or a regular job waiting, but she thought if she lingered one more day her nerves would unravel.

Nicky was in the kitchen, making a peanut butter sandwich, when Meg walked in. The weather had turned at the end of October. Before all the corn was in, the wind blew the rest of the leaves off the trees. Patches of frost covered the grass in the mornings.

132

Brownie, Rhubarb and Champion grazed in Dan's field. At first they had run and run. The goats had given up trying to catch them, running with them only when they galloped past and then only until they left them behind. Meg had watched worriedly. This was how horses injured themselves, skidding into things, like fences. After a while, though, they'd settled down to graze and she left them there, checking them only a couple times a day.

"Hey," she said, wrapping her arms around Nicky and leaning into her back. "You're home. I never heard Dan drive in."

Nicky turned in her embrace and hugged her tightly, burying her face in Meg's hair. "You're so cold. It's like winter here."

"Want me to warm you up?"

"Now? Don't you have a lesson or something? It's Saturday."

"God, yes. I forgot. Chelsea will be knocking on the door soon. I should have cancelled it."

"I can wait."

Chelsea was in the riding arena, trotting around the rail when she went out. She waved and Meg went in through the gate. Meg wore an old barn coat over her sweatshirt and jeans, yet she felt the cold, penetrating wind. She regretted losing Jack to the Healeys before she had a chance to show him at the big quarter horse shows. Although they wanted her to ride him in the Senior Western Pleasure classes, Tina had offered to pay her to show Sam—if she could hang onto the place long enough.

When Chelsea and Laura left, she went in the house. Allie was alone in the barn. She'd been sulky since Meg had put Rhubarb out on pasture. Meg found Nicky upstairs, enhancing photos on the computer—pictures of Nicky and her sisters and brother with Cleo.

"Nancy looks more and more like Cleo." She massaged Nicky's shoulders, looking over her shoulder at the screen.

"Yeah, they're both a couple of swans. Natalie and I are the ducks." Nicky laughed.

"You're just looking for compliments. You know you're damn cute." She ran her fingers through Nicky's dark hair.

"Not a beauty, though. That's you. Tell me, do blondes have more fun?"

"I'll show you how much fun. Come on, you can do that later. I have two hours before I have to go back to the barn. Let's get down and dirty."

Nicky grinned. "Sounds like fun to me."

Meg shut the door but left the back door unlocked. They shed their clothes, and Nicky released Meg's hair from its elastic band, spreading it out on the pillow. Their toes and bellies and breasts touched as they kissed. How she had missed this in the few days Nicky was gone. Scrappy, who was lying in his bed, let out a warning woof.

"Someone's in the house," Nicky whispered.

"Meg! The horses are loose." It was Lucy, her voice high and scared.

Meg and Nicky froze, but only for a moment. Meg was dressed and out the bedroom door while Nicky was pulling on her jeans.

"What do you mean loose?" She brushed past Lucy, grabbed her jacket off the hook in the mudroom and flew out the back door with Lucy on her heels.

"Look!" Lucy pointed toward the field.

Meg's heart leaped as a painful jolt of adrenaline swept through her. The horses were flowing through the field, galloping in one long multi-colored stream—Brownie in the lead, Champion and Rhubarb bringing up the rear, Tango and Jack and Sam bunched in the middle. In one fluid motion, Brownie jumped the creek and the others splashed through in his wake. As they rounded the corner, she threw herself over the fence, shouting, "Whoa, whoa, whoa." If she got in front of them, she thought maybe she could stop them.

It was when they were nearly upon her that she glimpsed Allie on Brownie's bare back, clinging to his mane, legs gripping. This was the real nightmare, not losing the stable, she thought. "Don't let them get hurt," she said aloud. She joined them briefly as they passed her—first Brownie, then Sam and Jack and Tango and lastly Champion and Rhubarb. As she watched, they bunched and squeezed through the open gate to Dan's field. If she could get to that gate before the horses rounded those fence lines, she could stand in the way. No horse would willingly run her down. She couldn't chance closing the gate, though. Brownie might jump it while the rest crashed into it. Rhubarb was the last to go through the opening. It was then she saw that one horse was down. She yelled "No" just before she tripped on a clod thrown by a hoof and went down herself.

Desperado shot past her, belly to the ground. He barked once when he reached the gate to the other pasture and sped through, his little legs covering ground at an astonishing pace. Pain ripped through her ankle when she jumped up, but she ran anyway.

Tango was struggling to his feet when she reached him. He'd apparently slipped and skidded into the open gate. His right hind leg was bleeding and he held it off the ground. He was blowing hard, his nostrils wide open and red. She closed the gate, separating him from the others.

She watched in awe as the dog turned Brownie, forcing him to break into a trot, making the others follow as he dodged their hooves. He worked them into a circle, stopping their headlong rush.

Her heart and lungs felt as if they no longer fit her chest. She leaned over with hands on knees, trying to breathe normally. The dog nosed her hand, and she dropped to her knees and tried to hug him. He moved away and barked once.

Briefly wondering if it was sprained or broken, she forced herself to put weight on her ankle and limped toward Brownie. She grabbed Allie's leg and pulled her off. "You nearly killed them, all of them, and Tango is hurt. Go get their halters and lead ropes." Then she made her way to the water tank to keep the horses from drinking deeply, knowing it could kill them when they were so hot.

Lucy was running with Allie toward the barn when Nicky reached Meg's side. Her phone was in her hand, and she was breathing hard. "I called the vet."

"Thanks." Meg cupped water in her hands, which Desperado lapped.

The horses in Dan's field were grazing as if a few minutes ago they hadn't been galloping mindlessly. Tango stood at the closed gate and whinnied.

"I dreamed this happened," Nicky said.

"You did?" Meg asked.

"In the dream the horses were running in one long stream, and you were running with them."

"You never told me."

Nicky had no jacket on and was shivering. Meg tucked her into her barn coat.

"It was only a dream. I never thought it would happen. What did happen, do you know?"

"No." Someone opened the gate. Had Allie let them all out of the barn? How had it begun, this mad race across the fields, tearing up the pastures? Her ankle throbbed. She looked at Tango. Her hope that he would be another Brittle or Jack or Sam looked blown, but she was too angry to cry.

"Champion is down," Nicky said and Meg only nodded. *What else?* she thought. When the girls returned with halters and led Sam and Jack to the barn, she was on her knees next to Champion. The horse was in distress, but she didn't know what to do with him except stroke his long neck and tell him he'd be all right. Desperado sniffed at Champion, ready to make him get up, but she told him no.

Lucy had tied Tango to the fence. He stood on three legs. Blood was clotting on the injured leg. His coat and mane stood on end in the wind. She nearly cried with relief when Dr. MacIverson drove across the field, parking at the gate.

Mac listened to Champion's heart, which Meg could hear booming without the stethoscope in her ears. The horse's sides had stopped heaving, though. Mac gave him a shot and motioned her to stand back. The old horse struggled to his feet.

The vet washed off Tango's leg, while Meg held the twitch tight on the horse's nose. He gave Tango a shot for pain and for tetanus and squatted to shave the skin clean of hair before stitching it together and wrapping the leg.

After that, he went to the other horses. He listened to their breathing and their hearts and said they would be okay. "Tell me what happened," he said.

"Somebody turned them out and opened the gate between the fields." She pictured Allie leaning forward over Brownie's neck, riding like she'd never seen anyone ride. "I thought they were going to run themselves to death or into a fence, but Desperado here herded them into a circle." Too late for Tango, of course, who had already hit the gate.

Mac looked at the dog. Desperado sat with his back to the wind, his coat ruffling, his tongue hanging out as if he were hot. "He's part border collie. I don't suppose you want to get rid of him now."

"Nope. He's a good dog," Desperado's tail wagged at the compliment. "Thanks, Mac, for coming so quick."

Nicky hitched a ride with Mac and drove Meg's truck back into the field. "Get in, Meg. I'll walk Tango back."

Meg gave Nicky her jacket and pulled herself into the driver's seat. She parked next to Tina's BMW. It must have been her Saturday to work at the clinic. Otherwise, she would have been there earlier and would never have let someone turn the horses out. She gritted her teeth when she put weight on the left ankle. She was running on rage when she sat down heavily on the bench outside the tack room. Since she'd pulled Allie off Brownie, she'd been thinking what to do with her.

"What happened to your leg?" Tina asked.

"I fell. Wait till you see Tango. And Champion nearly died. Where's Allie?"

Allie's head popped up. She was cleaning Tango's stall.

"Let me see your ankle," Tina said.

"Not yet. Come here, Allie."

"She didn't know they would all run," Lucy said.

She waved away Lucy as if she were a distraction and stared at Allie with eyes that were hot with anger. "What did you think you were doing?" she asked, knowing it didn't matter what Allie said. She'd send her home.

"You put Rhubarb and Brownie out," the girl said.

She waited, thinking she would calm down, but as the pause grew into a long silence, her anger grew. "And?"

"I thought the other horses should go out too." Allie lifted her head and met Meg's eyes, but only briefly. The girl looked down again.

"What were you doing on Brownie? I told you not to ride any of the horses unless I was around."

Allie toed the aisle floor. "I wanted to ride him like you did. I didn't know all the horses would follow us."

Meg took a deep breath to keep from shaking the girl, who seemed to have no fear and no sense. Just then Nicky led Tango into the barn. Both were shivering. She jumped to her feet, thinking to put a blanket on Tango, and let out a yowl of pain and rage. She sat down with a thump. "Somebody put a blanket on Tango. Please. Nicky, would you get us a couple of warm jackets?"

Tina took hold of her leg and gently but firmly put it up on the bench. "Keep it there for now."

Allie started to walk away and Meg called her back. "You're going home now, Allie. I'll bring Rhubarb over tomorrow. Don't come back. Do you hear?"

The girl flashed her an angry, pleading look, but said nothing.

"Do you understand you're not supposed to come back?"

"I didn't mean Tango to get hurt or Champion. I didn't make them run."

"Go." *Before I throttle you*, she thought. Throttle was a word her dad had used when he was angry.

As Allie left, taking her time before finally going out the door, throwing looks at Meg as she went, perhaps hoping she would change her mind, Nicky came back with the jackets. "Where's Allie going?" she asked as she put one of the coats around Meg's shoulders.

"Home."

"I better give her a ride."

"Go ahead. Make sure she doesn't come back."

"Let's get that boot off," Tina said, giving the cowboy boot a tentative pull. Meg grabbed the bench.

"Leave it." She clenched her teeth to keep from screaming.

"We'll have to cut it off," Tina said.

"No. These are my favorite boots."

"Lucy, will you go out and get my bag from the backseat of my car?"

Tina gave Meg a shot of Demerol and waited for Nicky to come back. Together they got the boot off. Meg's ankle and foot popped out, having grown to twice their normal size. Tina thrust Meg's foot into a pail of icy water, and Meg leaned against the wall as Nicky and Tina and Lucy took care of the horses.

Afterward Tina and Nicky helped her into the house, changed her dirty clothes for a clean sleep shirt and put her to bed. She stretched out gratefully, hardly feeling the pain when Tina wrapped her foot and ankle. Tina gave Nicky some pain pills to dole out every six hours or as needed. Lucy was already gone with her brother, roaring down the driveway. Meg shut her eyes and slept.

Chapter Twelve

The display on Nicky's cell showed Beth's work number. Her heart ticked faster as she put the phone to her ear. "Beth?"

"Patricia Robson. How are you, Nicky?"

She almost said "Busy," but rudeness had never been her forte. "Good. Well. And you?" They were like two dogs, sniffing around each other. She bent and stroked Scrappy, who was in her office with her.

"We're looking for people to give house parties to increase support for Beth's campaign. Would you be interested?"

What nerve. "I thought my life with Beth was being swept under the rug."

"We thought, Beth and I, that you would want to be a part of the election."

She knew what Robson was asking. "You mean you want the gay community's vote while denying Beth belongs in it?"

"I didn't say gay, did I? Of course, it would be great if there were some diversity." Patricia's voice was seductively persuasive. Was this how she talked to juries?

Beth had cut her off as if she never existed. "Why should I do her any favors?"

"Because you know she'd be a fair judge, without prejudice toward anyone, regardless of their sexual orientation or race."

"Sorry. This isn't my house anymore. I can't help you. I have to go now."

She went back to her computer but couldn't concentrate. *Nervy woman*, she thought. Robson had no doubt played a part in deciding Beth would never win if she were in a committed lesbian relationship. Yet that hadn't stopped her from asking Nicky to appeal to the gay voters. However, it had been time for her to move on before Beth shoved her out the door. She knew that now, but no one liked being dumped.

She took the steep stairs down to the first floor to see how Meg was doing. Meg had taken a few days of sick leave after spraining her ankle. Nicky, Tina and Lucy had been taking care of the horses. Close contact with the animals had made Nicky less nervous around them.

She had bought Meg a cane. The sprain was a bad one, but Meg had been restless once the pain pills wore off. She was not in the house when Nicky looked for her. She found her sitting on the bench with Desperado at her side. Neither Lucy nor Tina had arrived yet.

"He likes you," Nicky said, nodding at the dog. The weather had turned again in early November. It was not shirtsleeve weather, but it was unusually warm.

Scrappy nosed Desperado and put his head between his front feet and his butt in the air, tail wagging playfully. Nicky and Meg watched the two dogs roughhouse for a while. Scrappy tired first. Nicky told Meg about the call.

Meg was silent a few moments, and Nicky waited for her

reaction. "It might be fun," Meg said at last. "You'd have to clean, though."

"Wait a minute. You could dust. I could run the vacuum. You could clean the counters. I could wash the kitchen and bathroom floors." Using could, instead of can, because it wasn't going to happen. She recalled Allie saying she would clean for Rhubarb's keep, but Nicky knew better than to bring up Allie. Rhubarb was back home.

"And who would fix sandwiches or whatever?"

"I could look up some appetizers on the Web."

"Isn't the primary in February or April? Seems like a long ways off."

"I told Robson no anyway. It wasn't my house."

"You'd do it if Beth called, wouldn't you?"

"I'd like to see her win, but I'm still mad."

"As you should be." Meg sighed. "Am I your booby prize, Nicky?"

"Do you really think that?" She was shocked.

Meg nodded, looking at the dogs lying side by side.

"I love you, Meg."

"I know that, but you love Beth too."

"I *did* love Beth." When had that changed? "I chose *you*."

Meg smiled wryly, one corner of her mouth twisting upward. "Nicky, she asked you to leave, and you came here. That's not exactly a choice."

"Where else would I go? Why are you out here anyway?"

"Waiting for someone to hold the twitch while I dress Tango's leg."

"Why me?" She hated twitching Tango. She feared any minute he would fling his head and send the twitch flying.

"I don't see anyone else here but us."

"If you wait a little, Lucy and Tina will come."

Meg got up and limped with the cane's help to Tango's stall. She put on the horse's halter, tightened the rope over his soft nose and handed the wooden end of the twitch to Nicky. Careful not to hurt her own leg, she sat on an old milking stool to tend to Tango's wound.

It was Nicky's role to keep the twitch tight enough to make the horse pay attention to his breathing rather than what was being done. Nicky thought it a form of benign torture. Without it, though, there'd be no way to administer to the stitched leg.

As Meg was rewrapping, Nicky's cell rang. "You can take the twitch off. He'll be all right now."

Nicky moved away to answer the phone. Her heart jumped painfully when she recognized the caller's voice. "Hi, Beth." She glanced at Meg. There was no sign she'd heard. "What's up?" she said casually as if Beth was calling to ask her to pick up a loaf of bread or something.

"Hi, Nicky." The voice that had thrilled her for twenty-five years still had an effect on her. Her heart blipped faster. "How are you?"

"Good, and you?"

"Nicky, I need your help with the campaign."

"Now you want me in your life?"

"I want you to be part of my campaign. You could bring the gay community together."

Nicky sat down on the bench. Lucy was in the barn now. Soon Tina would arrive. She lowered her voice. "I didn't think you wanted anyone to know about us."

"There's a fine line here, sweetie, between being in a relationship and being gay friendly." Sweetie? Was that a slip from the past? Nevertheless, Nicky's heartbeat picked up speed, and she hated herself for it. "A house party would be a great start. I would even come and talk."

When had Beth become such a self-serving shit? "Why don't you talk to Meg? It's her house. I don't have one."

Beth never hesitated. "Is she there?"

Meg was talking to Tina, who had just walked in. Nicky motioned to her. Just before she handed over the phone, she said, "It's Beth about the house party."

Meg's eyebrows arched as if to say, I told you so. She put the cell to her ear. "Hi, Beth, what's happening?" A pause, while she listened. "Sure. How about the first Saturday in December? Say, eleven o'clock? Coffee and tea and appetizers." Another pause. "No problem. Do you want to talk to Nicky again?" A shorter pause ensued. "I'll tell her." She pushed the end button and handed the phone to Nicky. "She said to say thanks."

Nicky snorted. "How could you, Meg?"

"She didn't throw *me* out of the house." She squeezed Nicky's arm. "It'll be fun, except for the cooking and cleaning. I mean, we have to clean sometime anyway."

Nicky looked into Meg's gray eyes, annoyed almost to anger. Her heart plodded along—no leaps, no blips. Then Meg gave her a knowing smile and wink. Nicky was surprised by a surge of desire, and her resistance melted away.

Snow fell at the end of the month. Whenever Meg saw Brownie and Champion huddled in the shelter, tails to the wind, she wanted to bring them inside, give them a little grain and a clean stall they could lie down in and stay dry.

The day the Healeys came to take Midnight Jack away, Chelsea tied Jack outside his stall. "I'll clean it," she said, seeming in no hurry to leave.

Meg had two checks in hand, one for fifteen hundred dollars and one for eight thousand five hundred for Jeannette. Meg had told them to offer less and they had, but Tom insisted that she get ten percent of the original asking price.

"You promise to come over once a week to give lessons?"

"Chelsea is doing well. How about once every two weeks?"

"We're hoping you'll coach her at the bigger shows next year."

Before the Healeys arrived, Meg had put her arms around Jack's neck and whispered, "I'd buy you myself if I could." His ear had twitched. He'd blown dust out of his nostrils and continued eating.

"Are you ready, Chelsea?" Tom asked.

Chelsea threw her arms around Meg, surprising her. "Thanks. I'm sorry I was such a snot."

Laura said, "She wanted to leave Jack with you so that she could come here for lessons, but it takes too much time out of my day now that I'm teaching again."

Meg handed Chelsea Jack's lead rope. "I'll see you soon."

"Tell Lucy and Tina and Nicky goodbye. And Allie, if you see her."

Meg nodded, her throat thick with tears. Jack whinnied as Chelsea led him out of the barn. Sam and Tango answered, and from outside, Brownie and Champion took up the cry. They were saying goodbye.

When the truck and trailer were gone, she brought Brownie and Champion into the barn, rubbed them dry and put them each in a stall. Desperado had appeared at her side as soon as the Healeys left. When Meg sat on the bench, the dog leaned against her good leg.

"I've still got you, right, Desperado? Nobody's going to take you away." The dog's tail brushed the floor. She had coaxed him into the house on cold nights, but he slept in the mudroom on a horse pad and was out the door when she went to feed in the morning.

Cold air swept through the door when Nicky pushed it open. "He's gone?" She sat down next to Meg and put an arm around her.

Meg leaned into her. "Yep." The barn looked empty to her. "Where is Scrappy?"

"He didn't want to come."

"Smart dog. It's damn cold out."

"He's in his bed. Why don't we go to ours?"

Meg was thinking about all the horses bought and sold, like commodities, which of course they were. At least, Jack wouldn't be alone at the Healeys, although he'd been alone at Jeannette's. He would settle in pretty quick.

Another puff of cold air chilled Meg, and she looked toward the door. "Hello. Anyone there?"

Meg and Nicky stood and Desperado disappeared into Brownie's stall. "Mr. Poole," she said with surprise. The Pooles had moved into Dan's house. Meg was glad that Rhubarb had the barn for shelter.

"The name is Dennis." He nodded at Nicky. "You were one of the women who picked Allie up and brought her home."

"Nicky Hennessey." Nicky shook his hand. "How is Allie?"

"She never told me why she stopped coming over here. I thought maybe you would let me know. I know she's strong-headed. I figured she'd done something to displease you."

"Well…" Nicky began.

Meg limped forward and offered Dennis her hand. "Come on inside and have a cup of coffee."

Nicky made a fresh pot and poured the black stuff into three cups. Dennis sipped his. "Good and strong," he said, "just like I like it. I've got a favor to ask."

"What is it?" Meg said, sure he wanted her to take Allie back.

"I'd like to snitch those two goats to keep Rhubarb company. He's never stopped calling for the horses."

"They're Dan's goats, but he won't care. They came with the field."

His eyes, the same color as Allie's, looked troubled even as he thanked her. "What did she do?"

Meg told him, reliving it as if it were happening all over—the horses galloping in a multicolored stream, Brownie jumping the creek as if it were a puddle, Allie clinging to his back as if she were a part of him, Tango on the ground, injured.

He shook his head. "Is your horse healing? Are you?"

"I'm okay. Tango will always have a scar and a thickening, but the vet says there's no reason he won't be sound."

Poole looked relieved. "I'm not making excuses for her. She needs a mother or a father who isn't milking cows at suppertime."

Meg and Nicky exchanged glances. "She's a natural rider," Meg said, thinking again of Brownie and Allie looking like they were of one flesh.

"She belongs to the horse and pony 4-H club," he said. "That Rhubarb is a good pleasure pony."

"I think she could be going over jumps. She's got the best seat I've ever seen."

"Can you give her lessons?"

"On Rhubarb, yes. But not for jumping. There is a hunter-jumper stable over on Columbine Road."

He looked puzzled. "I've passed it."

"If you can take her and Brownie there, they'll give her lessons."

"I don't think I can afford that." He shook his head.

"I don't know what the lessons cost, but Brownie's free. My only condition is that you don't sell him."

"I couldn't take the horse without paying for him."

"Someone tied him to our fence. He was starving. Just take good care of him. If you don't want him anymore, bring him back." Would Desperado go with Brownie? She hoped not.

"I'll see you get hay when you need it."

"Good. I can help with haying," she said.

"Me too," Nicky added. "What we need is someone to plow us out in the winter."

"You got both—the hay and the plowing." He stood up. "Thanks for the coffee. Allie thinks the world of you people. I see why."

They looked at each other as he shut the door behind him. "I'm ready now," Meg said to Nicky.

"To go back to bed?" Were they already reading each other's thoughts?

When they lay down, though, she realized she wasn't ready. Only Sam, Tango and Champion would be left in the stable once she delivered Brownie to Poole's barn. There had been too many changes in too little time. Dan had moved, she'd sold Midnight Jack and now she'd given Brownie away.

"Hey, babe, this is not a time for crying." Nicky hugged her closer. "There is room now for other horses, paying ones."

"Except there aren't any, and I don't think I want any. Sam is enough."

"Maybe you can find a good home for Champion."

"Champion has a home." She thought the old horse deserved the right to die here. How often had he changed hands? The thought made her cry harder.

"You have to look at this place as a business, not a refuge, sweetie. You should be pleased with selling Jack to the Healeys and finding a home for Brownie. That was very generous of you, by the way." Nicky leaned back and looked into Meg's eyes, wiping away the tears with her thumbs.

"Did you see Allie ride? It was an incredible sight."

"Maybe she'll be in the Olympics." Nicky pressed her cheek against Meg. "Cheer up, darlin'. You just did a good thing."

Chapter Thirteen

The first Saturday in December dawned cold and sunny. Ten people were expected, twelve if Nicky and Meg counted. Beth would make thirteen. The house was clean, a joint effort. Meg hobbled around but without a cane. Nicky had borrowed folding chairs from Margo along with two big urns, one for coffee and one for hot water for tea. Around ten they set out hummus and pita bread, cheese and crackers, bean and corn salsa and taco chips, two bunches of grapes and a bowl of mixed nuts. Easy snacks. If anyone wanted pop, they'd bought Diet Pepsi and Sprite.

Margo would be there and Laura Healey and Tina. Meg asked her co-workers, but only Amelia said yes. Dennis and Dan pleaded work, as did Natalie. Saturday was one of the busiest days at the restaurant. Vicki was bringing four people besides herself and Callie. They were Kate Sweeney and Pat Thompson. She introduced the other two as Lillian Matheson and Ann Rutten.

"We saw the horses out there. Are they yours?" Lillian asked, her cheeks red from the short walk to the house.

Nicky said, "They belong to Meg and Tina."

"Meg as in Meg and Skippy's Peanut Brittle?"

Meg swung around and actually beamed. "Hi, Lillie."

Lillian climbed the few steps to the kitchen. "I was so sorry to hear about Brittle. You have a new horse?"

"Yes. The one with the wrapped leg."

"This is my friend, Ann. She had horses as a child."

"Workhorses. We were Amish." Ann's mouth twisted ruefully. "My father let me ride them out to the field. They were huge but gentle."

Meg smiled and Nicky guessed she too was wondering why Ann was here with Lillie. "If you want to go out to the barn afterward, we can do that," Meg said.

"I do. I have to meet this new horse. Is he as good a pleasure horse as Brittle?" Lillie asked.

"He's Brittle's little brother. He has potential. He got hurt."

"That old saw 'healthy as a horse' is just that—a saw," Lillie said. "If they don't colic, they find some way to get hurt."

"Isn't that the truth?" Meg said. "Help yourselves to food and drink."

Beth was last to show up. Somehow Nicky missed her arrival, even though she'd kept an eye on the door. She saw her with Meg and took a deep breath. Even now, her heart leaped when she saw Beth. She watched as Meg introduced her to their guests. Elegant and poised, Beth was talking, smiling and gesturing with her hands. She would make a good impression on everyone and they would vote for her. That was the whole idea, wasn't it?

She wore a pantsuit, which made Nicky think of Hillary Clinton, except Beth was trimmer, her hair perfectly groomed, so much so that Nicky wanted to mess it up. She knew the silky feel of Beth's hair between her fingers but thought maybe Beth had begun coloring it. Would that change the texture? Nicky

150

mentally undressed her. The feel of her body was etched in her mind.

Vicki edged over and said to Nicky, "Pretty classy lady, isn't she?"

"Yep. She reminds me of my mother," Nicky said. Cleo was chic too.

Vicki looked surprised.

Beth was working the crowd, shaking hands like a politician. Nicky moved away whenever she came near, until she accidentally bumped into Meg. "I'm sorry."

Meg's eyes were a dark, warning gray. "Why aren't you taking photos?" She wore a V-neck, long-sleeved fitted pullover and new jeans.

"Good idea." She galloped upstairs, grabbed her camera and came down.

Everyone was seated. "Thanks for coming," Beth said with a friendly smile and then looked down. Scrappy had risen from his bed and was nosing her leg. Nicky's flash went off. She caught Beth's expression, her attempt not to show any emotion as she bent to pat the dog.

Beth said she disagreed with some of Judge Hamner's sentences—giving drunk drivers a slap on the hand, not treating baby killers the same as others accused of reckless homicide, as if a baby's life were less important than an adult's, long sentences for first-time drug offenders. Was there anyone in the audience who hadn't smoked marijuana? The prisons were full of people who had been caught with a little dope. These offenders should be put on tracking bracelets.

She didn't talk long. Afterward, she stayed and conversed with those who hung around. Nicky leaned against an inner wall and took pictures. When Beth walked toward her, her first instinct was to run.

"Hey, thanks for the support." Beth smiled.

She cleared her throat. "It's not me you should thank. It's Meg."

"You must have invited some of these people."

"Vicki asked most of them. She should be your lesbian representative, not me."

Beth was searching her face. Her hazel eyes pinned Nicky to the wall. "You're my oldest friend, Nicky."

"A friend doesn't cut you out of her life for expediency's sake."

"You're not cut out of my life." Beth touched her briefly on the arm. "I'll be seeing you."

When Beth was gone, Meg took everyone out to the barn. Tina and Meg brought in the horses that had been standing in the weak sun. Nicky put Champion in his stall. "This summer we had more horses than stalls," she said.

Meg told them how what she had started as a stable had turned into a refuge. Now that Midnight Jack, Brownie and Rhubarb were gone, the barn seemed empty.

"Then there's room for one more boarder," Lillie said. "I keep my horse at the hunter jumper place. She's nearly sixteen hands and looks like a midget next to their jumpers. Is Brownie a big brown horse with no markings?"

Meg nodded, probably picturing again Allie stuck to his back as he flew over the creek and around the field.

"That girl who rides him takes him over the highest jumps. She looks like she's part of the horse. They're grooming them for the big shows. She could sell that horse and make a mint."

Just Meg's luck, Nicky thought, glancing at Meg, wondering if she was thinking the same thing. She rescues Brownie, gives him away and Allie gets all the glory, but Meg looked pleased.

Lillie asked, "What do you charge?" Meg told her and she said, "I'll bring my mare over at the end of the month. Is that okay?" Lillie handed her a card with her number on it. "Don't give the stall away."

"It's not as if people are standing in line," Meg said with an amused smile.

When everyone was gone, Desperado appeared at Meg's side.

"He's a shy one," Nicky said.

"He is. Where's Scrappy?"

"In his bed, I guess. I'm taking him to the vet Monday." She thought of how he'd heard Beth's voice and sought her out.

That evening they watched a movie and ate popcorn, sitting close on the old couch. Scrappy stayed in his bed, even though he loved popcorn. Nicky was alarmed enough to carry him to the couch and set him down between them. Even then, he ate no popcorn. She was so distracted by this that she paid little attention to the movie, *French Kiss*. She noticed instead that Scrappy's coat was no longer shiny, his eyes, when she lifted his head, were dull. She wanted to pick him up and rush him to the small animal emergency clinic, but her hope was that he'd be all right the next day.

Sunday morning Scrappy lay on the kitchen floor like a rug. He wagged his tail but didn't lift his head when she spoke to him. His food bowl was full from last night. She called the clinic where she took him for his health care and got the number of the vet on call. The woman said she'd meet her at the office. She wrapped the little dog in a towel and carried him to her car. Meg was in the barn, feeding, when she left.

When she placed Scrappy on the examining table, he neither raised his head nor tried to get up. She brushed the hair back from his eyes and saw that they were on her, trusting. The vet prodded him gently. How old was he? Nicky knew he was at least eleven or twelve or maybe even thirteen. The vet she'd first taken him to thought he was around two. That was at least ten years ago.

The vet asked if he had eaten anything that might have made him sick. Nicky had never seen the veterinarian before—there were several vets in the practice—but she seemed competent. Youngish, she looked at Nicky with kind, dark eyes behind glasses. Her nametag read Dr. Brenda Scott.

"No. He's been lying around the house. He didn't eat any food last night or this morning."

"There's a mass in his stomach," Dr. Scott said. "We'll take an X-ray."

"I want to stay with him," she said, her own stomach churning.

"Okay. You can wear a lead vest."

But there was nothing in his stomach except the mass. "Can you take it out?" Nicky asked.

"We'll biopsy it. We'll have to anesthetize him, though. Can you leave him here till tomorrow? He needs fluids."

She hesitated. She had never left him anywhere but home since she'd taken him in. Dr. Scott put her hand over Nicky's, which rested on Scrappy's shoulder.

"I'll take good care of him," she promised. "Come back in the morning."

Scrappy died anyway. The mass was cancerous. Nicky stroked him as Dr. Scott injected a tranquilizer and, after a minute or two, administered the dosage that would stop his heart. His eyes, which never left Nicky's, became lifeless. Meg had taken the morning off work. Her arm was around Nicky as they both wept. They had known Scrappy as long as they'd known each other.

Nicky took his small body, wrapped in a towel, and buried it deep in the ground next to the mound where Brittle and Tawny lay.

Two weeks passed. It was close to Christmas, and the lab was relatively quiet. Amelia stuck her head into Meg's cubicle. "Do you ever rent your horses?"

"Never have had any to rent. Why?"

"Nothing, really. I like those Budweiser commercials. The ones with the sleighs pulled by big horses."

"Yeah. Me too. You could ride Champion." Once, she had clambered onto Champion's bare back and ridden him to the barn from the far field. He had carried her as if she might break. In fact, he'd gotten down on his knees before she could jump off, which made her think he might have once been a circus horse.

At home, her gaze was always unwillingly drawn to the mound, to the fresh dirt that wouldn't support grass till spring. The sight brought back the long winter after Brittle died, when she couldn't bear to look at the mound.

Inside, the door to the upstairs was open. They kept it

closed except when Nicky was up there, because it sucked up the warm air. She changed and went out to the barn where Tina was grooming Sam. Rosita had been right. Tina did have a male friend, another doctor, Fred Bollinger. Dr. Fred they called him where Meg worked. He was one of the primary care doctors. He stood around with his hands in his pockets, looking cold.

"Give me something to do before my blood clots," he said to Meg.

"Why don't you take him for a spin on Sam, Tina? Use the longe line. That will get his heart pumping." She liked Dr. Fred and was happy for Tina, who she thought was lonely in that big house now that her mother was gone. Of course, Rosita would return in the spring.

After cleaning stalls, she went back inside. She would come out later to exercise Tango and turn Champion out in the indoor arena. Desperado followed her to the door. She let him in and he settled down on the pad in the mudroom. She fed him inside now. He came into the kitchen when she was there but never ventured any deeper into the house.

She doctored a pizza and popped it in the oven, made a salad and put it on the table and called Nicky, who came down the stairs one slow step at a time. The kitchen was warm and redolent. Desperado crept up the few steps and lay against the wall nearest the door. His dark eyes followed Meg's movements as she cut the pizza and sat down across from Nicky.

Meg took a deep breath and said, "I think you need to get away, Nicky. You can't bear to look at that mound any more than I could." The light had gone out of Nicky's eyes when Scrappy died. Meg knew that whatever was wrong with Nicky was caused by more than the dog's death. Perhaps winter was the culprit, the long dark nights and bitterly cold days or perhaps it had started with the house party. She had seen how Nicky had looked at Beth, how she'd tried to avoid her.

"Why don't you visit your parents? Go see the ocean and the Everglades. Take lots of pictures. Your dad is better. It's almost Christmas."

"You want me to leave you here alone?"

"Hey, maybe I'll go see my parents when you get back."

"You're kicking me out?" Nicky sounded incredulous.

"Only temporarily." God, she hoped so. It was possible that Nicky might not come back, but it was a chance she believed she had to take. She had once thought it was enough just to have Nicky with her. Not anymore.

The night before Nicky left for Florida, she huddled with Meg under the electric blanket. Outside the wind beat against the windows. The cold leaked through the old glass. Desperado had finally made his way to the bedroom. He'd sniffed at Scrappy's bed and made it his own.

Tinged with sadness, their attempts to make love were slow to take hold. Despite the cold they lay naked with only their hair poking out from the covers, their warm skin touching. Meg sniffed at Nicky's neck while kissing it. "You have your own scent, you know."

"So do you. I'm not showering till I get back," Nicky said.

Meg laughed. "Cleo will love that." She kissed Nicky's shoulder, her breasts.

"What will I do there?" Nicky buried her fingers in Meg's hair. "Come back up here."

"Photograph everything. I've always wanted to see a horseshoe crab." She brushed her lips over Nicky's eyes and eyebrows.

"Why don't you visit for a few days?"

"That would defeat the purpose." She kissed Nicky and said, "Shush now. We'll talk later."

Chapter Fourteen

Meg drove Nicky's car to the airport, letting her off at the doors. It was nearly six in the morning, and Meg had to feed and get ready for work. Nicky set her bags on the sidewalk and gave Meg a hug and a kiss on the cheek. She watched the taillights of the Saturn blink at the turn and disappear around the west side of the parking lot. Gusts of wind swirled a dusting of snow around her feet. The temperature was ten above zero, according to the car radio. She threw her backpack over her shoulder and rolled her suitcase through the automatic doors and to the Delta Air Lines counter.

She was in Florida and on the road in a Ford Taurus by early afternoon. She had decided to spend a few days with her parents before taking some side trips. Her elbow protruded from the open car window as the warm air rushed at her. She had popped an Eva Cassidy CD into the player and was singing along, in the wrong key of course, when she spotted the snake curled near the edge of the road.

This would be her first photo, she thought, pulling off the pavement and running back to the snake. Its tail rattled in warning. She took three shots from different angles before picking up a long stick and urging the snake away from the road. It struck at the stick, which broke, and she let out a little shriek before it slithered into the brush and was gone.

An old Mustang had parked behind her. A man leaned out the window and said, "That's nothing to fool around with. You should have run it over."

"Why would I want to kill something so beautiful?"

"Hug it and see how beautiful it is," the man said, turning to laugh with the driver. The driver, a youngish man, leaned over the older passenger. "She must be one of them stupid northerners who got their brains up their ass."

Before they peeled off, the older man said, "Go poke a gator, lady. Take one home with you." She heard their guffaws as the Mustang screeched past her.

She got back in the Taurus and drove on down the road. Her heart jumped when she came up behind the Mustang, which had slowed down, and tried to pass. The driver stepped on the gas and the old car leaped forward. Nicky took her foot off the gas pedal and coasted back into the right lane, hoping the men would keep going, but the Mustang slowed down even further, to thirty miles an hour. She again tried to pass, and it sped away. She fumbled for paper and pen in her backpack and wrote down the license plate number.

When she got to The Villages, she remembered where her parents' house was near the highway and parked in front of their garage, sure that she had lost the Mustang. She was covered with sweat. Even her hair was damp with it.

"You are so hot. Are you ill?" Cleo asked after a hug.

"She's okay, honey. She just thinks she's hot. It's ten degrees in Wisconsin. Aren't you glad you're here, Nick?"

"Yeah, Dad." She glanced out the front window, half expecting to see the Mustang.

She and her dad took a walk. Lights were strung on houses and trees. Wreaths hung on front doors. Christmas trees glowed behind front windows. Sometimes a Star of David or a menorah declared a different celebration. It all looked out of place in this warm climate. There should be snow or at least frost.

"Want to golf tomorrow morning?" her dad asked.

"Sure." It had been years since she golfed.

After a light supper of fish and salad and fresh fruit, Cleo said she was playing bridge the next afternoon. Would Nicky sub?

"Only if you need me. I think I'd like to sit by the pool and vegetate, if that's okay." She had several books with her and lots of sunscreen. "After Christmas, I plan to drive to the coast. Would you like to come with me?"

Cleo looked at her for a long moment. Nicky was sure Cleo was going to ask why she was here, but her mother's gaze shifted to the window. "What's that car doing in our driveway?"

Nicky sucked in air as her heart rocketed around her chest. The Mustang was parked next to the Taurus. She watched as the youngish man put something under the windshield wipers before backing out and driving slowly away. She was pinned to her chair with fear, but her dad jumped up and went outside to get the note.

It read—*Dear lady snake charmer, we got you a present. Look in your backyard.* Ward and Cleo glanced at each other and made their way to the windows that looked out on the space behind the house. Nicky followed. An alligator, maybe three feet long, was tied to a tree.

Ward called the people who removed alligators. Nicky took pictures—first of the alligator as it tried to escape and then of the two men who tied a small rope around its jaws and carried it away.

"The alligator's downward bite is powerful, but tie its mouth shut and it's helpless," her dad said. "The police are on the lookout for the Mustang. These guys have become a public nuisance."

How easy it was to terrify her. She wanted to call Meg. Maybe

Meg would tell her to come home. She went to bed early, while her parents watched *House Hunters International* on TV. The location was Costa Rica. Were they planning to move? she asked.

"No. We might visit, though."

She slept poorly. In the morning, she found her parents drinking coffee in the inner patio. A platter of fruit and a coffeecake were breakfast. She filled a small plate and ate, washing it down with strong coffee.

"We have a seven thirty tee time," her dad said.

"Let me take a quick shower. Fifteen minutes tops."

Her dad was backing his Escape out of the garage when he noticed the smashed taillight on the Taurus. He braked and they got out of the car. "Why would anyone do that?" he asked. "We'll have to get it fixed. Did you take out insurance?"

She had. She felt like she might puke.

"I'll phone the Ford place and see if they can fit it in today." He pulled his cell out of its case and made the call. When he stashed it away, he told her to follow him to the garage. "If they have the part, they'll fix it. You better call the car rental place and let them know it was vandalized."

The fear was turning to anger, and the rage blossoming inside her gave her a strong swing. She had always hit straight, right down the fairway. But now she got to the green a lot faster.

"Hey, girl, you're good," her dad said as they lunched at the country club.

She got through a quiet Christmas. Meg had told her not to call except in an emergency. Did the Mustang men qualify? She phoned Margo instead before she went to sleep. "Merry, merry and all that stuff."

"Same to you. Your prints are selling. Beth bought one."

Beth's name made a small blip in her steady heartbeat. "I'm in Florida at my parents. I got your message. I didn't have time to reply. Two guys in a Mustang are harassing me for trying to save a rattlesnake. I'm afraid to go anywhere." She told Margo the story.

"Come home. They won't follow you here," Margo said after a long pause.

Two days after Christmas her car was ready. She and her dad planned to pick it up after golfing. "I've been wanting to go to the coast," her dad said, lifting his ball out of the cup on the third hole. "I just needed someone to go with. We'll take the Escape and put your car in the garage."

Relief made her legs weak. "Thanks, Dad. Are you well enough to travel?"

"Never better." He winked at her and she smiled.

Cleo was readying the house for her bridge group when they left early the next morning. She shooed them out the door, promising to call if she heard anything about the Mustang.

Ward drove to the coast, and they walked on the beach. A cool, wet wind drove them further south, where Nicky found the horseshoe crabs. "Is that what they are, Dad?" She took several photos, worrying that they would look like no more than dark rocks to Meg.

"They're practically fossils they've been around so long."

Her dad found a bed-and-breakfast with a wraparound porch from which they ventured to the national seashore. It was warmer on Merritt Island, like they'd crossed an invisible line that separated northern and southern Florida. They watched the shuttle shoot into the sky, soaring out of sight while the rocket that propelled it fell into the ocean.

The Everglades were a wonder to her, teeming with life. Ibis and herons and egrets and ospreys fed in these waters, along with a myriad of other birds. Alligators looked like bumpy logs. She spied one huge snake her dad said was a Burmese python that someone had loosed into the wild. Everything she stored on her camera and in her mind to tell Meg.

"You see why they call the Everglades a sea of grass?" her dad asked. "The wildlife is in danger, though. There's a delicate balance here. When the freshwater is depleted, the salt water moves in. Too many people, too much agriculture."

In the car on the road that crossed southern Florida, her dad said out of the blue, "Neil is gay. That's what they say these days, right? Gay, not homosexual."

She looked out the window to hide the flush on her face. How had she missed something so obvious? Her handsome, witty, unmarried brother took after her. Had he ever brought home a girlfriend? She couldn't remember, but she'd been oblivious of her brother and sisters when she was young. She looked out at the pavement disappearing under them and said, "Stop, Dad, there's a turtle in the road."

Ward swerved and came to a screeching halt. The turtle scrabbled to escape, its toenails scratching her arms as she picked it up. It disappeared into its shell and peed on her as she carried it at arm's length across the highway and set it down. It plopped into the watery ditch and swam to safety.

"Rescuer of peeing turtles and poisonous snakes," her dad said as she climbed back into the car. He smiled ruefully at her. "You were the one who cried when a bird hit the window or you saw some dead animal by the side of the road."

"I must have been tiresome." She thought of Scrappy but was unable to talk about his death. "How did Neil tell you?"

"Your mother guessed years ago." Her mother had guessed about her too. "Cleo thinks you're another Annie Liebovitz, by the way." Her dad threw her a smile, his eyes crinkling.

"Don't I wish?" Although flattered, she snorted. "I'm back in that old farmhouse I once owned, only now I'm paying rent."

"I know. Your mom keeps track of you kids. I hear the barn has been turned into a stable by the woman who owned the peanut butter horse, the blonde with the great legs."

Nicky laughed. She'd tell Meg this too, along with all the other things she'd hoarded away. "That would be Skippy's Peanut Brittle and Meg Klein." But then she added, "Brittle died and so did Scrappy, my dog."

Her father pulled off the road to comfort her. He hugged her as best he could with both of them strapped in seat belts. "Your mother said something was wrong."

Her mother apparently knew her a whole lot better than she thought.

They drove through horse country. *Lots of quarter horse farms,* she noted. Her dad said, "I thought you could tell Meg. Maybe she'd want to move here."

"I don't think so, Dad. Meg doesn't have a lot of money." She told him how Meg had taken in abandoned horses and only now, after finding a home for one and selling another, was she getting on her financial feet. "Besides, this all seems alien to me." She gestured around her at the landscape.

Her dad was nodding. "It's the weather that draws people here, but it's so hot in the summer that your mom and I are thinking about buying a summer place on a lake in Wisconsin. Then we can see you kids."

When she flew home, her parents followed her to the airport, even though the men in the Mustang had been arrested and charged with reckless endangerment. Apparently, scaring tourists was how they got their thrills.

Ward and Cleo left her after she turned in the car. "We'll see you in the summer," her dad called as she wheeled away her suitcase.

Dan was waiting for her at the airport. He lifted her backpack off her shoulders, even as she protested. "That's what guys do," he said, meeting her eyes. "Meg left yesterday to visit her parents."

She had been so eager to get home, to tell Meg all that she'd seen and done. The disappointment was physical. She tried to hide it, and when Dan said right now he wished he were down south, she said, "I sort of forgot about the cold." By then they had picked up her luggage and stepped out into an icy wind.

"Meg will be home in ten days," he said when they shut themselves in the Volkswagen.

"She did say she was thinking about making that trip. How is Natalie?"

He grinned. "She looks like she's going to pop."

"When is she due again?" she asked.

"February." His grin was contagious.

"Do you know the sex?"

"Nah. We want to be surprised."

She liked their not caring whether they had a girl or a boy. When Dan turned into the driveway and parked near the barn, he jumped out and took her suitcase in one hand and her backpack in the other. "You can open the door."

She did and nearly fell over Desperado, who yelped and ran up the stairs into the warm kitchen, redolent with spices. Natalie stood at the stove, one hand on her belly.

"What is this?"

"A welcome home dinner," she said with a smile. "How are Mom and Dad?"

"Great. You look like the kitchen blimp."

Natalie laughed loudly. "I've got ten pounds of baby in my gut."

It helped, she admitted later. They wanted to hear what she had to tell them—about the Mustang and her trip with her father—and looked appropriately horrified and pleased. Cleo had told her to take lots of photos of the infant (her word), that they would be here in June to hold the baby. "She and Dad are going to buy a summer place on a lake in Wisconsin so that they can see us more often."

"No kidding," Natalie said.

The dinner was pasta with grilled vegetables and feta, fresh bread and a chocolate cake for dessert. "Cleo keeps track of us," she said, between bites. "She knows us frighteningly well, despite our best efforts to keep her in the dark." For some reason she found that comforting. She said nothing about Neil.

Natalie and Dan laughed. She laughed even though she ached inside. They would go home soon, and the diversion they'd created would go with them. The house would be empty, just like she was.

The next morning as she helped Tina pick up stalls and feed, she realized the horses were a connection with Meg. She kept expecting to turn around and see her. Lillian Matheson's horse had moved in. The dun mare, nicknamed Bunny, pinned her ears when Nicky put a halter on her.

"She's a bit nasty," Tina said.

"Great. Does she kick or bite or both?"

"She hasn't yet. She rubs against Champion's stall. Gets him all excited and then pins her ears and runs at him."

"Maybe she's a lesbian?" Nicky said as if Tina were Meg.

Tina leaned against the wall of Sam's stall and laughed helplessly. "Maybe she's on the rag."

The mare cow-kicked at her when Nicky put her back in her stall. "Hey," Nicky yelled, her heart knocking loudly. She shut the stall door and Bunny rushed after her, snapping the air. Nicky sprinted out of reach. "God, what a bitch." She looked at Tina. "What's so funny?" Then she succumbed, hands on knees, breathless with laughter.

"Bunny, what an inappropriate name," Tina said, when she could talk, and they broke down again in helpless laughter. Tina grabbed her crotch and dropped her pants in Sam's stall. "Don't look," she said.

Nicky did the same in Champion's stall and kicked the wet spot under the sawdust. *The power of suggestion*, she thought. When they came out of the stalls, they were in control again. Tina hayed and Nicky dumped grain in the corner feeders. They had already watered.

Meg's parents met her flight. Her mother's hair was more gray than blond, her skin a bit leathery and lined. She felt as if she were looking at herself twenty-five years down the road. Her dad had always been dark, skin and eyes and hair. His hair was now a thick steel gray, which she thought looked great. They both seemed smaller somehow. Her mother stood on tiptoe to kiss her and her dad hugged her without stooping.

She collected her bags and walked outside into a warm winter day. The heat of the sun felt welcome on her face. She happily shed her lightweight jacket.

On the drive to her parents' house, she noticed the trailers, some with tires on their roofs, placed along the side of the road with nothing around them, not even a cactus. She hoped her parents, who were asking her about her new place, didn't live in a trailer like one of these. She'd go mad in such a small place with nowhere to go. She knew they'd moved from the apartment they'd rented in Scottsdale to the edge of Sierra Vista.

So it was a relief when her dad drove the old Buick Regal into the driveway of a small ranch house. The yard was made up of stones with various cacti flourishing in them. "No mowing," he said.

"And no shoveling snow." She smiled at him, glad to see them both despite the underlying tension, the unspoken differences that separated them. She wondered what topic was safe to talk about, except the weather.

"We'll go up in the canyon tomorrow," her mother said. "It's a bird-watcher's paradise."

"Sounds like a plan." To her, the surrounding mountains looked like they could have been on the moon—dry, barren.

"We'll take some day trips," her dad said.

"Great." Touched by their attempts to entertain her, she made an effort to sound enthusiastic.

She sat outside with them as the sun slipped out of sight, leaving streaks of red and purple in its wake. The air cooled quickly, and stars popped out of the huge darkening sky. She wrapped herself in her dad's jacket and enjoyed the astronomical display while her parents watched television. She wished Nicky were here to film the sunset, the vast sky. It really looked bigger here. When her mother touched her shoulder, she looked around to ground herself.

Her parents were up at seven as was she. She wore jeans, a long-sleeved shirt, a warm vest and tennis shoes. Her parents had said she would need something warm. "This okay? I left my cowboy boots at home," she said, joking, and took the cup of coffee offered. "Thanks, Mom."

"You're so blond. I've been thinking about coloring mine." Her mother touched her hair. "Do you?"

"Nope. This is the hair I was born with. I just spend a lot of time outdoors." She grinned.

"It's beautiful," her mom said, "like you."

166

Her dad added, "You look like your mom did at your age."

Flustered, she actually blushed. They had never even told her she was pretty. Her mother had always stressed humility. "Well, thanks" was all she could think to say.

The canyon came alive with birds as they drove into it, parking where the road ended. In an open space, people had set up scopes.

"The birders," her dad said. "If you'd come in September or earlier you would have seen a ton of hummingbirds."

Ramsey Creek bubbled through the canyon, parting around rocks and speeding through narrows. They followed a path created by many climbing feet. Her parents stayed with her as long as she kept their pace. Everything she saw, from the strange looking raccoon-like creature to the small deer, to the birds that flitted around her, she stored away to tell Nicky.

"Lunchtime," her dad said, finding a flat rock big enough for the three of them. Her mom took sandwiches out of the backpack her dad had slung over his shoulders. Gray jays hopped near them.

"Don't give them anything," her dad warned. "It just makes them bolder."

She devoured the peanut butter sandwich and the apple and drank at least a pint of water. Then they started down the mountainside. On the way to the car, a woman stepped away from her scope and called to Meg. "Want to take a look?"

She did. They all did. Soaring high above was a pair of golden eagles. Nearer were smaller birds—nuthatches, kinglets and siskens. The woman pointed them out.

Her dad barbecued chicken on the grill that night. Her mom made potato salad. Meg put together the green salad with avocado and red peppers. They ate on the back porch as the setting sun again put on a jaw-dropping display. "Is it always like this?" she asked.

"In March after a rain the desert blooms. You should come for that, you and Denise," her mom said quietly.

She thought she misheard. "I haven't seen Denise in years."

"Oh." Her mom looked at her and away. "I see."

Of course she didn't see, but Meg wasn't about to say anything about Nicky unless someone asked.

After doing dishes, she grabbed a blanket and went outside. She stretched out on the chaise longue and fell asleep. This time the sun woke her as it blazed its way into the sky, wiping out the stars.

Her dad brought her a cup of coffee and sat with her. "Haven't done this since we moved here," he said.

Her mom joined them, her short hair wet from a shower. "We're taking a little trip to an artist's colony today."

"Can I look at your computer?" Meg asked.

"Of course."

She Googled Margo's Web site and showed her parents the photographs by Nicole Hennessey. Warmed by the connection, she looked over their shoulders as they clicked on one picture after another. She had none of these photographs on her walls. There was one of a ruby-throated hummingbird near a feeder that her mom pointed out. What kind of a schmuck was she to have ignored such talent, even if it was unintentional? Knee deep in horses, she'd forgotten to appreciate Nicky's passion—her photography.

She found Nicky's Web site, ashamed that she'd never looked at it or Margo's. There were several photos of her with Tango on Nicky's site. Even to her critical eyes, she looked good, and her parents were enthralled.

"Can we buy these two?" One was of her standing with Tango under the willow tree, taken the day she broke her ribs. Another was of her mounted on Tango, ready to show.

"You can have them." She put in a request for the two photos of herself and Tango, added the hummingbird, typed in her credit card number and sent the order to Margo. If Nicky was home, she'd print and frame the photos and Margo would send them. She had a brief attack of homesickness. How long had it been since she'd talked to Nicky? It seemed like months, not weeks.

At the end of the ten days, she wished her parents weren't

more than a thousand miles away. She remembered how she'd wondered what she would do during her visit. They'd only stayed home one day, the one before she left. Her parents seemed so different than she remembered. Perhaps it was she who was different—less defensive, more accepting.

"Don't be a stranger," her dad said at the airport.

Her mother cried as she hugged her.

"I'll be back. You could come visit me, you know."

"We will," her dad promised. "I want to see your stable."

"Well, it's nothing fancy."

She told them she loved them before she walked through security, then turned and waved on the other side.

Chapter Fifteen

Meg had asked that someone park her truck along the fence on the east side of the parking lot and lock the key inside. She had another set of keys on her. Even so, she looked for a familiar face, preferably Nicky's. There was none. She threw her backpack inside the cab and her suitcase in the back, glad that at least it wasn't snowing.

She had worn a light jacket to Arizona and was shaking with cold when she climbed behind the wheel. Perhaps Nicky had forgotten her arrival time. Maybe she was speeding now to get to the airport. When no cars were parked in her driveway, she opened the garage door and drove in next to the riding mower.

When she unlocked the door to the mudroom and Desperado jumped up from his pad, she was the one to yelp. Crazed with joy, he turned in tight circles in front of her as she made her way to the bedroom, where she dropped her baggage and knelt before him. He panted in her face as she stroked his coat and talked nonsense to him.

"At least someone is glad to see me."

She pulled a heavy sweatshirt over her head and stuffed her feet into her cowboy boots. The house was cold, and she turned up the thermostat before going upstairs. She flipped Nicky's computer open. The screen lit up and she saw herself astride Tango—the same print she'd ordered for her parents. She was the screensaver. It made her smile. Her finger hit the mouse and Nicky's schedule came up showing dates and times of meetings for Beth's campaign, most of them at Vicki's house.

In the kitchen she checked the fridge. Four cold beers sat next to a partially empty bottle of skim milk. Maybe Nicky would bring home a pizza. Meg's itinerary was under two magnets on the fridge. Her arrival time was highlighted in yellow. No way could Nicky have forgotten.

In the barn the horses' breath hung in the air as they nickered at her. She walked from one stall to the next, stroking muzzles, until she came to the last one. The mare's ears flattened as she approached. Lillie's horse had arrived the day before Meg left. She remembered her. Meg seldom forgot a horse. As she stood before the dun's stall, the mare lunged at her. Meg kicked the door and the horse whirled away and stood with her nose in a far corner. She knew who had trained this horse. He was quick to use a crop. Maybe Bunny just needed a kind, firm hand.

She cleaned stalls, turning each animal out in the indoor arena, telling Desperado to keep the horse there. How he understood what she wanted, she didn't know. She went from horse to horse. When she got to the mare's stall, she talked to her quietly as she put the halter over her flattened ears, which flicked forward as she listened. She would be all right. Meg didn't want anything around that might hurt Lucy, who was a little too fearless for her own good.

She glanced at her watch. Tina should have been here by now.

Nicky had to know Meg was home. Was she in no hurry to see her? She fed and watered, cleaning the buckets before refilling them. She hated to go inside the empty house, but Desperado was pushing her toward the door.

Outside, she paused to glance at the sky and saw only clouds spitting tiny sharp-edged bits of snow. She kicked off her boots in the mudroom and climbed the few steps to the dark kitchen. *What a lonely homecoming*, she thought as she fumbled for the switch and let out a little shriek. A mob of people stood in the kitchen and she took a quick step back, nearly falling down the steps. The dog gave a sharp bark and hid behind her.

She looked for Nicky and saw instead Tina and Lucy with Callie and Vicki and Dan and Natalie. Natalie looked like she was carrying triplets at least. A light flashed in her eyes as Nicky caught the expression on her face and then hugged her. "You look cute when you're scared," she whispered in Meg's ear as she handed her a glass of Beaujolais. "Welcome home."

"I could have had a heart attack, you know. But I would have died happy." She laughed, glad to see all of them. She had begun to think no one cared whether she came home or not.

Natalie was in charge of cooking. Boeuf bourguignon or in English, beef with wine, was the main dish. Garlic mashed potatoes, brussel sprouts drizzled with olive oil and baked in the oven and, of course, fresh bread completed the menu. The dessert was one of Natalie's chocolate sheet cakes decorated with IT'S YOUR TURN TO CLEAN THE STALLS.

Desperado crept back in the kitchen, lured no doubt by the smells. Meg's heart had settled into a steady beat after the scare. "How did you get here?" she asked.

"We ferried everyone over," Dan said, "and the food."

She answered their questions about the trip. She even tried to explain the sky, how big and magnificent it was, but ended up saying they'd have to see it themselves.

When the dishes were put away and the few leftovers stored in the fridge and everyone was gone but Meg and Nicky, they looked shyly at each other. "Was this your idea?" Meg asked.

172

"I was met by such a meal but not so many people," Nicky eyes were so dark they looked black. A smile played across her face. "We fooled you."

It had been a little heart breaking to feel so lonely, but she wouldn't tell Nicky that. "I wasn't sure you'd come home till I went upstairs and opened your computer."

"Where else would I be?"

"I don't know." Working on Beth's campaign maybe? Was that so terrible? That didn't mean Nicky was spending time with Beth. Did it? She couldn't ask, not just because Nicky might think she was spying on her but also because it made her look too needy. Needy wasn't attractive. "What did you say?" She'd seen Nicky's mouth move, had heard her voice but not her words.

"Are you still in Arizona, Meg? Did you like it there? My parents want us to move to Florida."

"They want *you* to move to Florida. Are you tempted?"

Nicky shook her head. "Not in the least, but my dad showed me the horse country. Did you know there are a lot of quarter horse farms there?"

"Yes. What else did your dad show you?"

"Later, Meg. Now we have more important things to do." She took Meg's hand and led her toward the bedroom. "God, I missed you. Why wouldn't you let me call you? I wanted to tell you what I was doing, what I was seeing. I was more scared of never seeing you again than of that Mustang with the crazy men."

"What crazy men?" When Nicky tried to pull her along, she dug in her heels, which didn't do much good since she had socks on. "Tell me."

"As soon as we get our clothes off. I want to look at you."

"You know what I look like."

"It always gives me a thrill." They were in the bedroom, and Nicky was attempting to pull Meg's shirt over her head.

"I can do that," Meg said, trying not to laugh. How could she resist?

They fell in a heap, their clothes tangled around their arms and legs, both of them laughing. "God, I'm horny," Nicky said.

"No more than I am." Meg kissed her.

They made love under the covers. Heat engulfed Meg toward the end. She threw off the blankets and breathed deeply. "I thought I was going to die under there," she said and broke into laughter.

Nicky's hair was wildly askew, her face beet red. "What a way to go, though. Think of the scandal. Two women suffocate in bed."

"Tell me about the Mustang," Meg said, thinking how difficult it would be to give this up—the sex, the talk in bed, the intimacy of sleeping with Nicky.

Nicky threw an arm around her and told her about her trip. "You know, I think Cleo even forgave me for loving women."

"That's the feeling I got too, although my parents didn't come right out and say so. They thought I was still with Denise." She shuddered. "My brother can carry on the name."

"I didn't know you had a brother." Nicky got up on her elbow and looked into Meg's face.

"My brother is ten years older than I am. I hardly knew him, and he's a bigot. I sent him a UNICEF Christmas card years ago, and he sent it back, saying he didn't believe in the United Nations."

"I didn't know you were political."

"You don't have to be political to support UNICEF. They help kids around the world."

"I know. What do you feel about helping Beth?"

"I thought we did that. We had a house party, remember?"

"What about knocking on doors and making phone calls?" Nicky gave Meg's forehead a reassuring kiss.

"I don't have time, Nicky. I get up early to take care of the horses, work eight hours, and come home to take care of horses again." Her life sounded boring even to her.

"I know." Nicky fell back on the bed. "I've made some phone calls."

Meg turned her back and her arm fell on Desperado. He

licked her hand. "You do what you have to do, Nicky." It was like she'd never left.

"You're the one who wanted to have the house party, not me."

"Let's go to sleep. I have to get up early."

"I always get up with you. I help you with the stable."

"You do." Meg rolled onto her back. "Nicky, why don't we have any of your pictures on our walls?"

"I didn't think you cared about stuff like that."

"Your pictures would brighten up the place."

"Okay, honey. You pick them out. I'll put them up."

"How is the photography business anyway?"

"About the same as the stable business. I'm keeping my nose just above the black line."

Meg turned toward Nicky and kissed her hard. "You are so talented."

In January and February, Nicky spent a lot of time at Callie and Vicki's house. Vicki had obtained lists of voters from the courthouse, and volunteers, like Nicky, were using their cell phones to make calls on Beth's behalf. Vicki thought that anyone running for an office other than a state or federal one was pretty much unknown to the general public. She organized meetings where Beth talked to the general public. Her opponent was invited to participate. Vicki put out snacks and coffee, called in notices to the paper and invited everyone she knew to come. She made sure there was coverage. Nicky helped with these meetings, which were held in every public library branch in the county. Nicky also went door-to-door, dropping off literature about Beth.

After the last meeting before the February primary, she helped Vicki cleanup and then drove home through a bitterly cold night. The dog let out a soft woof just as Scrappy would have. Undressing quickly in the dark, she slid between the covers and pressed her cold body against Meg.

"Sorry I'm so late. The meeting went on longer than usual and then we had to haul the food and literature out to Vicki's car."

"Was Callie there?" Meg asked.

"No. Something was going on at Lucy's school. You should have gone with me, Meg. I think some people come for the snacks. They're not your usual cheese and cracker..."

"Why have you thrown yourself into this thing, Nicky? And don't remind me of that house party."

She pulled Meg closer, wondering how to make Meg understand. Beth had not only asked her to move but had excluded her from all the brainstorming meetings that led to her candidacy—as if she had nothing to contribute. She was showing Beth how wrong she'd been. She said, "She never should have shut me out."

"You're doing just what she wants you to do, you and Vicki—energizing the gay community."

"Meg, I don't love her anymore. I love you."

"You could have fooled me. I'm hot, Nicky. Back off a little, will you?"

Stung, Nicky moved away. She shivered in the cold sheets on her side of the bed. "How was your day?"

"We can talk in the morning. I'm going to sleep."

"There's never time in the morning. We're always out in the goddamn barn, cleaning the goddamn stalls." The rush of anger surprised her.

"You don't have to help with the goddamn horses. Now I'm going to sleep."

"Don't, Meg. Don't shut me out," she said, moving closer.

"I'd like to shut you up."

Nicky curled herself into Meg again. "This will shut me up."

Beth won the primary, and Meg went with Nicky to the small party afterward. The election in April was virtually a shoo-in. Meg dressed in black slacks and a white fitted top. Her blond hair was piled high on her head. "You look good enough to eat," Nicky whispered in her ear before they entered the rented room at the Blue Ox.

"Take a bite and you're in trouble," Meg said.

Callie and Vicki stood inside the door. "Wow," Vicki said. Callie only looked, but her face told Meg she hadn't forgotten the few times they'd spent in the sack together.

Meg said, "I haven't seen Lucy since that little homecoming party.

"She's champing at the bit to come out there, isn't she, Cal?" Vicki said.

"It's the cold and school that are keeping her away. Tony will be dropping her off soon," Callie said.

"You look terrific, both of you," Meg said. Callie blushed and Vicki laughed. "We should have borrowed Bill this winter. Mice scamper under Desperado's nose and he herds them to safety," Meg added.

"Bill needs a few mice to chase. He's turning into a fat cat." Vicki put a hand on Callie's back. "Come with us, Meg. You need some good food to fatten you up."

Meg smiled. It was true she ate little when Nicky wasn't there to eat with her. She followed Vicki and Callie to the food bar. Beer was packed in ice, and she took one and filled a plate with appetizers.

"How are you, Meg?" Dan stood at her elbow, looking at the appetizers. "What a spread."

Natalie plunked down in a nearby chair. "I've got cabin fever. I haven't been at the restaurant for a week. Go socialize, Dan. I'll be right here."

Meg sat down next to her, a little uneasy. She had never quite forgiven Natalie for insisting Dan sell the farm and move into town. She put her plate on her lap and looked around the room. She saw Tina and Dr. Fred across the room talking to Nicky. Beth was deep in conversation with her ex, Mark, and Patricia Robson.

"Uh-oh," Natalie said. "I'm afraid I've made a mess. I knew I should have stayed home."

"What?" Meg stared at the water soaking Natalie's legs for a moment before comprehending. "I'll get Dan," she said.

"No, stay here." Natalie grabbed her arm, digging her nails into the flesh. "Take the tablecloth off the table."

"Let go and I will." Natalie released her, and she swept the white cloth out from under the food.

"Walk with me," Natalie said. "Dan is over by the door."

When Natalie stood, Meg wrapped the tablecloth around her. They took tiny steps toward Dan. The funny thing, Meg thought, was that people didn't seem to notice, even when Natalie stopped to clutch her abdomen and say, "Oh god, this isn't fun."

Dan ran to get Natalie's Volkswagen Golf as Meg continued walking her slowly toward the door. Meg had her eyes on the exit when Nicky showed up on the other side of her sister. "Take my arm, Nattie." Together, they sort of carried Natalie outside where Dan helped her into the car.

As Dan drove off, Nicky looked at Meg. "Let's go," she said with an excited grin.

After midnight, they stretched out on the couch in the waiting room and fell asleep. It was daylight before the baby cried. Meg sat up and Nicky jumped to her feet.

Dan came out of the delivery room and Nicky threw herself in his arms. He looked dazed as he smiled and said "a girl" over Nicky's shoulder.

Nicky let out a hoot and performed a little dance. "I want to see her."

"Aw. She is so cute," Nicky said, when Dan handed her the baby. "You did good, little sister."

The baby's fists were clenched under her chin. Her black hair was wet and her face wrinkled. She wasn't cute. "She's so tiny. Look at those fingernails. Amazing, isn't it?" Meg said to Dan, who nodded and grinned.

Nicky gave the baby to her sister and began to take pictures. Natalie looked whipped. Dan was still dazed. The baby opened its tiny mouth and began to wail. Natalie put her to her breast, but she only cried louder.

"Get the nurse," Natalie said. "Put that camera away, Nicky."

On the way home, Nicky called Vicki and Callie and asked

them to phone Beth with the news. Meg told her to call Tina, who said to tell Meg she had fed and watered the horses.

Meg grabbed the phone and said, "Thank you, thank you."

"Why don't you go to bed when you get home from work? I'll do the barn chores."

"I just hope I don't put a needle where it doesn't belong today." She gave the phone back to Nicky.

When her cell woke Nicky up, she was sprawled on the bed, still dressed. She looked at the display—Beth. "Hey, how was the rest of the party? I never got a chance to say congratulations."

"Congratulations yourself. You're an aunt."

"Yeah. They named her Danielle after her daddy."

"How about we do a celebratory lunch?" Beth asked.

"Today?"

"Yes. Can you make it? Riverview?"

"Sure." How could she politely say no? Besides, she was curious.

It was late February and grassy patches showed through the melting snow. The sun held some warmth as it shone down on her. If she took a deep breath, she could smell the earth.

She parked next to Beth's new Acura in the restaurant lot. A breeze off the river lifted her hair as she locked her Subaru. Inside, a wall of windows looked out on the river, which was running high and fast. She spied Beth sitting at a table for two near the windows.

"I know you like a good view." Beth smiled up at her, her hazel eyes lit from within.

Nicky pulled out a chair and sat down. When the waitress asked for their drink orders, Beth said, "Decaf."

"Regular." Nicky smiled. "I need some caffeine. I used to be able to stay up all night. Not any more."

"So did I," Beth said, smiling in turn.

The waitress poured the coffee and asked if they were ready to order.

"Soup," they said as one.

Beth laughed, but Nicky felt a terrible sadness. She was

suddenly close to tears, maybe because she was so tired. She could not let herself cry in front of Beth, but Beth knew her well enough to recognize the symptoms.

Beth looked at the river for a moment. She was dressed casually—slacks and a sweater. "I asked you here today to thank you for all your help." When she met Nicky's eyes, there was a slight frown between her eyes. "Why did you do it?"

By then, Nicky had pulled herself together. "Because you apparently thought I couldn't."

"I never thought that."

"You excluded me from your plans."

"Yes, because they weren't really my plans at first. They were Mark's and Patricia's"

"You don't want to be a judge?"

"Oh yes, but I never thought it was within my reach. They made me think it was possible."

"So you owed your loyalty to them." She heard the bitterness in her voice. Would she ever get over this?

"You could have put up a little resistance. Instead you moved in with Meg."

"After you said you couldn't win if people thought you were in a lesbian relationship, was I really supposed to stay?"

They assessed each other. Beth spoke first. "You couldn't choose between us, Nicky. Whether you want to admit it or not, I helped you make the choice."

Nicky nodded. "Yeah. Thanks." She pushed her chair back as the waitress brought their orders. Fishing around in her pocket, she put a twenty on the table.

"Sit down, Nicky." Beth's eyes flashed with anger. "Thank you," she said to the waitress, who quickly left. "I didn't ask you here to argue. Can't we remain friends? That's how we started."

Nicky remembered when their friendship turned into love or was it lust? "Not yet," she said. "I can't eat this, Beth."

"Take it home." Beth gave her a leveling look.

"It's soup."

"Then eat it."

She did, swallowing past the narrowing in her throat.

Beth hugged her in the parking lot. "Say hello to Meg. You're a lucky woman, Nicky."

She wasn't sure she was going to tell Meg anything. Her thoughts swirled before her eyes as she drove away. She got home without incident and stepped out into the slush. Although there was room for one vehicle in the garage, most of the time neither parked in it.

By habit, she climbed the stairs and loaded her pictures on the computer and on Margo's Web site. She looked around the room. It was uninviting—cold in the winter, hot in the summer. The walls were bare like those in the rest of the house. Meg had yet to pick out the photos she wanted printed for downstairs. Since Meg's return, they seemed to cross paths only in bed and in the morning. She had thrown herself into Beth's campaign for all the wrong reasons. And she was deceiving herself thinking she could make a living with her photography. The money for her share of the condo had given her a false sense of security. She had no real job, she'd just made a fool of herself and she'd neglected the person who mattered the most.

Doreen had called her saying the Tech had a job opening for a photography instructor. "Go for it, Nicky," she'd said. That had been a week ago, before the primary. She found her old portfolio in the closet, dusted it off and looked at the prints. They were faded. She went back to the computer and selected the photos she wanted for the portfolio. She was working on them when Meg appeared in the doorway.

She put her chin on Nicky's shoulder. "Nice picture."

"Yeah? Do you think it's sharp enough—the colors, the focus?" It was a monarch butterfly on a milkweed plant.

"I think it's beautiful."

"Hey, do you want to pick out some pictures for the downstairs?"

"Tomorrow. I'm going out to the barn and then to bed. I can hardly function."

"I'll go with you. Is Tina here?"

"Her car is. You don't have to go out. All that melted snow is freezing. I'll just check to see if she needs help."

"I'll help."

"You could bake a pizza instead. That would be great."

"Okay." But then she got caught up again in what she was doing. When she went downstairs, Meg was putting the pizza in the oven.

"I'm sorry. Time got away from me." She put her arms around Meg, and Meg leaned into her.

"I'm pretty much wiped out."

After a few bites, though, Meg perked up and asked about Nicky's day.

"Not much happened," she said, deciding it was easier to say nothing about her meeting with Beth. Maybe later she would tell Meg, when they were less tired, when she could talk about Beth dispassionately. This wasn't that moment.

Meg took her at her word. "I don't even remember mine."

After cleaning up the few dishes, Nicky went back upstairs. She saved her photos on a flash drive and printed a few for the portfolio. Those she slid into plastic sleeves when they were dry. She would go to the Tech first thing in the morning.

Meg was asleep when she climbed in bed. Despite her exhaustion, Nicky lay awake a long time. She was nervous about tomorrow. She wanted this job badly, if only to feel vindicated. She was a damn good photographer. It shouldn't matter that she had no paper that said so. Experience was her degree.

She got out of bed when Meg did, went out to help her feed and water and took a shower with her. "I could get used to this routine very quickly." Meg kissed her wet face and Nicky's eyes popped open.

"Turn around," Nicky said. She scrubbed Meg's back, kissing her soapy shoulder.

After Meg left, Nicky gathered her computer, the flash drive and portfolio and put them in her car. She'd read the Tech's ad again. She fulfilled every requirement, except the bit about having a bachelor's degree.

182

The Tech's campus was spread over several acres. She parked in front of the administration building. For at least fifteen minutes, she sat in the car repeating her spiel. She told herself that all anyone could say was no, and she had lived through their no once before. Now she was a well-known photographer. If they turned her down, it was their loss.

She stepped into a quiet hall. Was this an early spring break? She knocked on the door marked Administration and tried the doorknob. It was open.

A woman was walking toward a desk, carrying an armful of paper copies. "Sorry, I was away from my desk. What can I do for you?"

Nicky stammered a little until she found her voice. "I would like to interview for the photography job opening."

The sign on the woman's desk read Janet Tyler. She was forty-something with kind eyes and dishwater blond hair tied into a knot at her neck. "I'm so sorry. They interviewed at the beginning of the week for that position." Perhaps she saw the disappointment on Nicky's face, because she said, "They haven't decided yet, though. Would you like to fill out an application?"

Nicky unloaded the things in her arms on Janet's desk. She untied the portfolio and showed Janet the prints.

"Oh, my," the woman said. "These are good." She looked up at Nicky. "Who are you?"

"I should have said. I'm doing this back to front." Janet laughed and Nicky stretched out her hand. "I'm Nicole Hennessey."

"Even I've heard of you."

"I've got more photos that I'd like to show you." Nicky set up the computer, plugged in the flash drive and clicked open the photos stored on it. They were among her best. "I could show you all of my pictures, but that would take hours." She took the flash drive out and turned off the computer.

"I'll tell you what. No one but me is in today. If you leave the flash drive and portfolio here, I'll make sure your work gets seen by the right people." She handed Nicky an application.

"I have college credits, but I don't have a degree."

"You have experience and talent."

Nicky left with a good feeling that began to leave her the further she drove. If it had been up to Janet Tyler, she was sure she'd be hired, but of course, it wasn't. She drove to Margo's to see if she'd sold any more prints.

"Meg ordered three while she was in Arizona and had them sent to her parents' address. I had all the prints here, framed. I mailed them."

"Why didn't you tell me?"

"I didn't see much of you. You were so busy campaigning."

"I've been such a dope. You didn't charge her, did you?"

"How else do we make a living? We can't be giving away photos."

"But Meg?"

"I asked. She wanted to pay."

"I took some prints over to the Tech. They have a position open for a photography instructor."

"You're the best photographer in the area."

She grabbed Margo by her broad shoulders and gave her a kiss on the cheek. "Well, thanks."

Margo touched her cheek and smiled. "Go on, get out of here. I've got work to do."

Chapter Sixteen

The second Saturday of March was deceptively warm. A robin sang fervently from a bare branch on the maple tree. Doves cooed at each other. They nested early and were busily pecking at the hay in the loft. Spring wasn't here yet, Meg knew. This was a bit of promise that could be buried under several snowstorms till the real thing arrived in April or May, but she welcomed it anyway. The ground was slushy and slippery. It wasn't safe to ride outside.

The boarders were out in full force, though—Tina and Lillie and Lillie's friend, Ann, who had bought a horse dirt cheap—Lillie's words—which was in the stall next to Bunny. Bunny lunged at Ann's gelding, an appaloosa with a large head, which rubbed against the wall between the two stalls and nickered at the mare through the wire. Bunny was in heat. The horses were still in their stalls. Tony had dropped off Lucy, who was getting ready to groom Tango.

Meg sat on the bench outside the tack room, cleaning her saddle. Despite the relatively warm day, the barn felt chilly. Tango was sound. She was grateful for that. There was a scar and a thickening of his leg below the hock, but since he wasn't born that way, he could be shown at halter.

Nicky handed Meg an envelope. She was smiling, her dark blue eyes happy. "Take a look."

"Good news?" Meg asked, noting the Tech's address on the front corner. Inside was a letter from the president, Gordon Blair. She read a few sentences and looked up at Nicky. "You never said…"

"I know. Last time I applied for a job there, they said I needed a college degree."

"But this is wonderful, Nicky."

Nicky grinned sheepishly. "It's just one class three evenings a week, but it's a foot in the door."

"That's great, sweetie." She handed back the letter and envelope. "Have you told anyone else?"

"Margo. I saw her right after I applied for the job."

"Why not me?"

"I care too much about what you think," she said.

"They'd be stupid not to hire you, Nicky. Come with me." She got up to put her saddle away and heard someone yelling. "What the…" She wheeled.

Allie was standing inside the door, shouting. Meg was so surprised to see her that it took her a moment or two to understand what the girl was saying. "The house is burning."

She stared at Allie for a few heartbeats before beginning to run. She pushed Allie aside and rushed into the yard, nearly falling over a bike. Heat was sucking the oxygen out of the air. "Where, where?" she asked, taking Allie by the shoulders.

"The back, by the creek. I was riding my bike and saw it. Look!" The girl pointed at the roofline. Flames appeared like waves, licking at the shingles. She heard crackling.

"Oh, God." She fumbled for her cell and called 911.

Nicky, who had followed Meg outside, bolted back into the barn. "The hose," she yelled, but the hose barely made it out the door. "We need another hose."

Meg sprinted for the garage and came back, dragging a long hose. She screwed it to the first and hollered for someone to turn the water on. Nothing came out of it and Meg threw it on the ground. "Frozen." She rushed into the barn and unscrewed the first hose, dragged it to the house and screwed it on that faucet.

"Somebody come hold it," she screamed. Tina took the hose, spraying the thin stream of water at the flames that were eating up the roof. "Where did Nicky go?"

"I don't know," Tina said.

"I've got to get the horses out of the barn. Somebody should move the cars. Do it," she said to Lillie and Ann, who were staring at the fire. She ran into the barn, Lucy and Allie on her heels.

With shaking hands she put halters on Sam and Tango and gave the lead ropes to Lucy and Allie. "Leave the door open," she said as they trotted toward the door that opened onto the pen and field. Desperado was trying to herd her out the door. She went down the aisle, putting halters on Champion and the appaloosa, which were nervously circling their stalls. The smell and sound of the fire had drifted into the barn. She led Champion toward the open door to the pen and smacked him on the rump. Desperado did the rest, chasing him outside and coming back in to do the same to the appaloosa.

The mare was kicking and whirling in her stall. Meg spoke quietly to her, dodging her feet. She put a rope around her neck and tried to lead her into the aisle, but she reared, and the rope burned through Meg's hands. "Easy, girl," she said, managing to get a halter over her ears by hanging on as the horse reared again. Desperado got behind the mare and did the rest. Bunny leaped forward, squeezing Meg against the post that held the stall door. The dog herded the mare out of the barn.

Meg walked to the door, holding her sore arm close to her

side. The horses were racing across the field as they had when Allie turned them loose. They blurred into one line as she watched. She shut the door so that none could return. Desperado was already beginning to circle them.

The cars and truck had been moved to the road. Lillian and Ann stood near them. Tina was still aiming the water at the roof in a vain attempt to stop or slow the fire. Sparks fell around her. Lucy and Allie were helping her hold the hose. The screams of sirens drowned out their voices.

"Where's Nicky?" Meg yelled again, knowing as soon as she asked where Nicky was. She had gone into the house to get her computer, of course, the one that held all her photographs. Meg raced toward the side door. Tina dropped the hose and tackled her. Lucy and Allie picked up the hose. Meg freed herself of Tina's weight and managed to stand, but Tina grabbed her leg and held on, calling for Lucy to help. Lucy took hold of Meg's other leg, and Meg went down again. Her gaze remained on the open door as she pulled herself and Tina and Lucy toward it, using her arms and elbows.

Nicky appeared in the smoke-filled mudroom door as two fire trucks screamed into the driveway. She stumbled toward Meg, who got to her feet with Tina's help. Nicky's face was smudged with dirt and tears. "I couldn't get up the stairs." She leaned on her knees and coughed horribly.

A fireman and Tina tended to Nicky while Meg stood nearby, watching her house burn to the ground. They had been shooed into the field, where Meg shivered as afternoon turned into night. Allie's dad was there, his arm around his daughter's shoulders. Dan parked out by the road, talked to a fireman and hotfooted it across the yard to the field. He carried blankets, which he put around Meg, Nicky and Tina, who stood nearby. Tony must have called him, Meg realized. Callie and Vicki had been allowed to go to Lucy.

The firemen had turned the hoses on the barn, wetting it down, even though there were no sparks leaping through the air anymore. The water turned to ice as the ground quickly cooled.

"I'm sorry, Meg," Nicky said, seeing tears on Meg's face.

"I don't give a fuck about the house," Meg said. "I thought you were dead, Nicky. How could you do something so idiotic?" They were huddled with the others, seeking warmth.

"It was stupid. I wasn't thinking."

Meg felt Desperado leaning against her. Had he been with the horses all this time? She enclosed him in her blanket. "Good dog," she said and he wriggled close.

A fireman was talking to Dan, who gestured for her to come over. "Is it out?" she asked the man, whose face was red. "Are you burned?"

"Nah." He asked her questions, like did she leave anything cooking on or in the stove? She shook her head. He said, "We're putting yellow tape around the place. A couple of inspectors will come out tomorrow to check out what might have started the fire. You better call your insurance agent if you haven't already."

"Can we put the horses back in the barn?" she asked.

"I'd wait till morning," he said.

She thought to thank him.

"We have to move the horses," she said to Dan.

"I'll get a flashlight."

Lucy and Allie both begged to help with the horses. Lucy said, "They're out in the cold. Can't I stay here with you? Are you going to sleep in the barn?"

"Both of you, listen," Meg said firmly. "The horses will be fine. And we'll be sleeping at Tina's tonight, not in the barn. It might not be safe." The girls were heroines in her mind. "Thanks, both of you."

"C'mon." Tony tugged on Lucy's sleeve. "You can ride with me."

"In that noisy old piece of junk? I'll ride with Mom and Vicki."

"I won't ask you twice," Tony said, winking at Meg.

She laughed, startled that she found anything funny, but she was older than his mother.

They separated the mare from the others. Once Desperado

understood, he kept the mare in the field closest to the barn as Meg, Dan and Tina led the others into Dan's field and Nicky closed the gate.

Dan patted her on the back before getting into his truck.

"Want your blanket?" she asked.

"Nope. I'll be out soon. You two get some sleep."

Meg lifted Desperado into the truck with her. Nicky drove her Subaru. They followed Tina home. When they got there, Tina gave them each a bathrobe and washed and dried their clothes while they took turns showering. It was wonderfully warm in the queen-size bed in Tina's guest bedroom. Nicky fell asleep almost as soon as she shut her eyes. Meg wrapped herself around Nicky and listened to her labored breathing. It had seemed almost a miracle when Nicky appeared in the doorway of the house. She had been so sure Nicky wasn't going to come out, so desperate to find her, so angry with Tina and Lucy for holding her back.

No matter how tightly she closed her eyes, no matter how heavy her limbs, no matter how much she wanted to forget for a few hours, she couldn't sleep. Finally she realized it was no use, she wasn't going to sleep until she assured herself that the barn wasn't on fire and the horses were all right. A digital clock read three a.m. when she got up and dressed. She tiptoed down the stairs to the first floor with Desperado on her heels and quietly slipped outside into the cold, clear March night. After helping the dog onto the passenger seat of the F250, she backed out of the driveway, turning the lights on only when they were on the road.

The barn stood as they had left it. The ruins of the house, burned to the basement, stank. She walked with the aid of the moon's pale light to the gate where the mare called to the horses, which were standing in a huddle.

Assured that they were all right, she went back to the barn. She made a mattress of horse pads for herself and the dog, wrapped up in Dan's blanket and fell asleep. That's where Nicky and Tina found her the next morning.

"Wake up, sleeping beauty," Nicky said. "Talk about *me*

scaring *you*. What about you disappearing in the middle of the night without telling me where you were going?"

Tina handed her a thermos of coffee.

Nicky helped Tina and Meg bring in the horses. They balked when they smelled the remains of the fire, but Desperado urged them forward.

When the horses were in their stalls, Nicky and Meg finally went to see what remained unscathed by the fire. There wasn't much. They stood near the edge of the stinking rubble that had been the house, amazed that the nearby garage was still standing, as was the maple tree—although both were scorched on one side.

Nicky was just beginning to realize the full extent of their losses, especially her own. It wasn't just her computer that was gone and all the images stored on it. Her expensive printer was burned up too. Thankfully, her camera with all its lenses had been in her car. She never went anywhere without them. Also tucked in her camera bag was some cash and her credit card. Meg had a few dollars in her jeans.

Tina had invited them to stay with her indefinitely. But neither she nor Meg had any extra clothes, much less toothbrushes, shampoo or anything else. When Nicky told Meg she was going shopping for them, Meg said, "Okay. I'll pay you back." She wouldn't budge from the barn.

Nicky made a quick trip to town. She threw the bags of clothes and personal necessities, like toothpaste and floss and ibuprofen, in the backseat of her car and hurried back to the barn. The inspectors had arrived by then and were poking around the ruins of the house. Meg's insurance agent was hovering around the edges too. He also handled Nicky's rental insurance.

The agent was saying, "We'll get you a check as soon as the inspectors are done. You too, Nicky," and Nicky was glad she'd had the foresight to change her residence on her policy.

"Mice," Meg told Nicky as soon as she knew. "They were chewing up the wiring. If we'd had Bill, that wouldn't have

191

happened." When Nicky looked confused, she said, "Callie's cat, Bill, is a mouser. He probably kept the house from burning down when she lived here."

"I lived here before she did," Nicky said. She shivered. "It could have happened at night. God, what a disaster!"

They were alone in the barn. Meg shrugged. "Well, it didn't. And no one died. That's all I care about."

Nicky had realized belatedly that Margo had all of her photos stored on her Web site. Her insurance would cover everything else, which, except for the computer and printer, wasn't much. She could have died trying to rescue things that could be replaced. How stupid was that?

"Will you go with me to look at trailers?" Meg asked.

"Why are you looking at trailers?" she said, thinking Meg was talking about horse trailers.

"We need a place to live. We can't stay at Tina's forever."

"You're not going to build?" Nicky knew her parents would be appalled if she moved into a trailer. "They're fire hazards, you know, and they're the first to go in strong winds."

"In Arizona they put tires on the roofs. I suppose it's to hold them down."

Nicky grinned. "We don't want to look like trailer trash, do we?"

Meg lifted one eyebrow. "Wouldn't that frost Cleo?"

"I don't know which Cleo would consider worse, my living with a woman or staying in a trailer." Although she thought her mother had pretty much resigned herself to her sexual orientation. She laughed. "Wait till she hears I'll be doing *both*!"

When the yellow tape was removed, Nicky and Meg scoured through the remains of the house. They wore cowboy boots and leather gloves to protect themselves from nails and other sharp objects. Parts of the appliances and bedsprings were recognizable. Everything else had melted beyond identification. Dan was coming over soon with a bulldozer to push the wreckage into the basement and cover it with dirt.

He drove into the driveway and unloaded the heavy machinery. "Find anything worth saving?" he asked before he climbed onto the dozer.

"No." Meg gave him a faint smile. "What do I owe you for this?"

"A friend let me use the dozer and trailer."

"C'mon, Dan," Meg said skeptically.

"No, really," he said. "A buddy of mine owns it. He let me use it in exchange for some welding."

"Let me pay for the welding."

"Do you have to be so goddamn proud, Meg? Give it a rest, woman. Okay?"

"Wow. Listen to the man," Nicky said. Dan rarely got riled up.

Meg's mouth twitched. "Okay, big guy. Have it your way."

Dan grinned. "Besides, it's fun."

Meg disappeared into the barn, but Nicky leaned against Dan's truck and watched. After a few minutes she got her camera out of her car. The roar of the diesel engine and the fumes it belched faded into the background as she took pictures. *"Man at Work,"* she thought. Maybe she'd give one of the prints to Dan for Christmas.

When her phone vibrated in her pocket, she glanced at the display. Beth again. She let the call go in with her other messages from Beth. If Beth wanted to know how she was, she could come out and see.

The bulldozer pushed what was left of the house into the basement and Dan drove back and forth over the wreckage, crushing it. By mid-afternoon, he covered it with the dirt that had been dumped in the yard. He loaded up the bulldozer and waved at Nicky as he drove out. The place almost looked like a park. She could see all the way to the creek that ran behind the house.

The sun warmed her as she took an old lawn chair out of the garage and lay back in it. Her mind was occupied with the course at the Tech. She had been asked to submit a curriculum but had been given an extension because of the fire. What would she say? What would she do? This was her first teaching position, something she'd coveted for years.

"Hey." Meg's voice woke her. "You okay?"

She shaded her eyes and looked up at Meg. The sun made a halo of Meg's blond hair. "You look like an angel."

"Yeah, sure. I'll show you how much I'm not an angel."

"Ah, something to look forward to. Don't you ever get bored with these horses?" She got to her feet and looked into Meg's eyes.

"No more than I'm bored with you."

"You're comparing me to Tango?" She walked with Meg to her car.

"Tango never gives an opinion." Meg opened the back door and Desperado jumped in.

"Horses are high maintenance. They can't even brush their hair or clean up after themselves."

Meg ran her fingers through Nicky's hair. "This is what you call brushed?"

She would have said Meg's hair didn't look much better, but she loved it loosely piled on her head, just like it was. She changed the subject. "How are we going to thank all these people? Especially Tina and Dan?"

"I don't know. I've been thinking, though. We could take them out to dinner, but that seems so not enough. I think we should throw a big party when we get our new home."

"Except then they'll bring house-warming gifts and think the party is for us."

"You're right. We'll have to think some more. Right now I'm hungry."

Tina was no cook either. The three of them bumbled around the kitchen doing different things and getting in each other's way. Tina had decided they would have creamy rigatoni. She was making the sauce. Nicky was cooking the rigatoni and Meg was putting together a salad.

"When is your mom coming back?" Meg asked.

"A week from Monday. I can't wait. She's a great cook."

194

"Why aren't you?" Nicky asked.

"I could ask you the same question. Probably disinterest."

They sat at the kitchen table, where they could look out the windows at the birds on Tina's feeders. The goldfinches were turning bright yellow. Tina asked. "When is the first show?"

"The shows started a long time ago. We just didn't go. We weren't ready and they were too far away. People who show all the time keep their horses under blankets and lights. We haven't done either."

"The lights would probably burn down the barn," Nicky said. She was thinking that mice had to be populating the barn too. Maybe it was wired differently. Maybe the only wires were those exposed for them to see. Still, it might be a good idea to get a cat.

Meg said, "I'm aiming for May. We'll show Sam in Amateur and Senior Pleasure and Tango in Junior Pleasure."

"What about Lucy?" Nicky asked.

"She'll be our gofer. She needs a good little horse."

"What about Allie?" Nicky persisted.

"She has Brownie. That's a whole different thing."

In bed that night, Nicky snuggled close to Meg. The spring peepers were singing outside the open window. Desperado was curled into a ball on a clean horse pad. "You promised."

"What did I promise?" Meg asked sleepily.

"To show me how much not an angel you are."

Meg laughed softly. "You already know that."

"It's Saturday." Nicky stroked Meg's arms, feeling the long muscles.

"That feels good."

"How does this feel?" With a gentle touch Nicky caressed Meg's shoulders, her breasts, her belly, her hips. She traced the strong muscles of her thighs.

"Okay."

"Just okay?" She'd been looking forward to this. Meg's tepid response was a turn-off.

Meg pulled her back when she started to turn away. She kissed her face, her shoulders and breasts. "How does this feel?"

Nicky gave a low lustful growl, but said only, "Okay." To her, making love was something of an art. She pictured them through the photographic lens in her brain. Meg's blond hair contrasting with her own dark head, their mouths as one, legs and arms wrapping their long slender bodies together. When she buried herself between Meg's legs, she pictured that too.

"Shhh, Tina might hear us," Meg whispered, just before pulling Nicky down.

Chapter Seventeen

The doublewide trailer was delivered on a Saturday. Meg had it unloaded and jacked up on a slab she'd had poured next to the garage, near the maple tree. She believed the tree would recover and, indeed, it had buds. She and Nicky had painted the garage, so that it gave the illusion of newness. She liked the trailer, the way every little extra space was put to use. She thought it was cozy. After they moved in their new furniture, she threw open the windows, sat in the chairs and lay on the beds. There were three bedrooms, one of which Nicky was setting up as her office.

Nicky arranged her new Mac and high-end Epson printer on the computer desk she'd also bought. When Meg stuck her head in the door, she told her she was downloading new software off the Web and putting together a file and backup system that would preserve her work in the event of another disaster. "Actually," she said, "Margo is my backup system of last resort."

"That's good," Meg said absently. Although she knew and cared little about computers, she realized Nicky had to have good equipment for her photography.

Nicky had finished the curriculum for the Tech and practiced what she would say to her class in bed at night, waking Meg when she fell asleep.

Meg came into the office and put her arms around Nicky and leaned into her. "You just keep working. Your ideas for class are good. Really. Your students will be giving you competition soon."

Nicky reached up and pulled her head down for a kiss. "You're a sweetie. If nothing else, I'm good at putting you to sleep."

"I'm sorry. I'm just so tired at night. See you when you're done. I'll be in the barn."

"I'll be out soon."

The stable was not making money, but it was not losing it either. As soon as the grass got a head start, Meg would put Champion out on pasture. Laura Healey had called after the fire to say they had room for a couple horses if Meg was short on space. She'd told Meg then that they'd kept the palomino because Jack would be lonely without a companion. She'd said, "Sometimes I ride him when Chelsea is working Jack."

At the first horse show the next weekend, Laura came over to say hello. "I've got something I want to talk to you about when you have time, maybe tomorrow." She was shading her eyes, looking up at Meg.

"Sure." Meg was sitting on Tango next to her old stock trailer, ready to go to the arena for Junior Western Pleasure. She had a sinking feeling in her gut, because Tango was craning his neck and moving sideways like he'd never been at a show.

The vet rode past on his young stallion. He too had offered help after the house burned down. He had never billed her for administering to the abandoned horses and Desperado. "Hey," he said. "Is this Tango's first time out this year?"

"Yep. He's acting like it too. Hope he doesn't make a fool of both of us." What she really hoped was that he wouldn't disrupt the class.

"No horse can make a fool of you, Meg." It was a rare compliment.

"Thanks," she said and called, "Good luck."

He touched the brim of his hat and wished her the same.

Tango actually made the cut, which made her think the judge liked the way he looked and moved. If he had worked better, he probably would have placed. She rode him around in the field after the class until his gaits and transitions were smooth.

She was currying the sweat off him when Mac walked over. "Want to sell him? There's a guy willing to pay eight thousand for him."

"Well, he's a fool then and I'm one too for not taking the offer."

"I think he's a keeper too, Meg."

Tina came around the trailer, lugging her saddle. She opened the tack room door and put it on one of the saddle racks. "You made him look good, Meg."

Meg laughed. "Not good enough. I think I'm going to burn up a lot of entry fees before he wins anything." But she felt good—about the offer and about Mac's comments regarding her and Tango.

When Nicky showed up with her camera and lenses stowed in their bag, Tina and Meg loaded the horses in the trailer and drove out of the fairgrounds for home.

Tina sat between them, because Nicky claimed she suffered from claustrophobia. "Look at all those ribbons," Nicky said. "You're stars."

"Sam and Meg are the stars. I'm just a passenger on the horse."

When they turned into the driveway, Meg said more with annoyance than surprise. "Who owns that?" A matching truck and trailer were parked out by the barn. All Meg wanted was to unload, take care of the horses and relax, and here was some stranger parked in her way.

Tina cleared her throat. "Me. They belong to me."

"What?" Nicky and Meg said at once. For a moment Meg

thought Tina was taking Sam out of her barn. Why else would she have bought a truck and trailer?

"Well, do you want to move it?" Meg asked.

"Don't you want to see it?"

"Later." Her truck had well over a hundred thousand miles on it and the trailer was at least as old. She had been thinking about buying a used truck with fewer miles on the odometer and an enclosed trailer.

"Come on," Tina said. "Take a look inside. I got a great deal." She showed them the living quarters with the big bed in the gooseneck, the tack room with its saddle racks and hooks, and finally the padded stalls for four horses.

"How great a deal?" Meg asked grudgingly. Sienna Sam and Tango deserved a trailer like this.

"I bought the pair from the bank at less than cost."

"Somebody loses and somebody wins," she said ungraciously, and Tina looked stunned.

"They're really nice," Nicky said, looking from Tina to Meg.

Meg sighed and crossed her arms. She glanced away and back at Tina. "I can't afford a truck and trailer like these."

"And I can't park them in my driveway. The subdivision doesn't allow vehicles that won't fit in the garage." Tina was not cowed. "Listen, Meg, you're my trainer. You can drive my truck and pull the trailer with my horse in it."

"Let's unload the horses and talk about this later." Meg turned on her heel and there was nothing to do but follow her.

Before Tina went home, she tried to park the truck and trailer out of the way. "I don't know how to back this thing," she said, giving up. "Can you put it out of the way? Maybe at the next show someone will buy it."

"You're behaving badly, Meg," Nicky said when Tina drove off in her car. "You need a new truck and trailer. For god's sake, I drove that truck of yours ten years ago and it wasn't new then. What if you break down with horses in the trailer, all because of your stupid pride?"

Meg whirled on her. "I will buy a newer truck and trailer, but

I'll do it."

"Why not let Tina help if she wants to? She's got a fifteen-thousand dollar horse to think about."

"Let it go, Nicky. It's my decision."

"Then I'll pay for part of it. I've got insurance money left over. I've got the condo settlement."

"No, you won't. Did you let Beth pay all the bills?"

"Of course not," Nicky said angrily. "Go ahead and keep driving that rig until the transmission goes out or a wheel rolls off the trailer."

"I told you I was going to look for a good used rig."

The dog had disappeared. "We're scaring Desperado."

That silenced them both. Nicky reheated Friday night's dinner—chicken and mashed potatoes and green beans. When they sat down, Nicky said, "Look, do what you have to do. I can't stand the silence."

Meg nodded and began eating. The dog lay near the door, keeping a wary eye on them. "I'm sorry. I wish she'd said something to me first."

"Would it have made any difference?"

"Maybe. I worry that someone is going to dump another horse on us. I have to have money in case that happens."

Nicky stared at her. "I think the odds are against that."

Meg chewed and chewed and swallowed, like eating was a chore. "Every time I go out the door or drive in the driveway I see another Brownie tied to the fence."

"Well, if that happens we'll deal with it, but you have to be safe when you're on the road."

Meg nodded. "I'm going to bed," she said. "Do you mind cleaning up?"

Yes, Nicky minded cleaning up. The rule was whoever made dinner got out of doing dishes, but she sighed and said nothing. It was still light out and after she was done in the kitchen, she went to her office and looked at the pictures from the horse show. She had taken some orders.

201

When she climbed in bed, Meg was sleeping. She curled against her and fell asleep, listening to the croaking of frogs coming from the creek.

In the morning, Meg was gone. It was unusual for one of them to rise before the other. Most mornings they spent a few minutes lying together, talking. But there was another show that day. They were going only for the performance classes that started at noon. Meg must be out feeding.

Nicky's phone rang and she cradled it between her shoulder and chin as she poured water in the coffeemaker. It was Tina.

"Will you tell Meg I'll be over around ten?"

"Well, sure, but why don't you tell her yourself?"

"She's probably out in the barn."

Lucy arrived with her mother and Vicki. Tina got out of her car armed with FOR SALE signs. Wowed by the rig, Lucy looked in every door, until Meg said, "Why don't you help load stuff in the trailer?"

"Okay," she said enthusiastically and ran toward the barn, her brown hair flying.

Vicki and Callie were standing together, admiring the truck and trailer.

"I bought them for my horse," Tina said, carrying her chaps and hat. "I was hoping Meg would drive the truck for me, because I've never towed a trailer, much less backed one, but hey, I can learn."

"Well, we're taking it today," Meg said, "and I am driving."

Nicky and Tina exchanged looks, eyebrows lofted.

"Looks like the truck has a backseat. Can we go with?" Vicki said.

The show was at the same fairgrounds as the day before. When Tina started to tape FOR SALE signs to the truck and trailer, Meg took them down. "We'll use it," she said in a low voice to Tina. "I'll buy in. Sorry about yesterday. I don't like people making decisions for me. Do you?"

"Let me tell you something I learned the hard way. You have

to look successful if you want people to knock on your door. People often judge your abilities by how much money they perceive you to have."

"Well, I guess I better finish painting the barn then," Meg said with a sudden grin.

The make-up and show arena had been watered down, but before long, dust hung in the air. Lillian had come with them this time. Her mare was tied to one side of the trailer. Tango and Sam were on the other. Meg helped her saddle the mare, which was no longer in heat but cow-kicked anyway when Meg tightened the girth. She slapped its belly. "Quit that."

"Let me get Tango, and I'll ride with you." Meg threw a leg over Tango and rode toward an open space. Lillie and Tina followed. "Let's just pretend we're in the show arena. Keep your distance from each other and do what I do, but don't jump into a trot or canter. Take your time. And talk to that mare, Lillie. Don't let her pin her ears."

Before long, others joined them—Chelsea on Jack, Mac on his horse. They rode to get the horses working well, but not long enough to work up a sweat. The mare worked well, but she pinned her ears and swished her tail. Even so, she got a sixth in Amateur Western Pleasure, the class Tina and Sam won.

After Meg won the Senior Pleasure on Sam and placed fourth in Junior Western Pleasure, she rode back to the trailer and began taking Tango's tack off.

Lucy had been the gofer—the one who carried the fly spray, who pinned on numbers, who did a last-minute brushdown before the horses went into the show arena. She was sitting on the fender of the trailer.

Meg thanked her for her help and she shrugged it off, but Meg knew how she longed to show. She carried her saddle into the tack room, where there was plenty of room to stand up and hang four saddles. When she came out, Laura and Chelsea were talking to Lucy.

"Congratulations," Meg said. She had been going over to their house to give lessons every other week.

"Can I talk to you, Meg?" Laura said, moving out of earshot of Lucy and Chelsea.

Meg followed. "What's up?" she asked, unzipping her chaps.

"Remember yesterday when I said I wanted to talk to you about something? Our palomino needs someone to show him. We thought maybe Lucy would do that for us. We'd put his papers in her name and would take him to the shows, and she could come over to our place to ride when you give lessons."

Meg was so taken by surprise that she stared at Laura as if she hadn't understood.

Laura stumbled on. "Do you think Lucy would do that for us?"

"What do you mean 'for us?' You're offering her a horse to show and you act like she's doing you a favor?"

"Well, Sunny needs someone to show him. I'm not good enough. She is."

"Yes, she is." Meg smiled and touched Laura's arm. "Thanks. Why don't you ask her mother first? You know Callie."

When they left the fairgrounds, Nicky said, "I can hardly believe how things have fallen in place. Every disaster has had a plus. Allie took Brownie. We have a new house, a new rig and everyone has a horse to ride. And I have a new job."

Meg pictured the horses running across the field in a stream of color, Allie and Brownie in the lead. "It seems too good to be true, doesn't it?"

Tina patted Meg's leg. "You deserve it."

She didn't believe in just desserts. So she wasn't too surprised to see a horse in the pen outside the barn when she drove slowly down the driveway. Before unloading the horses, she walked to the fence with Nicky and Tina.

This time the horse was a paint—white and black that blended into brown. He was gaunt, his tail chewed short, his mane standing on end. He put his head over the fence and nickered. "Poor guy," she said, her heart aching as it had for Brownie and Champion and Desperado. How many unwanted animals were out there? How many would end up here? "I better call Mac. He'll need shots and worming."

In bed that night, Meg said, "I'll never come out ahead. I felt so good when we left the fairgrounds. It seemed like everything was coming together. I should have known better. No one is going to buy Champion or the paint except for meat. We're back where we started when someone dumped Brownie." She lay on her side, facing Nicky.

"Oh, I don't know. What's one more horse? He can go out on pasture with Champion. We're not at the end of our rope yet. How about a little appreciation for what we do have?"

"I have you and Tango." Wasn't that all she ever wanted—a good horse and Nicky?

"Thanks for putting me first. Love me, love my horse."

Meg laughed softly. "No, it's not that way. I love you, Nicky—more than anything or anyone." She kissed Nicky's chin.

"Yeah, me too."

"You too what?"

"I love you, Meg—from the top of your wild blond hair to the tips of your old cowboy boots." She loosened Meg's ponytail, releasing her hair.

Meg smiled and moved closer. This was the ultimate comfort for her, the feel of Nicky's warm skin against her own. It was better than winning any pleasure class.

Epilogue

Nicky talked to Rosita about throwing a party for those who had helped with the fire. "Can you teach us to cook for all these people?"

"How many?" Rosita asked.

"Well, let's see—Dan and Natalie, Tina, Lucy and Callie and Vicki, Allie and her dad, Chelsea and Laura and Tom Healey, the other boarders and Dr. Fred and Tony and Dr. MacIverson and his wife and you and me and Meg."

"What?" the older woman exclaimed. "Nineteen people?"

Nicky looked chagrined. "Of course, that's too many. How would we squeeze them in the trailer anyway?"

"We will do it here. This house is big enough. Tina will help. It will be a tapas party," Rosita said confidently.

The tapas turned out to be a huge amount of work but incredibly good. Grilled grape leaves stuffed with cheese and sun-dried tomatoes, shrimp ceviche, mini barbecued ribs, stuffed tomatoes, bean and chicken enchiladas, margaritas and on and on. Meg thought the variety and number of tapas were endless and more than once regretted their decision to do this. Tina grumbled too but never managed to shorten her mother's menu no matter how many times she said, "Mama, no more."

The party was a great success. Everyone showed up. They filled Tina's house with conversation and laughter. They even stayed around to clean up the dishes. And when they were gone, Rosita, Tina, Nicky and Meg collapsed on the couch and chairs.

"Now we should have a dinner for you, Rosita," Meg said. "You were a star. Your tapas won the blue ribbon."

"It was fun," Rosita said. The other three looked at each other with bemusement, and Tina rolled her eyes. "You all done good."

"Did you know what Laura was up to, Meg?" Tina asked.

"Nope. I never had a clue."

Laura Healey had set up a legal charity for rescued horses. She was collecting donations to support Champion and the paint and any other horses that might be left at Meg and Nicky's barn. She had also offered pasture and shelter on their property when and if the horses became too many, and Dr. MacIverson had agreed to provide care to abandoned animals at cost.

"She and Mac deserve trophies too," Nicky said.

"You all do, everyone who was here does. I can't even begin to thank them or you," Meg said.

On their way home, Nicky told Meg how she could thank her, and Meg laughed. "Dream on, sweetie. Not tonight. I'm worn out."

"So am I," Nicky said. "There's always tomorrow."

"And the next day and the next." She believed, finally, that the luxury of time was on their side.

Publications from Bella Books, Inc.
Women. Books. Even better together.
P.O. Box 10543 Tallahassee, FL 32302 Phone: 800-729-4992
www.bellabooks.com

TWO WEEKS IN AUGUST by Nat Burns. Her return to Chincoteague Island is a delight to Nina Christie until she gets her dose of Hazy Duncan's renown ill-humor. She's not going to let it bother her, though...
978-1-59493-173-4 $14.95

MILES TO GO by Amy Dawson Robertson. Rennie Vogel has finally earned a spot at CT3. All too soon she finds herself abandoned behind enemy lines, miles from safety and forced to do the one thing she never has before: trust another woman.
978-1-59493-174-1 $14.95

PHOTOGRAPHS OF CLAUDIA by KG MacGregor. To photographer Leo Wescott models are light and shadow realized on film. Until Claudia.
978-1-59493-168-0 $14.95

SONGS WITHOUT WORDS by Robbi McCoy. Harper Sheridan's runaway niece turns up in the one place least expected and Harper confronts the woman from the summer that has shaped her entire life since.
978-1-59493-166-6 $14.95

YOURS FOR THE ASKING by Kenna White. Lauren Roberts is tired of being the steady, reliable one. When Gaylin Hart blows into her life, she decides to act, only to find once again that her younger sister wants the same woman.
978-1-59493-163-5 $14.95

THE SCORPION by Gerri Hill. Cold cases are what make reporter Marty Edwards tick. When her latest proves to be far from cold, she still doesn't want Detective Kristen Bailey baby-sitting her, not even when she has to run for her life.
978-1-59493-162-8 $14.95

STEPPING STONE by Karin Kallmaker. Selena Ryan's heart was shredded by an actress, and she swears she will never, ever be involved with one again.
978-1-59493-160-4 $14.95

FAINT PRAISE by Ellen Hart. When a famous TV personality leaps to his death, Jane Lawless agrees to help a friend with inquiries, drawing the attention of a ruthless killer. #6 in this award-winning series.
978-1-59493-164-2 $14.95

A SMALL SACRIFICE by Ellen Hart. A harmless reunion of friends is anything but, and Cordelia Thorn calls friend Jane Lawless with a desperate plea for help. Lammy winner for Best Mystery. #5 in this award-winning series.
978-1-59493-165-9 $14.95

NO RULES OF ENGAGEMENT by Tracey Richardson. A war zone attraction is of no use to Major Logan Sharp. She can't wait for Jillian Knight to go back to the other side of the world.
978-1-59493-159-8 $14.95

TOASTED by Josie Gordon. Mayhem erupts when a culinary road show stops in tiny Middelburg, and for some reason everyone thinks Lonnie Squires ought to fix it. Follow-up to Lammy mystery winner Whacked.
978-1-59493-157-4 $14.95

SEA LEGS by KG MacGregor. Kelly is happy to help Natalie make Didi jealous, sure, it's all pretend. Maybe. Even the captain doesn't know where this comic cruse will end.
978-1-59493-158-1 $14.95

KEILE'S CHANCE by Dillon Watson. A routine day in the park turns into the chance of a lifetime, if Keile Griffen can find the courage to risk it all for a pair of big brown eyes.
978-1-59493-156-7 $14.95

ROOT OF PASSION by Ann Roberts. Grace Owens knows a fake when she sees it, and the potion her best friend promises will fix her love life is a fake. But what if she wishes it weren't?
978-1-59493-155-0 $14.95

COMFORTABLE DISTANCE by Kenna White. Summer on Puget Sound ought to be relaxing for Dana Robbins, but Dr. Jamie Hughes is far too close for comfort.
978-1-59493-152-9 $14.95

DELUSIONAL by Terri Breneman. In her search for a killer, Toni Barston discovers that sometimes everything is exactly the way it seems, and then it gets worse.
978-1-59493-151-2 $14.95

FAMILY AFFAIR by Saxon Bennett. An oops at the gynecologist has Chase Banter finally trying to grow up. She has nine whole months to pull it off.
978-1-59493-150-5 $14.95

SMALL PACKAGES by KG MacGregor. With Lily away from home, Anna Kaklis is alone with her worst nightmare: a toddler. Book Three of the Shaken Series.
978-1-59493-149-9 $14.95

WRONG TURNS by Jackie Calhoun. Callie Callahan's latest wrong turn turns out well. She meets Vicki Brownwell. Sparks would fly if only Meg Klein would leave them alone!
978-1-59493-148-2 $14.95

WARMING TREND by Karin Kallmaker. Everybody was convinced she had committed a shocking academic theft, so Anidyr Bycall ran a long, long way. Going back to her beloved Alaskan home, and the coldness in Eve Cambra's eyes isn't going to be easy.
978-1-59493-146-8 $14.95